HUSH NOTE SERIES

Devney Perry

USA TODAY BESTSELLING AUTHOR
DEVNEY PERRY

RIFTS AND REFRAINS

ISBN: 978-1-950692-23-1

Editing & Proofreading:

Karen Grove

www.karengrove.com

Julie Deaton, Deaton Author Services

www.facebook.com/jdproofs

Karen Lawson, The Proof is in the Reading

Kaitlyn Moodie, Moodie Editing Services

Cover:

Sarah Hansen © Okay Creations

www.okaycreations.com

ALSO BY DEVNEY PERRY

Jamison Valley Series

The Coppersmith Farmhouse

The Clover Chapel

The Lucky Heart

The Outpost

The Bitterroot Inn

The Candle Palace

Maysen Jar Series

The Birthday List

Letters to Molly

Lark Cove Series

Tattered

Timid

Tragic

Tinsel

Tin Gypsy Series

Gypsy King

Riven Knight

Stone Princess

Noble Prince

Runaway Series

Runaway Road

Wild Highway

Quarter Miles

Standalones

Rifts and Refrains

CHAPTER ONE

QUINN

"The funeral is Saturday."

I nodded.

"I know you're busy, but if you could come, your father would . . . I know he'd appreciate the support."

Beyond my dressing room door, a dull roar bloomed. Hands clapped. Voices screamed. The beat of stomping feet vibrated the floors. The opening act must be on their last set because the crowd was pumped. The stadium would be primed when Hush Note took the stage.

"Quinn, are you there?"

I cleared my throat, blinking away the sheen of tears. "I'm here. Sorry."

"Will you come?"

In nine years, my mother had never asked me to return to Montana. Not for Christmases. Not for birthdays. Not for weddings. Was it as hard for her to ask as it was for me to answer?

"Yeah," I choked out. "I'll be there. Tomorrow."

Her relief cascaded through the phone. "Thank you."

"Sure. I need to go." I hung up without waiting for her goodbye, then stood from the couch and crossed the room to the mirror, making sure my tears hadn't disturbed my eyeliner and mascara.

A fist pounded on the door. "Quinn, five minutes."

Thank God. I needed to get the hell out of this room and forget that phone call.

I chugged the last of my vodka tonic and reapplied a coat of red lipstick, then scanned the room for my drumsticks. They went with me nearly everywhere—Jonas teased they were my security blanket—and I'd had them earlier, on the table. Except now it was bare, save for my plate of uneaten food. The sticks weren't on the couch either. The only time I'd left the dressing room was when I'd gone to get a cocktail and a sandwich.

Who the fuck came into my dressing room and took them? I marched to the door and flung it open, letting a rage brew to chase away some of the pain in my heart.

"Where are my sticks?" I shouted down the hallway. "Whoever took them is fired."

A short, balding man emerged from behind the door where he'd been hovering. He was new to the crew, having been hired only two weeks ago. His cheeks flushed as he held out his hand, my sticks in his sweaty grip. "Oh, uh . . . here."

I ripped them from his hand. "Why were you in my dressing room?"

His face blanched.

Yep. Fired.

I didn't allow men in my dressing room. It was a widely known fact among the crew that, unless you were on a very short list of exceptions, my dressing room was off-limits to anyone with a penis.

The rule hadn't always existed, but after a string of bad experiences it had become mandatory.

There'd been the time I'd returned to my dressing room to find a man in the middle of the space, his jeans and whitey-tighties bunched at his ankles as he'd presented me his tiny glory. Then there'd been the show when I'd come in to find two women making out on my couch—they'd mistaken my dressing room for Nixon's.

The final straw had been three years ago. I'd been drenched from a show and desperate to get out of my sweaty clothes. Pounding on the drums for an hour under hot lights usually left me dripping. I'd stripped off my jeans and tank top, standing there wearing only a bra and panties, and reached for the duffel I brought with me to every show. When I opened my bag to take out spare clothes, I'd found them coated in jizz.

So no more men—short, tall, bald or hairy.

"S-sorry," Shorty stammered. "I thought I'd hold them for you."

Beyond him, my tour manager, Ethan, came rushing down the hall, mouthing *sorry* with wide eyes. Ethan was the peacemaker, but he'd be too late to save Shorty.

In a way, I was glad this guy had snuck into my dressing room and taken my sticks. I needed a target, somewhere to aim this raging grief before it brought me to my knees, and this asshole had a bull's-eye on his forehead.

I almost felt bad for him.

"You wanted to hold them for me?" I waved my hand, Zildjian sticks included. The crew bustled around us, keeping a wide berth as they prepped to switch out the stage configuration. "Were you also going to hold Jonas's

Warwick? Or Nixon's Fender? Is that what your job is today? Holding stuff for the band?"

"I, uh—"

"Fuck you, creep." I pointed my sticks at his nose. "Get the fuck out of my sight before I use your head as a snare."

"Quinn." Ethan collided with my side, putting his arm around my shoulders. He gave me a brief squeeze, then spun me around and nudged me into the dressing room. "Why don't you finish getting ready?"

Behind my back, I heard Shorty mutter, "Bitch."

Why was a woman a bitch when she didn't let a man off the hook for this kind of shit behavior? If a guy were standing in my shoes, Shorty wouldn't have dared enter the dressing room in the first place.

"He's fired, Ethan," I shot over my shoulder.

"I'll take care of it."

I kicked the door closed and took a deep breath.

Damn it, why was our tour over already? Why was tonight the last night? What I really needed was a packed schedule of travel and shows so that going to Montana for a funeral was impossible.

Except there were no excuses to make this time. There was no avoiding this goodbye, and deep down, I knew I'd hate myself if I tried.

Somehow, I'd find the courage.

Tears threatened again, and I squeezed my eyes shut. Why hadn't I grabbed more vodka?

After this show in Boston, I'd planned to return home to Seattle and write music. The summer tour was over, and we had nothing scheduled for a month. Except now, instead of Washington, I'd fly to Montana.

For Nan.

My beloved grandmother, who I'd spoken to on Monday, had died in her sleep last night.

"Knock. Knock." The door inched open and Ethan poked his head inside. "Ready?"

"Ready." I clutched my sticks in my hand, drawing strength from the smooth wood. Then I followed him outside and through the crush of people.

The crowd's cheers grew louder with every step toward the stage. Nixon and Jonas were already waiting to go on. Nix was bouncing on his feet and cracking his neck. Jonas was whispering something in his fiancée Kira's ear, making her laugh.

"Are you okay?" Ethan asked as he escorted me toward them.

"Change of plans for tomorrow. I'm not going to Seattle. Can you make arrangements for me to go to Bozeman, Montana, instead?"

"Um . . . sure." He nodded as confusion clouded his expression.

In all the years Ethan had been our tour manager, he'd never had to arrange for me to take a break from the show lineup for a trip to my childhood home. Because since I'd walked away at eighteen, I hadn't been back.

"I want to leave first thing in the morning."

"Quinn, are you—"

I held up a hand. "Not now."

"There she is." Nixon grinned as I approached, his excitement palpable. Like me, he lived for these shows. He lived for the rush and the adrenaline. He lived to leave it all on stage and let the audience sweep us away for the next hour.

Jonas smiled too, but it faltered as he took in my face. "Are you okay?"

Where Ethan was the peacemaker and Nixon the entertainer, Jonas was the caretaker. The designated leader by default. When Nixon and I didn't want to deal with something, like a Grammy acceptance speech or hiring a new keyboardist, Jonas was there, always willing to step up.

Maybe we relied on him too much. Maybe the reason it had been so hard to write new music lately was because I wasn't sure of my own role anymore.

Drummer? Writer? Token female?

Bitch?

Shorty's damn voice was stuck in my head. "Some guy from the stage crew came into my dressing room and took my sticks. He was 'holding them' for me."

It was better they think that was the reason I was upset. Ethan wouldn't ask questions about my trip tomorrow, but Jonas and Nixon would.

"He's fired." Jonas looked to Ethan, who held up a hand.

"It's already done."

"Good luck, you guys." Kira gave Jonas another kiss and waved at Nixon. She was a little less friendly toward me— my fault, not hers—but she smiled.

I hadn't exactly been welcoming when she'd gotten together with Jonas. I'd been wary, rightfully so. His taste in women before Kira was abhorrent.

"Thanks, Kira." I offered her the warmest smile I could muster before she and Ethan slipped away to where they'd watch the show.

Jonas held out one hand for mine and his other for Nixon's. As we linked together, we shuffled into a shoulder-to-shoulder circle.

This was a ritual we'd started years ago. I couldn't remember exactly when or how it had begun, but now it was something we didn't miss. It was as critical to a performance as my drum kit and their guitars. We stood together, eyes closed and without words, connecting for a quiet moment before we went on stage.

Then Jonas squeezed my hand, signaling it was time.

Here we go.

I dropped their hands and, with my shoulders pinned back and my sticks gripped tight, walked past them to the dark stage. The cheers washed over me. The chanting of *Hush Note, Hush Note* seeped into my bones. I moved right for my kit, sat on my stool, and put my foot on the bass drum.

Boom.

The crowd went wild.

Nixon walked on stage and lights from thousands of cameras flashed.

Boom.

Jonas strode toward a microphone. "Hello, Boston!"

The screams were deafening.

Boom.

Then we unleashed.

The rhythm of my drums swallowed me up. I escaped into the music and let it numb the pain. I played like my heart wasn't broken and pretended that the woman who'd supported me from afar these past nine years was clapping in the front row.

Tonight, I'd be the award-winning drummer. *The Golden Sticks.*

Tomorrow, I'd be Quinn Montgomery.

And tomorrow, I'd have no choice but to go home.

———

"WHAT ARE YOU DOING HERE?"

Nixon shrugged from his seat on our jet. His eyes were shaded with sunglasses, and he was wearing the same clothes he'd changed into after last night's show. "Heard you were taking a trip. Thought I'd tag along."

"Have you even been to sleep yet?" I walked to his seat and plucked the glasses off his face, and the sight of his glassy eyes made me cringe. "Nix—"

"Shush." He took the sunglasses from my hand and returned them to his face. "After nap time."

I frowned and plopped into the seat across the aisle. His partying was getting out of hand.

The attendant emerged from the galley with a Bloody Mary. "Here you go, Nix."

First-name basis already? This one wasn't wasting any time.

"I want an orange juice," I ordered, drawing her attention. "And a glass of water, no ice. And a cup of coffee."

"Anything else I can get you?" she asked, her question aimed at Nixon, not me.

He waved her off with a grin.

"Do not get any ideas of taking her to the bedroom," I said after she was out of earshot. "She's probably already poked holes in a condom."

Nixon chuckled. "So cynical this morning."

"Helpful, not cynical. Think of how many skanks I've chased off with my prickly attitude. Think of how many 'accidental' pregnancies I've help you avoid. You could say *you're welcome.*"

He laughed, sipping his drink. "So where are we going?"

"I assumed Ethan told you since you're sitting here."

"Okay, let me rephrase. Why are we going to Montana? You *never* go home."

I stared out the window, watching the ground crew motioning to our pilots. "Nan died."

Voicing the words was like a hammer to my chest, and every ounce of my strength went to keeping the tears at bay.

"Fuck." Nixon's hand stretched across the aisle, and his fingers closed over my forearm. "I'm sorry, Quinn. I'm so, so sorry. Why didn't you say anything? We could have canceled last night's show."

"I needed it." Of all people, Nix would understand the need to disappear into something for an hour to avoid reality.

"What can I do?"

"Don't fuck the attendant until after you drop me off."

He chuckled. "Done. Anything else?"

"Help me write a song for her. For Nan," I whispered.

"You got it." His hand tightened on my arm, then fell away as the attendant returned with my drinks. She set them on a table, leaving us to relax in the plush leather seats as the pilot came back to greet us and confirm our flight schedule.

When he disappeared into the cockpit, I put on my headphones and closed my eyes, listening to nothing as we prepared to depart. Nixon saw it as my signal that I didn't want to talk and settled deeper into his chair. He was snoring before we were wheels up, soaring above the clouds.

And I was flying home, dreading the return I'd put off for nearly a decade.

The last time I'd seen Nan, or any of my family members, had been nine years ago. I'd left home at eighteen, ready to break free and chase my dreams. The first year had been the hardest, but then I'd found Jonas and Nixon and our band had become my makeshift family. With every passing year, it had been easier and easier to stay away from Montana. It had been easier to avoid the past.

Except the easy way out had also been the coward's path. I'd missed the chance to tell Nan goodbye.

She wouldn't call me on Mondays anymore. There would be no more cards in the mail on my birthday, stuffed with a twenty-dollar bill. Nan wouldn't boast to her water aerobics class that her famous granddaughter had won a People's Choice Award, then call to tell me exactly what she'd bragged.

Tears welled as the sunlight streamed through my window. I blinked them away, refusing to cry with the flight attendant checking on us constantly, waiting for Nixon to wake up. I turned on my music and cranked the volume so loud the sound was nearly painful. Then I tapped my foot, matching the tempo. My fingers drummed on the armrests of my chair.

I lost myself in the rhythm, like I had last night, only this was someone else's beat.

My own seemed fragile at the moment, like a pane of glass that would shatter if I hit it too hard. I was tiptoeing around my own talent, avoiding it, because lately I'd been questioning my ability to craft something new.

This creative block was crushing me.

Nixon's deepening love affair with cocaine, alcohol and whatever other substances he was putting into his body had hindered his creative prowess as of late too.

Our record label had been hounding us for months to get going on the next album. Jonas was flying home to Maine to write new lyrics. Since he'd found Kira this past year—his muse—most of his recent songs were fluffier than we'd recorded on previous albums. Nixon and I had both vetoed a couple of his drafts, but some of it had great potential.

If we could match them to a tune.

That's where Nixon and I came in. Jonas had a gift with words. Nixon and I wielded the notes.

Jonas's recent lyrics needed the right amount of love in the melody. They needed a hint of angst to keep them interesting and an edge to be rock and roll. Explaining what I wanted in each song was simple. Stringing together something tangible was proving to be a challenge.

Things had been so much simpler when he'd only written about sex.

Now that we had a break in our schedule, I was anxious to get home to Seattle, where I could hole up in my apartment and sit behind my piano until it clicked.

But first I'd spend a week in Montana saying goodbye.

I loathed goodbyes, so I avoided them.

Not this time.

The knot in my stomach tightened with every passing hour. When the pilot announced we were beginning our descent, I shot out of my seat, raced to the bathroom and puked.

"You okay?" Nixon asked, handing me a piece of gum as I emerged and took my seat.

"Yeah, thanks."

"Sure?"

"Just nerves."

Hell, I hadn't been this nervous since Hush Note's early days. I didn't get keyed up before shows anymore, not after years and years of practice. Besides, the moments on stage were the best part of this life. Playing for thousands of people live or playing for millions of people on television, my hands never shook. My stomach was rock solid.

But this? Returning home to my family. Returning home for a funeral. Returning home to him.

I was terrified.

Nixon's hand closed over my forearm once more, and he didn't let go until the plane touched down.

"I don't want to be here," I confessed as we taxied across the runway.

"Want me to stay?" His eyes, clearer after his nap, were full of tenderness.

He'd stay if I said yes. He'd be miserable and bored, but he'd stay. A part of me wanted to use him as a buffer between me and my family, but his presence and fame would only make things harder.

My face wasn't as recognizable on the street as his, and I didn't get half of his attention because I wasn't one of the guys. I wasn't the lead on stage, singing into a microphone as I played a guitar. Nixon had been *People Magazine*'s Sexiest Man Alive three years ago. This year's reigning man was Jonas.

The last thing we needed this week were swooning fans wanting autographs.

I wanted to get in and out of Montana without much fuss. I was here to pay my respects to Nan and then I was going home.

Alone.

"No, but thanks." The plane stopped and the pilot came out to open the door as I collected my things. "Where will you go? Home to Seattle?"

"Nah. I'm feeling somewhere tropical. Hawaii's close."

"Please don't drink so many dirty bananas that you forget to pick me up. Next Monday. Should I write it down?"

"No, but you'd better make sure Ethan has that in his calendar."

"I will." I laughed, bending to kiss his stubbled cheek. "Thanks for flying with me."

"Welcome."

"You're a good guy, Nix."

He put a finger to his lips. "Don't tell. It's easier to get women into bed when they think you're the bad boy."

"Annnd you're also a pig." I frowned as the attendant came over, batting her eyelashes as she handed Nixon a cocktail. When had he even ordered that drink? Maybe I should make him stay with me and force him to be sober for a week. "Don't go crazy. Are you going to be okay?"

"I'm a rock star, baby." He flashed me a smile, the devilish one he saved for his fans and women. It was the stage smile that masked his demons. "I'm fucking awesome."

Lies. He was far from awesome, but I wasn't sure how to help him. Not when he was on a mission to lose himself in sex and booze and drugs like he did every summer.

"Thanks again." I waved. "Enjoy your flight attendant."

"Enjoy your time home."

My stomach pitched at his parting words. I slung my backpack over my shoulder and headed toward the door. At the base of the jet's stairs, my suitcase was waiting with the pilot.

I nodded a farewell and fished a pair of sunglasses from my bag, sliding them on before crossing the tarmac. The path from the private runway to the terminal was marked by yellow arrows on the charcoal asphalt.

The sunshine blazed hot on my shoulders as I pulled the

hood on my black jacket over my blond hair. It was the best way to keep from being recognized, and with the mood I was in, it would do no good to be spotted by a fan today.

The summer breeze blew across my face, bringing that clean mountain air to my nose. We'd spent too many days breathing recycled air in buses and planes and hotels. I might have traded my country upbringing for a life in the city and preferred it as such, but this fresh, pure air was unbeatable.

Montana had a wholly unique smell of mountains and majesty.

I reached the terminal door too soon and stepped into the air conditioning. Ethan had reserved a rental car and a hotel suite for me, and as soon as I was checked into my room, I was planning on a long, hot shower. Then I'd unpack and go through the hotel move-in routine I'd perfected over the years.

My toiletries would be lined up beside the bathroom sink. I'd put my clothes in drawers and stow my suitcase in the closet. Then I'd search for a TV channel in a foreign language. I didn't speak a foreign language, but I liked the background noise to drown out any sounds from the hallway.

It was a trick I'd learned in Berlin on our first European tour. These days, I couldn't sleep in a hotel room without the TV blaring some drama in Spanish, French or German.

If it was loud enough, I'd be able to cry without fear someone would overhear.

I spotted the rental car desk, but before I could aim my feet in that direction, a familiar face caught my eye.

The world blurred.

Standing in the lobby of the airport was the boy I'd left behind.

Graham Hayes.

Except he wasn't a boy anymore. He'd grown into a man. A handsome, breathtaking man who belonged on the cover of *People* beside Jonas and Nix.

He stood motionless with his eyes locked on me. The airport had been remodeled since I'd left, but the spot where he stood was almost exactly the place where I'd left him nine years ago. He'd been standing at the base of a staircase, watching me walk away.

I wouldn't fool myself into thinking he'd been waiting here for my return.

What the hell was Graham doing here? I wasn't ready to face him yet. I wasn't ready to face any of them yet, but especially Graham.

He broke out of his stare and unglued his feet. His strides were easy and confident as he walked my way. His square jaw was covered in a well-trimmed beard, the shade matching the brown of his hair. It was longer than how he'd worn it as a teenager. Sexier. The man he'd become was beyond any version that I'd imagined during many lonely hotel nights.

I gulped as he neared. My heart raced.

This was not the plan. I was supposed to rent a car, go to my hotel and regroup. I needed time to regroup, damn it, and time to prepare.

Graham's long legs in dark jeans ate up the distance between us. The sound of his boots on the floor pounded with the same thud of my heart.

Before I was ready, he stood in front of me.

"Quinn." His voice was smooth and deep, lower than I remembered. He used to say my name with a smile, but there wasn't a hint of one on his face.

"Hi, Graham."

He wore a Hayes-Montgomery Construction T-shirt. My mother had sent me one of the same for Christmas two years ago.

He was the Hayes.

My brother, Walker, was the Montgomery.

The black cotton stretched across his broad chest. I'd spent many nights with my ear against that chest, but it hadn't been as muscled back then. It had held promise, though, of the man he'd become.

The man he *had* become.

Everything about Graham seemed to have changed, even those golden-brown eyes. The vibrant color was the same as I saw in my dreams, but they were colder now. Distant. A change I couldn't blame on time.

No, that one was on me.

"Let's go." He ripped the handle of my suitcase from my grip.

"I have a car reserved." I pointed to the rental kiosk, but Graham turned and walked toward the doors. "Graham, I have a car."

"Cancel it," he clipped over a shoulder. "Your mom asked me to pick you up."

"Fine," I grumbled, yanking my phone from my pocket. Texting Ethan while keeping up with Graham's punishing pace was difficult, and I looked up just in time to stop myself from crashing into a wall.

Oh, hell. It wasn't just a wall. It was a wall holding a framed Hush Note poster, and there I was, in the center. My hair was thrown back as I pounded on the drums. Jonas was singing into a microphone while Nixon riffed on his guitar.

It was the poster our label had made for tour promo last

year, and the airport had embellished it with a banner strung over the top.

Welcome to Bozeman.

Home of Quinn Montgomery, Hush Note's Grammy Award-Winning Drummer.

Graham paused and looked back, likely wondering what was taking me so long. When he spotted the poster, he shot it a glare that might have incinerated the paper had it not been protected behind glass. Then he marched through the door, his strides even faster.

I jogged to keep up but was too far away to stop him from throwing my suitcase into the bed of a truck—an actual throw far more damaging than I'd ever seen from airline personnel.

"Get in." He jerked his chin to the passenger door.

"Okay." I bit my tongue.

Since my rental car was out, my new plan was to survive this ride to the hotel. Graham was upset, and I'd let it blow over. Ten minutes, fifteen tops, and we'd go our separate ways. I was here this week for Nan and causing drama with Graham would have upset her.

So I climbed in his truck and took a deep breath.

Graham's scent surrounded me. As a boy, he'd smelled fresh and clean. It was still there, familiar and heartbreaking, but with a spicy undercurrent of musk and cologne and man. The heady, intoxicating smell wasn't going to make this trip to the hotel any easier.

Before I had my seat belt buckled, Graham was behind the wheel and racing away from the curb.

I swallowed and braved conversation. "So, um . . . how have you been?"

His jaw ticked in response, but thankfully the radio filled the silence.

The Sirius XM Countdown continues with "Sweetness" by Hush Note. A song that's been number one on our countdown for—

Graham stabbed the off button with his finger.

I faced the window.

So Graham wasn't just upset. He was furious. Clearly nine years apart hadn't turned me into a fond memory.

"I have a reservation at the Hilton Garden Inn. If you wouldn't mind dropping me—"

"You're going home."

Right. End of discussion. Graham was doing a favor for my mother since my family would be busy on a Sunday morning. He'd been sent to retrieve me before I could disappear to my hotel.

Maybe I shouldn't have been in such a hurry to leave the East Coast.

The drive through Bozeman was tense. I kept my gaze fixed outside, taking in the new buildings. The town had boomed over the years. Where there had once been open fields, there were now office complexes, shopping centers and restaurants.

It wasn't until we approached downtown that the streets became more familiar and I was able to anticipate Graham's turns. When we reached my childhood neighborhood, I marveled at the homes. Had they always been this small?

Then we were parked in front of my parents' home. My home.

Finally, something that hadn't changed. Slate-blue siding, white trim, black shutters and Mom's red geraniums planted in a whiskey barrel by the front door.

"Thanks for dropping me off," I told Graham, risking a glance his way. "Just like old times."

He'd always insisted on dropping me off at my house even though he lived next door.

Except back then, he would have smiled and kissed me goodbye.

But that was before.

Before I'd broken his heart.

Before he'd shattered mine.

CHAPTER TWO

GRAHAM

Nine years and I still wasn't ready to see her.

Maybe if I'd actually had nine years without constant reminders of Quinn, facing her in the airport wouldn't have felt like a goddamn sucker punch. But there'd been no escaping her, not with Hush Note's music everywhere. No matter how quickly I turned off the radio or flipped the television channel, it was there, haunting me.

Now she was here to torture me in person. There'd be no compartmentalizing her memory and shoving it into a dark corner this week. Especially not today as she climbed out of my truck.

I'd known this day would come. That eventually she'd return to Montana and we'd have to face each other. Instead of coming to terms with that inevitability, I'd built up nine years of dread.

Every Thanksgiving or Christmas, I'd wonder if this would be the year she'd come home. I refused to ask her family, but my mother or her mother would deliberately drop comments to make sure I knew that Quinn had found some reason to stay away.

She's dropped out of school to join a band.

They're playing in Australia for the holidays.

She's working on an album.

Bullshit excuses. Quinn hadn't wanted to come back. She had her rich and famous life to live—her and that fucking band.

Quinn had turned her back on everything from her youth. Her family. Her friends.

Me.

She'd forgotten us. Nine years was a long damn time to hold on to anger, but try as I might, I just couldn't let it go. The rage simmered under my skin; no cooler now than it had been when she'd first left.

I shoved open the truck's door and slammed it hard before going to the back and hefting out her suitcase.

"Thanks." She gave me a faint smile, reaching for her luggage.

I walked past her to the sidewalk, dismissing her as I strode to the front door, her suitcase in my grip.

Her footsteps followed. "I can take it."

"No." My lip curled at her musical voice.

In our years apart, I hadn't forgotten that smooth, sultry sound. It was a siren's call, alluring and charming. Irritating. I willed myself to block it out and walked faster.

There was no point in knocking at the front door. It was always unlocked because only a sick and demented individual would break into Pastor Montgomery's house on a Sunday afternoon.

Chatter filled my ears and the smell of a charcoal barbeque drifted from the kitchen.

Son of a bitch. Wasn't everyone supposed to be busy? That was why I'd been stuck with the job of retrieving Quinn, wasn't it? Because the Montgomery crew would be long at church, talking with everyone who wanted to pay their respects. Mom and Dad wanted to stay too, for moral support.

This house was full of liars. Well, one meddler.

My mother.

I threw Quinn's suitcase down and stalked past the living room toward the back of the house where the kitchen and adjoining dining room were teaming with people. The patio door was open, and Dad was manning the grill.

"Oh, Graham." Mom smiled when she spotted me, then her eyes darted over my shoulder. "Where is Qui—Quinn!"

The room went silent and all eyes swung my way, sweeping past me to where Quinn was hanging back.

"Hi." She lifted a hand and gave an awkward smile.

No one moved.

Quinn's hand hung in the air as everyone stared. The smile on her face fell as seconds stretched into what felt like hours.

Guess I wasn't the only one not prepared for today's reunion.

I cleared my throat and the room sprang into action.

"Welcome home." Quinn's mother, Ruby, flew across the kitchen, tossing a towel aside before pulling Quinn into a long hug. "You look . . ." Ruby let Quinn go, and a flash of regret crossed her face. "You look beautiful."

"Thanks, Mom."

Bradley appeared in the hallway beside Quinn. His eyes were glassy, like he'd excused himself from the crowd to weep for his mother in private.

"Hi, Dad." Quinn repeated her awkward wave.

"Quinn." Bradley's voice was hoarse and rough as he scanned her from head to toe, like he didn't believe she was really standing here.

Just like I'd done at the airport.

"I'm sorry about Nan," Quinn whispered.

"She's in a better place." Bradley hesitated a step, then another, before pulling Quinn into a stiff hug.

Ruby swiped at her eyes and placed her hands on their shoulders.

This was a private moment, a reunion that didn't need an audience. Why were we here? I shot a frown to Mom.

She shrugged and made her way toward Quinn, waiting until Bradley and Ruby released her. Then she pulled Quinn into a firm hug. "You look so beautiful. All grown up. And that nose ring is so cute."

I forced my gaze away from Quinn's button nose. Cute was not the word. Sexy. Tempting. Those were the words to describe the tiny silver loop in Quinn's left nostril.

When had she gotten it pierced? Before or after the phone call that had crushed my heart?

That nose ring was going to be my reminder. It would do me no good to fall into Quinn's orbit. Been there, done that. She wasn't the same girl I had known. She wasn't eighteen anymore. She wasn't perfect in every way. So what that she'd gotten more beautiful?

My Quinn was gone. This was the Quinn I saw on TV.

A stranger.

And I'd been forced to watch her transformation from afar.

As a young man, I'd planned for Quinn to be by my side.

We'd shared the naïve dream that high school sweethearts could grow old together.

When the youthful softness of her face faded to a womanly grace, I was supposed to have had a front-row seat, watching through a shared bathroom mirror. When her hair had reached toward the small of her back, I should have been the man to toy with the ends. When her body had tightened, when she'd become this lithe *woman*, she was supposed to have been in my bed.

Naïve wasn't strong enough a word.

"Hi, sweetheart." Mom stood on her toes to kiss my cheek.

"Everyone was too busy to pick her up, huh?"

"We *were* busy. Church ended earlier than expected."

"Uh-huh," I deadpanned, sweeping my hand toward the room. "And this?"

"Ruby thought it might be easier with, um . . . you know"—*Quinn*—"if there was some activity. And she thought Bradley might want everyone close today."

Bradley had given the sermon this morning, even though his mother hadn't been in her usual seat. He'd stumbled through a few parts but had mostly kept his composure. I hadn't been surprised to see him at the pulpit because he was a man who drew strength from others, especially from his friends and family.

Or maybe he gave us strength when we needed it.

He'd lost his mother, but we'd all lost Nan.

How was he still standing? My mother made me crazy with her meddling and pestering and constant intrusion into my personal life, but if I lost her, I'd be a wreck.

Yet here he stood stiffly beside Quinn in silence. Both of

their gazes were cast to the floor, and their discomfort was beginning to infect the room.

"Hey," Walker said as he came through the patio door, slapping my shoulder. "Colin's out back playing."

"Thanks for bringing him over."

"No problem," he muttered, then his eyes locked on his sister.

Quinn spotted him and crossed the room. She shot me a cautious glance before smiling up at her older brother. "Hey, Walker."

"Hi, Quinn." He gave her a polite nod.

Her arms raised slightly, like she was going to hug him, but when he didn't move, they fell to her sides.

For fuck's sake. I didn't want to be here for any of this. Bradley might want people around as he mourned his loss, but I wanted the peace and quiet of my own home. Standing here just made Nan's absence more noticeable.

At functions like this, she'd been the one to make light jokes and break the tension. Nan would have made Quinn's return into a party, chasing any awkwardness from the room. Without Nan here to smooth things over, this lunch was going to be insufferable.

"Walker . . ." His wife, Mindy, leaned her head inside the house. "Oh, hey, Graham. I didn't know you were"—her eyes locked on Quinn—"here."

"Come on in, babe." Walker waved her inside. "Mindy, this is my sister, Quinn."

Mindy forced a smile and shook Quinn's hand. "Nice to meet you."

"You too." It was stifling outside, but Quinn was dressed for winter in that jacket, hood and a pair of ripped jeans tucked into thick-soled boots. Her blond hair, the golden shade of wheat fields in August, hung nearly to her waist. Her eyes, the color of the Montana summer mountains at dawn, blue and gray and flecked with snowcap white near the iris, were lined in black.

The rock star.

I wanted to hate her new look, like I wanted to hate her voice.

I didn't.

"Our kids are outside." Mindy hooked a thumb over her shoulder. "I'll, um . . . I'll go get them."

"Thanks." A flash of regret crossed Quinn's eyes. "I'd love to meet them."

Quinn hadn't met her niece or nephew yet. They were six and four. Mindy and Walker had been married for seven years.

Those numbers, the years she'd missed, erased any shred of pity I had at her discomfort. She should be miserable. She should regret her choices. She hadn't just left me behind when she'd disappeared to Seattle and never looked back.

She'd abandoned us all.

"Mom, do you—" Brooklyn came downstairs with her baby in her arms. She must have been upstairs nursing when we'd arrived. She took one look at Quinn and her face hardened.

"Hi, Brookie." Quinn turned and gave her a smile.

Brooklyn scoffed. "No one calls me that anymore."

"Oh, sorry." Quinn's face fell and her attention went to the baby named after their father. "This is your son? Bradley?"

"Yeah." Brooklyn didn't spare her another glance before marching past us and storming outside.

Quinn's eyes closed and she blew out a long breath. "Wow."

"She'll come around," Ruby said, walking to Quinn and putting an arm around her shoulders. "It's good to have you home."

"I'm ready for the burgers and dogs!" my dad bellowed from outside before poking his face through the door. "Oh, hey there, Quinny."

Quinny. With one word, my dad erased the tension in her face. She smiled, bright and so goddamn beautiful I had to look away. "Hi, Mr. Hayes."

"Mr. Hayes." Dad huffed a laugh. "You haven't changed."

No matter how many times Dad had insisted Quinn call him Don, she'd always refused.

But Dad was wrong. Quinn had changed.

Too much had changed.

"Dad!" A bolt of light shot inside, racing past my dad to collide with my legs. My son smiled up at me, both his front teeth missing. Those had cost the tooth fairy five bucks apiece—I was a generous fairy.

"How's it going, bud? Were you good for Walker and Mindy?"

"Duh. Will you play catch with me?"

"After lunch." I ruffled his brown hair, a shade that matched my own. "Go wash up."

He spun around, ready to blast off because he was a run or run faster kind of kid. Colin Hayes didn't understand the concept of walking. When he launched, he bumped into Quinn. "Oh. Sorry."

She blinked at him, her gaze bouncing between the two of us.

Colin's eyes widened, recognition washing over his face, and I tipped my head to the ceiling, stifling a groan. *Shit.*

"What the what? You're Quinn! Quinn Montgomery, the drummer for Hush Note. You're The Golden Sticks."

Quinn's nose scrunched at the nickname, but Colin kept rambling, his arms flapping in the air as they tried to keep pace with his tongue.

"Hush Note is my favorite band ever, but 'Sweetness' isn't my favorite song, because Dad's right, they overplayed it and now it's ruined. My first favorite is 'Torchlight.' My second favorite is 'Passive Aggression.' My third favorite is tied with 'Hot Mess' and 'Fast Hands.' What's your favorite? Are you allowed to pick one? I bet it's 'Torchlight' too, huh?"

"Um . . ." Quinn's mouth fell open.

"I want to be a drummer. I have a drum set in the basement and everything. Maybe you can come over and we can play." Colin whirled. "Can she, Dad?"

I was tempted to say yes and leave Quinn to Colin like a lamb to the wolves. My seven-year-old son would eat her alive with his perpetual commentary.

Asking questions was Colin's super strength. From the minute I picked him up at the bus stop to the time I tucked him into bed at night, the kid was a string of question after question, and most of the time he didn't wait for an answer between them.

Once, about a year ago, I'd asked him to give me five minutes of quiet and he'd told me that if he didn't speak, he wouldn't be able to breathe.

That was my son.

Unless you were prepared for it, unless you had years of built-up stamina, the kid could zap your energy in under an hour.

It would be fun to sic him on Quinn and see how she held up.

But the way the color had leeched from her face, the way she was staring at him, unblinking, hit me square in the chest. It hit that part of me, the part I couldn't ignore, that would always protect Quinn.

Seeing my son for the first time was causing her pain.

"Go wash up." I turned Colin's shoulders and gave him a gentle shove in the direction of the bathroom.

As he walked, he mouthed *oh my gosh* and fist pumped.

I grinned. My son was fucking awesome.

Most seven-year-old boys didn't care much about rock bands. They were into basketball and baseball. Colin loved sports, but he devoted an equal amount of time practicing dribbling or his throw to playing on the drums I'd bought him for Christmas.

He was awful. Truly, awful. But it made him so happy I didn't care about the noise.

"You have a son," Quinn said, barely over a whisper.

I nodded. "He just turned seven. You didn't know?"

"No, I, uh . . ." She shook off the surprise. "Nan told me about him."

"They were close." For Colin's sake, I was grateful that Quinn was here. She'd be a distraction from the death of a woman he'd loved nearly as much as his grandmother.

"He knows a lot about me," she said.

"That's Nan's doing. Not mine." I wanted to make it crystal clear Colin's infatuation had nothing to do with me. "I banned Hush Note music in our house a long time ago, but Nan was proud of you. Whenever she'd spend time with Colin, they'd play your music, and she'd tell him all about her famous granddaughter."

Tears flooded Quinn's eyes, but she blinked them away. "'Torchlight' was her favorite song too."

Because it was a good song, something I wouldn't admit out loud.

And Nan had had impeccable taste when it had come to music. She'd taught Colin about the classics, not just Hush Note.

My God, we were going to miss her. Yesterday and today had been such a flurry of activity that it hadn't sunk deep that Nan was gone. I expected to walk onto the patio and see her in the chair beneath the umbrella, sipping a huckleberry lemonade and reapplying the hot-pink lipstick she'd worn at all times.

"Let's eat," Mom called.

Quinn kept her head down as she walked to the sliding doors, then slipped outside.

I raked a hand through my hair, finally able to breathe now that she was out of sight. Everyone had better eat fast because I was not sticking around long.

What I wanted was a quiet afternoon with my son at home, answering his questions and playing catch and remembering the woman who'd been just as much a grandmother to me as she had been to Quinn, Walker and Brooklyn.

I waited for Colin to come running from the bathroom and led him outside, getting him seated at the kids' picnic table in the yard before I sat down on the deck with the adults.

Nan's chair was empty.

I pulled out the chair beside Dad, three seats away from Quinn, but before I could sit, my mother, carrying a bowl of her famous potato salad, hip-checked me and plopped down in the seat.

"Nice, Mom," I muttered.

She smiled and her eyes darted to the empty seat beside Quinn. "Sit down so we can eat."

My jaw ticked as I sat, inching away from Quinn as far as possible. Walker was on my left and I was practically sitting on his lap.

"Let us pray." Bradley held out his hands.

Quinn stared at my hand, keeping her own beneath the table, until everyone was linked and waiting on her. She extended one hand across the table to Ruby and the other slipped into my palm.

A shiver ran up my arm to my elbow, and my mind blanked as Bradley prayed.

Quinn's hand fit in mine no differently than it had when we were fifteen and going on our first date. Or when we were sixteen and lost our virginity to each other. Her skin was smooth and warm. Her fingers were too dainty to make such loud music. Her palm was too familiar to belong to this beautiful stranger.

"Amen," Bradley said, and Quinn's hand slipped out of my hold, much like when we were eighteen and she'd walked away from me at the airport and cut herself out of my life.

I wiped my palm on my jeans, erasing her touch.

Quinn stiffened.

"Your room is a little different than the last time you were here," Ruby told Quinn as she dished salad onto her plate. "We put a queen-size bed in there and got rid of your old desk. But I think you'll like it."

"Oh, um . . . thanks, Mom, but I have a reserva—"

I bumped her knee with mine. Hard.

"Ouch," she muttered, scowling up at me.

I glared right back. There was no way she was hiding in a hotel after being away from her parents for so many years.

"Fine," she grumbled through gritted teeth.

"What was that?" Ruby asked.

"Nothing." Quinn shook her head. "I hope it won't be too much trouble."

"We're just happy to have you home." Ruby looked at her daughter like she was trying to memorize her face in case Quinn went another decade before returning home.

Throughout the meal, I caught Bradley looking at her in the same way, though his stares were full of apology.

He'd messed up with Quinn. He'd pushed her too far. Yeah, she'd screwed up too. She'd made a stupid decision at eighteen, but her punishment had not fit the crime.

Bradley and Ruby loved their children. They were good parents who'd always done their best to protect their kids from harm. I tried to do the same with Colin. It wasn't until he'd been born that I'd learned true fear. Maybe if I'd been in Bradley's position, I would have reacted the same way. I would have let my fears get the best of me too and put blinders on to my child's own desires.

There was a fine line between protecting your kids and stifling them.

Bradley had crossed it.

And he'd been paying for that mistake for nine years.

The meal passed quickly because there wasn't much conversation like we normally had at Hayes-Montgomery get-togethers. There was too much sorrow in the air. Too much grief. The empty seat under the umbrella weighed heavily on us all.

When the meal was over and the dishes were done, I waved Colin inside from the yard and bid my farewells.

"Do we have to leave, Dad?" Colin asked.

"Yeah." I put my hand on his shoulder. "Let's go home and play catch. Go say goodbye."

"Okay." He hurried through the house, giving hugs and high-fives before racing to the front door, leaving it wide open for me to follow.

I didn't search for Quinn as I strode down the hallway. I didn't glance at her suitcase. I kept my eyes on my son. The best thing in my life. Quinn might have wrecked me years ago, but it was the reason he was in this world. No matter the hurt, my kid was worth it in spades.

"Graham," my mother called as I cleared the doorway.

"Damn," I muttered. "What's up, Mom?"

"You're leaving already?" She hurried to catch up, walking with me down the sidewalk. "What about Quinn?"

"What about her? She's not long for Montana. I picked her up. Now I'm going to go home and get on with my life."

She frowned. "Maybe you two should talk."

"No."

"She's a beautiful woman."

I rolled my eyes. "I'm not interested, so please, don't go there."

"But—"

"Eileen, would you leave him alone." Dad stepped out of the Montgomery house, closing the door behind him. "He's a grown man."

"Fine." She pouted, then crossed the grass to the house next door.

"See ya later." Dad shook my hand and followed his wife home.

My childhood home and the Montgomery house were mirror images of each other. The Hayes's house was a sage green instead of slate blue. Both homes were simple but nice with sprawling front lawns and yards big enough for kids to have adventures. Above the front door on each, the pitch of the roof was interrupted by a dormer window to a bedroom.

At my house, that room had been mine. At the Montgomerys', it was Quinn's. A curtain flickered, and I looked up to see Quinn standing in her window.

Her eyes were aimed at me.

Once upon a time, I would have smiled up at her. I would have waved. I would have silently motioned for her to sneak down and meet me on the sidewalk for a midnight kiss.

That was a different lifetime.

Now she was just a woman in a window, and once the funeral was over, the woman would be gone.

I just had to avoid her for a week.

Easy enough.

CHAPTER THREE

QUINN

I woke up with a splitting headache and the sun streaming on my face.

The latter was likely responsible for the former. I preferred to wake in sheer darkness and let myself adjust before braving the light. There were times when I'd shower in the dark at my penthouse, relying on fumbling and muscle memory because the sunshine seemed to trigger these morning skull-splitters.

But with the noise drifting up from downstairs and the brightness beaming through the window, there'd be no rolling over and sleeping until noon. When my parents had redecorated my former bedroom, they'd replaced more than just the bed. The blackout curtains I'd had as a teenager were gone, and in their place were light gossamer coverings.

Why hadn't I insisted on the hotel?

Because at one time, I'd been a part of this family, and now I was an outsider. So I'd deal with the morning headaches for one week because, at the moment, I didn't want to rock the boat. My goal was to survive Nan's funeral, spend a little time with my parents, then get the hell out of Montana.

I slid from bed and shuffled to the bathroom I'd once shared with Brooklyn and Walker. The shower didn't help my headache, and I winced blow drying my hair. There was no need for my normal heavy eyeliner and shadow since I wasn't planning on leaving the house, so I opted for a light coat of makeup. Maybe if I looked more like the teenage version of Quinn than Hush Note's Quinn, my family would relax.

By some miracle, I'd survived yesterday's lunch, but I wasn't sure if I had the energy to sit through another.

Dinner had been marginally less painful simply because it had only been Mom and Dad across from me at the dining room table. Dad had opened his mouth about fifteen times, ready to say something only to clamp it shut. Mom had attempted small talk for a few minutes before giving up.

Conversation had been nearly nonexistent through the meal, and I'd excused myself early to settle into bed, blaming my sudden fit of fake yawns on the travel and the time change. Mom had seemed sad to see me retreat up the stairs. Or had she been relieved?

Avoid. That was the plan for this week. I'd stay out of everyone's way, not spark any conflicts or discussions of the past, then retreat to my life.

Dressed in a pair of jeans and a simple black tee, I swallowed three Advil down with a guzzle of water, then braced to go downstairs.

"Morning," I said, announcing my arrival in the kitchen.

"Good morning." Mom was buzzing around, pulling out colorful, plastic bowls for cereal, much like she'd done when we were kids. Except there were wide swaths of gray in her blond hair now. When she smiled, wrinkles formed by her blue eyes. "How did you sleep?"

"Great," I lied, putting on a happy face despite my throbbing temples. Coffee. I needed caffeine.

"Isn't that bed comfortable?" she asked.

"Very." I nodded at the truth.

It was nicer than the bed I'd had as a kid. It was soft. The blankets were warm and heavy. But it was strange to sleep in my old room without my twin bed. I'd woken up a few times, not exactly sure where I was.

That didn't happen when I traveled. Maybe it would take me a minute to remember what city I was in or where we were headed next, but I always knew I was in a hotel bed and could sleep.

Last night, too many memories had played through my mind, and despite the cozy bed, I hadn't been able to relax.

"Would you like coffee?" Mom nodded to the full pot in the corner of the kitchen as she poured orange juice into three little cups. Were those for us?

"Yes, please. I can get it." The coffee mugs were in the same cupboard where they'd always been. Everything about the kitchen seemed the same. The familiarity was comforting.

Maybe that was why I hadn't slept. My room hadn't been *my* room. Now it was for guests.

I was a guest.

"Would you like some?" I asked after filling a mug to the brim.

"No, thanks. Your father and I gave up caffeine a few years ago. But I figured you'd want some, so I dug out the pot."

"Thanks, but you don't have to do that. I can go grab coffee every morning."

"It's no trouble." She stared at me for a long moment. She'd done that during dinner too, like she was worried I wasn't really here. Or maybe that I'd leave again and not come back.

Her worries were justified.

Though in all fairness, it wasn't like they'd made an effort to visit me.

Seattle was a long day's drive from Bozeman, but the flight was easy. I'd offered to fly them out countless times and get VIP tickets to one of our shows. But there'd always been an excuse. There was always something happening with the church that kept them busy. Dad had to preach on Sundays. He couldn't be at a rock concert on a Saturday night.

The man didn't take vacations, not even the Sunday after his mother had passed.

"Where's Dad?" I asked, sitting in a chair in the dining room. The table was set with three plastic green bowls, each filled with cornflakes.

"He's gone already. They had a men's Bible study early this morning."

Thank God. I sighed into my coffee. A morning with just Mom would be much easier to handle.

If Dad was at the church, he'd probably stay all day. Maybe Mom and I could go out and explore. It would be nice to spend a day with her. The last time we'd been alone together had been on our trip to Seattle when she'd driven me out to visit a college campus.

A day alone might help me remember how it had been once, before the bitter resentment had driven me away and the awkwardness had settled into every phone call and text.

"What's all this?" I asked, waving a hand at the bowls. If Dad was gone, why were there three? "Breakfast?"

"Yep. The kids will be here soon."

"Kids?"

"Your niece and nephews." She frowned, but it quickly disappeared. Apparently, I wasn't the only one not wanting to rock the boat. "I watch them in the summer. It saves Brooklyn and Walker from having to enroll them in year-round daycare and summer camps. Plus, it gives me time with them while I'm on summer break."

"Ah." We'd have to find another day to catch up. If there was time before I left.

Mom was a first-grade teacher at the same elementary where we'd gone to school three blocks away. Dad's church was only one block from home.

My entire childhood had taken place in this quiet neighborhood. Other than trips to the grocery store, we hadn't ventured out of our safe haven much. Everything we'd needed had been here and within walking distance.

Even Graham.

I pushed his name out of my head, not wanting to dwell on how cold he'd been yesterday or the fact that he had a son. Replaying it over and over again last night had been enough.

Nan had told me about the boy. *Colin.* But knowing he existed and seeing Graham's mini in person were two entirely different experiences. Colin was the evidence that Graham hadn't waited long to find my replacement in his truck bed. I, on the other hand, had waited three years before dating, if you could call two dinners and lousy sex with an executive at my label dating.

I hadn't bothered much with men since then. They were

a distraction and required energy I just didn't have, not when I was pouring myself into the music.

Nan had been hounding me lately to wade into the dating pool. Every week, it was the same question. *Found a man who can keep up with you yet?* I'd laugh, tell her no, and she'd change the subject, usually to tell me about whatever gossip was running through her canasta club.

She had been the only person in my family who'd kept in touch regularly. The only one from home who'd seemed to miss me.

"Nan used to call me on Mondays," I told Mom, toying with the plastic spoon beside my coffee mug. "Every Monday. Did you know that?"

Maybe that was the root cause of my headache. A heartache. There'd be no call from Nan today. For the first time in nine years, my Monday wouldn't include her voice.

"I know." Mom sat down across from me. "She'd report to me each week and tell me how you were."

"You could have called me yourself," I snapped, instantly regretting my tone.

"I'm sorry, Quinn."

"No, it's fine." The phone worked both ways. "I have a headache and it's making me irritable."

"I thought about calling you. Often." Her shoulders fell. "The truth is, I think I forgot how to talk to you once you left. After the fight and everything . . . I wasn't sure what to say."

During the fight, she'd said plenty. So had Dad.

After I'd left the next day for Seattle, it had taken her three weeks to call me. We'd gone from daily talks to silence for three, miserable, hard weeks. The woman who'd been my hero, the one who'd walk me to and from school, who'd set out cereal for me each morning and who'd play with me in the evenings, had let me run away to college without so much as a check-in to make sure I was safe.

Her silence had sent a message. It had broken my heart.

If not for Nan, I might have hated Mom. But Nan, she'd had this way of bridging the gap. She'd never taken a side. She'd never spoken of the fight and the day I'd left. She'd simply asked about me and how I was settling into school. She'd made sure I had everything I'd needed and cash if I'd been running short. Later, when I'd realized that college wasn't the right fit and found a job at a bar, she'd laugh at my stories of drunk patrons. She'd been overjoyed when Jonas, Nixon and I had started our band.

Year after year, Nan's Monday phone calls had made the anger and hurt I'd held against my family slowly fade.

Now she was gone. She wasn't there to hold us together.

When I left this time, there was a real chance we'd all drift apart for good.

An awkward air hovered over the table and stifled any other attempt at conversation. I sipped my coffee as Mom sat across from me, watching but attempting not to stare. The tick of the wall clock grew louder and louder as the moments stretched, until the front door burst open and little feet pounded down the hallway.

Praise Jesus, the kids were here to rescue me.

"Nana!"

Nana. They called her Nana. It was so close to Nan that my heart squeezed. Nan had used her first name as her grandmotherly title. Even Dad called his mother Nan, per her insistence.

The kids came running but slowed when they spotted me at the table. They herded toward Mom, cautious of the stranger beside their cereal bowls.

I stood and smiled. "Good morning."

They didn't smile back.

"Hey, Mom." Walker came into the kitchen, carrying backpacks on each arm, one decorated with pink princesses and another with red and blue puppy cartoons. "Quinn."

"Hi, Walker." I smiled.

He didn't smile back. "Their swimming suits are in here for lessons at two. Mindy has a meeting that might run late, is that okay?"

"Fine." Mom took the backpacks, setting them against the wall. "We'll be here."

"Thanks." Walker dropped a kiss to her cheek, then helped his children into their seats, kissing them as Mom poured milk into their bowls.

Evan and Maya.

They looked so much like Walker with his gray-blue eyes. They both had blond hair a few shades lighter than his sandy curls. Walker was the only one who had curly hair in our family. None of us knew where he'd gotten it from, but as teenage girls, Brooklyn and I had both coveted his curls, teasing him that they'd been wasted on a boy.

He'd made them useful. Walker had caught the eye of every girl in our high school, especially when he'd stood beside Graham. Even two years apart, they'd been best friends and fodder for teen fantasies.

My fantasy had become reality the day Graham had asked me on a date, despite Walker's disapproval that his best friend had the hots for his sister. But he'd gotten over it eventually. Walker had been the only one in this house who hadn't once told Graham and me that we were too young to know love.

While Graham and I had been exclusive for years,

Walker had been the playboy, stringing along girlfriend after girlfriend. But then he'd gone to college and met Mindy his junior year. *Head over heels*, that was how Nan had described it to me on one of our calls.

And now his children had his beautiful hair.

My fingers itched to touch the soft strands, but Evan and Maya would probably run away screaming *stranger danger* if I got too close.

"What?" Walker asked, his gaze darting between me and his children.

"They have your hair."

"Yep," he clipped. "Have their whole life."

Which I'd missed. The unspoken reminder clung to the air.

"I'd better get to work," he said. "Be good for Nana, guys. Love you."

"Bye, Daddy." Maya waved brightly as her older brother inhaled his cereal, saying goodbye with milk dripping down his chin.

I took a seat at the island, watching as the kids ate breakfast and Mom fussed over them, until Brooklyn arrived.

"Hi, Brookie, uh . . . Brooklyn," I said as she handed baby Bradley to Mom.

She didn't return my greeting, speaking and looking only at Mom. "He already ate, but he's been up since five thirty. He'll probably need a longer morning nap."

"No problem." Mom kissed his chubby cheek.

"See you tonight." Brooklyn kissed her son goodbye, then spun for the door.

"Have a good day," I said to her back.

She kept walking.

Nice. I was the bad guy, right? I clapped my lips shut so I wouldn't remind her that I'd reached out plenty of times to say hello and all my voicemails had gone unreturned.

Mom cooed at the baby, bouncing him on her hip. Did six-month-old babies eat cornflakes? That seemed young, but there was that third bowl at the table.

"When is Colin getting here?" Evan asked Mom.

As if Evan had conjured him with his question, the door burst open once again and running feet came our way.

My stomach dropped when a familiar mop of brown hair came into view. It was going to be hard avoiding Graham if Mom was babysitting his son every day this week.

"Hey, Evan." Colin dropped his backpack on the floor beside the others before his eyes caught on me. "Quinn!"

I gulped and waved. "H-hey."

My God, he looked like Graham. He looked so much like the boy I'd been friends with at seven. Then crushed on at twelve. Then loved at sixteen.

Graham came down the hallway and my racing heart jumped into my throat. Why did he have to look so good? Why couldn't he have grown a beer belly or a big nose over the past nine years? His white T-shirt stretched across his broad shoulders, and the sleeves fit tight around his corded biceps. His faded jeans hugged his strong thighs as they draped to his scuffed work boots.

His jaw hardened when he spotted me, and those warm eyes turned to ice.

What the fuck? What gave him the right to be so goddamn angry? He'd made his position clear all those years ago. He'd stood beside my parents after the fight.

He hadn't believed in me.

If anyone got to be mad, it was me.

Because I might have been the one to leave, but he'd abandoned me when I'd needed him most.

"Thanks for watching Colin this week, Ruby," he said, his voice gravelly and low and so frustratingly sexy.

Damn him and his appeal.

Mom ruffled Colin's hair as he sat to eat his cereal. "My pleasure. He actually makes it easier. He and Evan will entertain themselves for the most part."

"Call me if there's any trouble. I'll be here around four."

"We'll be here." Mom nodded.

"See ya, bud." Graham bent to kiss Colin's head.

"Bye, Dad."

Then Graham was gone, not sparing me another glance, like I wasn't even in the room.

He only had to wait a week and I wouldn't be.

Avoid. Seven days and counting. Now that I knew Colin would be coming over each morning, I'd sleep late or find somewhere else to be. There had to be a coffee shop within a ten-block radius of the house.

The kids seemed to inhale their cereal and were out of their chairs minutes later, begging to play outside.

"You boys make sure to include Maya," Mom told them, opening the sliding glass door for them to fly out. "Well, I guess we'll do the dishes."

"Would you like me to hold him?"

"Oh, uh . . . that's okay." She took the baby to the bouncer in the corner. "We'll let him jump around."

"Okay." I pretended like that didn't sting. Had Brooklyn told Mom under no circumstances was I allowed near her baby? Was I really such a monster?

Maybe that stagehand had been right. Maybe I was a

bitch. Maybe Mom and Brooklyn were afraid I'd rub off on the innocent.

"Can I help?" I asked as Mom opened the dishwasher.

"No, we're good. We'll just play and have fun until the kids have swimming lessons this afternoon."

Outside, the kids' laughter rang loud. Colin and Evan were chasing each other around the playhouse while Maya sat on a swing, kicking her legs.

My God, Colin was like Graham. They had the same features. The same laugh. Nan hadn't told me just how much son resembled father.

Nan had been the one to call and tell me that Graham had a baby. A boy. Everyone, including her, had kept the pregnancy a secret. At the time of her call, I'd had an airplane ticket to fly home and surprise everyone for a weekend visit. I'd saved up for months.

Then she'd called, and the minute we'd hung up, I'd ripped those tickets in half.

And I'd spent the past seven years pretending like that phone call hadn't happened. That Graham hadn't made a child with another woman.

A beautiful, sweet child who might have been mine in another life.

My headache came roaring back with a vengeance as I stared at them through the glass. The caffeine and pain pills had kicked in, but the thought of an awkward day with Mom, around Graham's tiny clone, was too much.

"Mom, can I borrow your car?" I asked, turning away from the kids.

"Uh, sure. Why?"

Because I'm suffocating. "I just wanted to explore town a little. See what's different."

"Well, I, uh . . . I need the car—"

"It's okay." I waved my hand, already walking through the room. "Never mind. I'll just take a walk."

"Quinn . . ."

She spoke, but I was already dashing upstairs to get some cash from my purse and a pair of sunglasses. I swiped a black hoodie from my suitcase and tied on my favorite pair of Chucks. I shoved my drumsticks into my back pocket, then I was gone.

The moment the door closed behind me, I let the air rush from my lungs. The tension in my shoulders eased with every step away from the house, and after a few blocks, the pain in my head was nearly erased. I wandered downtown, leisurely strolling up Main Street. Only two or three shops from my youth were still in business. Most had been replaced and renovated with kitschy stores geared toward the tourists who came flocking to Bozeman each season.

My hometown wasn't as rugged as it had once been. There was a primness to the quaint atmosphere, likely driven from the influence of outside money. But it was still home, peaceful and charming.

The air was cool and crisp, not yet hot this early on a June day. I let the sunshine warm me as I walked up one side of the street, then down the other, exploring slowly until hours had passed and I steered my feet toward home.

My phone buzzed in my pocket on the way, and I pulled it out to see a text from Harvey.

Progress?

"No, Harvey. No progress." I shoved it away without a reply.

I loved our producer, Harvey, but lately he'd been driving me insane with his constant check-ins.

Once I got home, I'd lock myself in my bedroom and attempt to write something, anything, to appease him for the rest of the week. I didn't need his stress on top of my own.

The sidewalks were empty and I hummed a melody to myself, matching its rhythm to my strides. It was crude and I only had a few notes, but it was a start. While Mom was at the kids' swimming lessons, hopefully I could tinker with it on the piano.

I hummed it over and over, committing it to memory by the time I reached home.

"Hello?" I called without a reply as I wandered to the kitchen.

Mom had left me a note on the island.

Went to the park to play before swimming. Be back by three thirty.

I sighed and went to the piano in the living room, glad for the solitude. The Yamaha upright was clean but seemed lonely. It was no longer the focal point in the living room, having been shoved into the far corner to make room for a larger TV. The tall, black back held photos on top. The bench seat that slid under the keys looked to have been hiding under there since I'd left. Didn't anyone play anymore?

I sat down and raised the lid, running my fingertips across the smooth ivory. A shiver ran down my spine. There was magic here. There was music. It danced in my hands as I splayed them over the keys and pressed down slowly to play C major.

There was a tang to the chord. A slight hitch that reminded me of countless hours of practice. This piano didn't have the smooth tone of my concert grand, but I liked that it gave the notes character and a bite.

Its edge fit my mood and I dove in, playing song after song. My eyes drifted closed as the melodies filled the house and consumed my mind.

I didn't bother flushing out my new song in favor of the old, familiar songs I'd written with Jonas and Nixon in the early days. We'd had so much freedom and fun back then, so I played the songs that had never found their way onto an album. The songs the label had deemed not within our brand. They were rough and raw and fun. They reminded me of simpler times. Of easy laughter and gigantic dreams.

So lost in the music, I didn't realize I had an audience until a throat cleared behind me.

I spun around, gasping, and found my father's face. "Oh. H-hi."

"That was . . ." His expression stiffened, only slightly, but I'd seen that look enough to notice the censure.

"That was what?" *Loud. Harsh. Noise.* Those had been his favorite words to describe my music.

"That was, uh . . . different."

Fair enough. He wasn't wrong.

Dad walked to the couch and took a seat, his shoulders slumping forward like the weight on them was too much to hold up any longer.

The clock beside him showed it was nearly four. I'd been playing for hours. "Mom must have run long with swimming lessons, huh?"

"I'm sure she'll be here soon."

"How are you?" I asked.

He lifted his head and gave me a sad smile. "I wish your Nan was here to help make this easier."

Me. He meant to help make it easier with me. Nan had

always been our go-between and mediator, long before I'd moved to Seattle.

"I wish she was here too," I confessed. So, so much.

"I met with her attorney today and went through her will."

"Alone?" If Mom had been watching the kids, who'd been with Dad?

"Walker and Brooklyn came with me," he said. "I stopped by to see if you were here but . . ."

I'd been on my walk, and he hadn't bothered to call.

For nine years, my grandmother had called me every week without fail, sometimes numerous times in a week. After those first three weeks, my mother had found a way to dial my number, breaking her silence.

But my father hadn't spoken to me in nine years. Until I'd walked into his home yesterday, I hadn't heard his voice.

All because I'd refused his cage.

God, what I wouldn't do for a drum kit for my sticks. I wanted to spend hours drumming out the anger and frustration. Because the only other thing that would help ease this resentment toward my father was a phone call with Nan.

Knuckles rapped on the front door before it opened and Graham stepped inside. "Just came to pick up Colin."

"They aren't back quite yet." Dad waved Graham into the living room. "Come on in."

As if I didn't have enough emotional turmoil to deal with, I also got to put up with Graham. I aimed my eyes at the floor, not wanting to witness his glare as it burned into my profile.

"I'm glad you're both here," Dad said. "I was just about to tell Quinn, but I went through Nan's last requests today.

She's outlined some specifics for the service, and she's asked that you perform."

A lump formed in my throat. "Is there something in particular she wanted me to play?"

"No, uh . . . sorry. Not just you. Together. She'd like you both to play together."

"What?" My eyes whipped up to Graham leaning against the wall.

His shirt was damp with sweat and his jeans smudged with sawdust. If he was affected by the request, he gave nothing away. "No problem."

No problem? This was a huge, damn problem. How was I supposed to play at my grandmother's funeral beside Graham? Alone would have been hard enough.

Now avoiding Graham for the week would be nearly impossible.

And somehow, I had a feeling that was exactly what Nan had intended.

CHAPTER FOUR

GRAHAM

"Heard you got roped into playing at Nan's funeral," Walker said as he positioned a two-by-four stud on the wall we were framing.

"Yeah." I barked a laugh, driving a nail into place with the gun. Nan made my mother's meddling look amateur. Hell, even after her death she'd made sure that the spoon in her pot was still stirring. "It'll be fine. How are you holding up?"

He lowered his arm, nail gun in hand. "She was ninety-one, but . . . it feels like she was taken too soon."

The same thought had crossed my mind the morning Mom had called to tell me of Nan's passing. We should have had more time.

Nan had died in her sleep. There'd been no signs of failing health or diminished mental capacity. Nan's mind had been as shrewd at ninety-one as mine was at twenty-seven—probably sharper.

But for Nan's sake, I was glad the end of her days had

come without pain or suffering. It was bittersweet, knowing it was exactly how she would have wanted to go. In the comfort of the home she'd lived in for over fifty years, surrounded by photographs of her children, grandchildren and great-grandchildren. I was fortunate enough to have been a family member, Colin too, though our tie had been by love, not blood.

Nan Montgomery would be missed.

"I'm sorry." I put a gloved hand on Walker's shoulder. "If I can do anything, let me know."

"Same for you. She was as much your grandmother as she was mine."

My own grandparents had passed when I was young, and Nan had filled that void as I'd grown older. Mostly because I'd blended so well into the Montgomery family, much like Colin did today.

Walker and I had been best friends as kids, neighbors and buddies. Though he was two years older, the age gap hadn't stopped us from playing together at recess or going to the same functions in high school. And where we'd gone, Quinn had followed.

The one and only time Walker and I had fought had been because of Quinn. One day, I'd noticed that our shadow wasn't just another buddy, but a girl. A damn pretty one at that. Walker had seen the glint in my eye and had warned me away.

But it hadn't done any good. I'd been too far gone.

It hadn't been easy for Walker to accept that I'd had more than lusty intentions for his sister, but once I'd proved my motives were pure—mostly pure—he hadn't stood in our way. He'd gone so far as to drive Quinn and me to the movie theater before I'd earned my driver's license when we hadn't wanted our parents to chauffeur us to a date.

Walker hadn't bitched when my Friday nights with him had been cut short so I could spend time with my girlfriend. Though, he'd been too busy chasing girls of his own to mind when Quinn and I would disappear in my ramshackle and rusty Chevy.

It was Quinn's fault that I'd had to sell that truck. I'd loved it, but she'd ruined it. There'd been too many memories in that cab to live with daily.

And it hadn't been safe for a car seat.

"So . . ." Walker lifted his gun and set a nail. "How's it seeing Quinn?"

"You tell me. She's your sister."

"She ghosted us." He pounded a fist on the board to make sure it was secure, using a little more force than necessary. "And that's not what I meant."

"Yeah," I muttered, adjusting the ball cap on my head to stall. Keeping Quinn locked away in a dark corner of my mind had been more difficult than I'd expected. I'd hit my thumb twice with a hammer this week, so distracted by her image that I'd lost track of my senses. "She looks good. Looks like she's doing well."

Walker raised an eyebrow.

"I'm not interested in starting things up with your sister. She'll be gone again in a flash."

Less than a week, if she left after the funeral as I expected her to do.

"I just want to get through this week," I said. "Say goodbye to Nan."

Say goodbye to Quinn.

Maybe after she leaves this time, I'd finally be able to send some old ghosts to their graves.

Quinn hadn't been at her parents' place this morning when I'd dropped off Colin. That, or she'd stayed away from the kitchen to avoid a run-in with me. Like yesterday, I'd been prepared to face her when I'd walked into the house. My expression had been schooled so she wouldn't know just how much power she held over my emotions.

It had been wasted effort, which was probably for the best. I'd save my energy to guard against her this afternoon at rehearsal.

"I need to take off around four," I told Walker. "That all right?"

"Fine by me. I'll be dead by then anyway." He rolled his shoulders. "I'm ready to be done framing this place."

"Same." I shot in the final nail, then went to the stack of boards to pick up another stud. Board after board, nail after nail, we worked side by side until my arm was a limp noodle and an early lunch beckoned a much-needed break.

Walker and I sat down on the subfloor and cracked open our lunch pails.

We were framing out a new build in the foothills of the Bridger Mountains. This place would be enormous when we were done, nearly ten-thousand square feet, and the cost of the windows and doors alone was more than I'd spent to buy my entire three-bedroom house.

On some projects, we'd subcontract out the framing, but since this project was our cash for the year, we were doing it ourselves, making sure it was perfect. Walker and I had started Hayes-Montgomery Construction four years ago and had made a reputation for ourselves in the area. We did high-quality work and delivered keys to homeowners on time. Normally, we came in on budget too because a satisfied customer meant referrals, and referrals were our bread and butter.

I'd dropped out of college at Montana State after Colin was born. I'd managed to stay in school for a month as a single dad, but sleepless nights and erratic schedules didn't lend well to study and when my first round of Fs had come in, I'd called it quits.

With the housing boom in the Gallatin Valley and a labor shortage, construction had been the obvious choice for income. Along the way, it had become a passion too, crafting and building from the ground up with my own hands.

For two years I'd worked for a local builder, learning and soaking up everything he'd teach me. When Walker had graduated from MSU with a business degree, he'd planned to find a job with a bank, but entry-level positions paid shit and desk jobs weren't his style. So he'd hired on beside me to work construction.

Four years ago, we'd decided to start our business. Hayes-Montgomery Construction was smaller than the outfit where we'd been working. Our vision was for a family company, the two of us along with one or two trusted employees who we never had actually hired. We built custom homes, focusing on quality not quantity.

Jobs had been hard to come by that first year, but we'd stuck it out. Mindy worked to help keep Walker's household afloat, and my parents had loaned me money when things had been tight.

Then we'd caught our break. Walker and I had been out drinking a beer with one of his friends from college. The guy had become a real estate agent and found some success in town. He'd wanted us to build his own house plus a real-estate office on his property, so we had. When one of his wealthy clients couldn't find the right home but had landed on the right property, Walker's real estate buddy had recommended us as the builder.

One house for one satisfied customer had led to another, then another, then another. Neither of us could believe it when we'd received a call from a well-known architecture firm last winter to do this Bridger project that would be valued at over five million dollars when it was complete.

Walker and I were looking at one hell of a payday, clearing six figures each for our labor.

This would be more money than I'd ever had, and every dime was going toward paying off my mortgage, then my truck, then stockpiling Colin's college fund.

Our families knew how important this job was for our business, so they were helping. Colin was enrolled in a few summer camps and he'd be participating in the Vacation Bible School at church, but during the weeks when he was free, Ruby had agreed to babysit. Nan had watched him the week after school got out.

Colin had loved Nan with a wild passion, so much so that it reminded me of how Quinn had been with her grandmother. Their relationship had always been easy and full of laughter. They'd both loved music and rocking out to the stereo cranked too loud. It had been exactly the same with my son.

It was Nan who'd insisted I buy Colin a drum set last Christmas, threatening to do it herself if Santa dropped the ball.

"When I pick up Evan and Maya, want me to grab Colin too?" Walker asked before taking a drink of water.

"If you don't mind. I'll come over and grab him when I'm done at the church."

"Sounds good." He shoved up from the floor, ready to get back to work.

I wiped my mouth of the crumbs from my peanut butter and jelly sandwich and chased the bite down with the cold dregs of my morning coffee. Even after a break, sweat dripped down my back. By the afternoon, I'd reek and would have to swing home for a shower before meeting Quinn.

Though maybe if I arrived dripping like a pig and smelling like one too, Quinn would stop staring at me with those stormy eyes like she was expecting to find the boy she'd left behind.

That boy had vanished the moment he'd become a father.

Walker and I put in a hard afternoon before calling it quits. I went home to take a cold shower and change into clean clothes. He went to do the same, then pick up the kids.

Colin would be more than happy to spend a few added hours with Evan. Those two were as close as their fathers had been at that age. The only difference was they didn't live next door.

Clean and cool, I climbed into my truck and drove the couple of miles to church, where Quinn and I had agreed to practice before Nan's funeral on Saturday. With the window rolled down, I let the hot breeze dry my hair, something I'd been meaning to cut for weeks.

The lot beside the church was nearly empty when I parked, and I let myself into the building through the side door, breathing in the smell of wood, must and weak coffee.

Like the scent, the church building hadn't changed in decades, though we were getting new faces all the time. The stuffy, traditional views on right versus wrong were beginning to bend and break.

It was about damn time.

The labyrinth of hallways leading to the sanctuary were empty, and when I reached the vast, open room, it was dark except for the light shining through the stained-glass windows. The pews were empty of all but a few Bibles strewn on the wooden seats. The wall tapestry above the pulpit was a green felt appliqued with pastel summer blooms of irises, lilacs and pansies.

Someone had swapped out the spring banner for summer since I'd been two Sundays ago. I'd missed service last week because I'd been at home, staring at a wall, trying to figure out how the fuck I was going to face Quinn at the airport.

And there she was, sitting at the piano on stage. Her long hair trailed down her back in a smooth, shining sheet of gold. Her hands were poised above the keys, but she didn't play. She stared down at her hovering fingers and sat motionless.

Would she play? I lingered by the doors to the sanctuary, leaning against the wooden frame. She looked so intently at the piano it was like she wanted to play but couldn't break past an invisible barrier keeping her fingers from touching the keys.

Play. Just one note.

"Hi, Graham." Bradley appeared by my side; his voice low enough that Quinn didn't hear.

He probably could have shouted and been unable to break her concentration. Her hands remained frozen and her spine rigid as she fought her internal war.

"It's nice to see her there again," Bradley said.

I hummed, though not in agreement. Quinn had never fit in that space. She'd played countless times on that piano, beautifully and effortlessly. And she'd been bored out of her mind. The music here wasn't her style, or at least, it hadn't been. Maybe she'd feel differently if she knew how things had progressed lately.

Not that she'd stick around to find out.

"Did you think about what you'll play?" Bradley asked. "I can get you a list of Nan's favorite hymns."

"I don't think that was what Nan had in mind."

"No, you're probably right. Though that music doesn't seem quite right for a funeral."

That music. Meaning, Quinn's music. It was loud and most of the lyrics dripping with innuendo, but it was hers. It was Quinn's.

"There's millions of people around the world who would love *that music* at their funeral. Nan included." I shoved off the door frame, not sparing him another glance.

Bradley had come a long way from the pastor he'd once been, but despite his sermons on tolerance and keeping an open mind, he had a blind spot when it came to his daughter. And damn, the man was stubborn.

My footsteps were muffled on the carpet and I was twenty feet away from Quinn when she dropped her hands to the piano. Her shoulders curled in on themselves.

"Hey."

She looked up and her face was etched with anguish, like the piano keys were made of needles. Her hands flew off the keys, finding safety in her lap. "Hi."

I stepped up on stage and sat on the bench at her side, my hip forcing hers to scoot over. She moved so far away that one leg was completely off the seat and there was a visible inch between us.

I set my keys on the music desk, beside a pair of drumsticks, and put my fingers where hers had been. "I'll play piano."

"Thanks," she whispered.

"What do you want to play?" I asked.

"I was thinking 'Amazing Grace' or 'How Great Thou Art.' Nan always liked those two."

"What?" I gaped. "No. What song of *yours* do you want to play?"

"I don't think we should play one of mine. I think that will only cause problems."

"Nan would have wanted one of yours."

"She loved hymns too."

"How about 'Torchlight'?"

"I don't think a song about sex and heartache is going to be well-received by anyone on Saturday."

"Who cares?" I barked. "This isn't their damn funeral."

She winced.

"Sorry." *Fuck.* I took a long breath and gentled my tone. "I think Nan would have wanted something you wrote."

"And I think she just wanted to have us sharing this bench seat." She wasn't wrong.

"Well, while we're here, we might as well sing something she loved."

"A hymn she loved."

"Quinn—"

"Graham, please"—she held up her hands—"I'm just trying to make it through this week."

And then she'd be gone.

I'd gone to bat for her with Bradley for no damn reason.

Quinn wasn't going to ruffle any feathers while she was here. She wasn't going to push her parents or confront the past. Their rift would stay as wide as ever.

"Fine." I pounded the first chord of "Amazing Grace," making her jump as it reverberated through the hall. The pounding didn't stop there. It was maybe the angriest, most rushed version of the classic hymn played in history.

Damn it.

The last note faded and her eyes were glued to my hands, just like they'd been through the whole song.

I didn't want to do this. I didn't want to sit up here with Quinn and sing a song that was a farewell to a woman we'd both loved. The truth was, it didn't matter what song we played. This wouldn't be easy.

This time when I played the first chord, it was soft and gentle. The piano's clear chime eased the tension from my shoulders and the frustration melted away.

Quinn's voice joined in, hesitant at first. She closed her eyes and lifted her chin, singing the words she'd memorized long, long ago when Ruby had taught us both to play.

This was where we'd had our lessons. From kindergarten to fifth grade, Quinn and I had spent our Thursday afternoons at this keyboard with Ruby, taking turns playing the scales and songs we'd practiced separately all week.

Ruby had wanted the quiet of the sanctuary instead of teaching us at her house, and she'd loved the acoustics of this sanctuary. So we'd play, and we'd sing. The lessons and practice had never seemed like a chore, for either Quinn or me.

Then one day, Quinn began writing her own songs. She'd play them for me when her mother was out of the room, self-conscious that they were different, faster and louder, than the music Ruby had preferred.

Every song she'd written had captivated me, like the girl herself.

Quinn's voice became more confident with each pass of the chorus. Her singing was magic, smooth and soulful with the slightest rasp when she let the emotion show. It consumed her. Did she even feel me beside her as she sang?

Quinn Montgomery had always been destined for greatness. It was in her soul and it came out through her music. Quinn's music was this enormous, living, untamable beast that she'd unleashed upon the world. But it shined especially bright when she was singing.

So why didn't she sing for Hush Note? The question had bothered me from their first album and had continued to plague me since. She'd settled behind the drums and seemed content in her place there. Had that been by choice? Did her bandmates even know how much of a waste it was to have her sitting in the back?

I let muscle memory take over as we reached the last part of the song. My mind was so lost in her voice that if I thought about what my fingers were supposed to be doing, they'd falter. So I listened and didn't sing along. And when the last note was done, I stood from that bench and walked for the door.

"Graham?" she called to my back.

"That's . . . it's good enough for today." I had to get the hell out of this place. I had to get the hell away from the woman who'd shattered my heart. Because if I listened to her sing once more, I'd forgive her for leaving me.

My anger, something I'd been nursing for a long time, was the only thing keeping my broken heart whole. I'd clutch it close all week and add fuel to its fire.

Quinn Montgomery had always been destined for greatness.

She'd leave again without a backward glance. She was too big for this small place. That was a fact I hadn't realized or acknowledged as a younger man. But not this time.

This time when she left, I'd be prepared to watch her go.

CHAPTER FIVE

QUINN

One tear streaked down my cheek.

I swiped it away, but another took its place.

This church. I hated this church.

Not for what it represented, my beliefs and faith had always been my own, but for the memories.

I hated this piano. I hated that I was scared of an instrument that used to bring me so much joy, and now it was painful to touch.

How many years had I spent in this seat, side by side with Graham as we'd practiced and performed? How many laughs had we shared in this spot? This used to be my favorite place in the world. A place where I could sing and play.

Some kids dreaded piano lessons, but practicing had always been the best part of my week. Performances had been easy here when I could look into the congregation and find Nan's bright eyes waiting and her hot-pink lips stretched in a smile.

She used to sit in the same seat every Sunday. Her space

was in the middle swath of pews, second row, first seat in from the right. Who would sit there now? Maybe it would stay empty for a time, but eventually someone would take it. Someday, even in a congregation of people who love her, she'd be forgotten.

The tears streamed as the dam I'd built against the grief broke. My shoulders shook, and the immense sadness of losing my grandmother, my cheerleader, my confidant, came rushing out.

Dad was somewhere in this building. The acoustics from the hall would reverberate toward his office, and I didn't want him to know I was breaking down. So only when my face was buried in my hands to muffle the noise did I let loose the sobs clawing at my throat.

I didn't want his comfort, not in this. If he found me crying, he'd do his duty and offer me some sage words of wisdom. But I didn't need a pastor today, and I'd given up a long time ago on my father.

"Shit."

I dropped my hands and my head whirled at the deep, muttered curse, finding Graham standing beside the stage.

Yeah. Shit. I would have preferred Dad over Graham.

"What?" I barked, drying my face with angry swipes. I should have saved the crying for my bedroom tonight so no one would have caught me unaware.

"Forgot my keys." He pointed to the music desk, where sure enough a bundle of silver and brass keys rested.

Graham stepped on stage, swiped them off the ledge and turned. The movement sent another wave of his soap and spicy scent wafting my way.

That fucking soap. Was he trying to torture me? He must have showered before coming here because the smell was fresh. In all these years, he hadn't changed his brand of soap, and the onslaught of memories that came with it were excruciating.

Him, sitting in his truck to drive me to school each morning. Him, standing beside my locker before second period, waiting to walk me to class. Him, coming over after football practice to study.

Graham still smelled like that boy I'd loved.

But the boy, the love, was gone.

He stepped off the stage and I held my breath, wanting him to disappear and leave me to my misery, but he paused. His shoulders twisted. He looked back. "Are you okay?"

I opened my mouth to lie, but the truth escaped. "No."

He stood there, his body conveying his conflict, and debated whether I was worth another moment. His feet were aimed toward the door, but his shoulders were poised to stay.

Before we'd broken up, Graham would have never let me cry alone.

The sigh he let slip free sounded a lot like *son of a bitch*. Maybe it was history that made him stay, maybe it was obligation to a friend of his family's, but his feet lost the battle and he came up on stage, sitting down on the bench at my side.

His arm grazed mine and our thighs touched, but neither of us spoke.

The gesture was enough.

The air in the room swirled from the vents and a soft hum drifted over our heads. Whoever had played during Sunday's service had left a booklet of sheet music behind, and I kept my eyes fixed on the black and white.

What was there to say? It was much too late for *I'm sorry*. The awkwardness between us was crushing. Talking to Graham used to be so natural. We'd always been able to trust each other. To open up and share our fears and truths.

Before.

I was seconds away from making a lame excuse and bolting when my phone rang. I grabbed it off the piano and saw Nixon's face on the screen. The photo was ages old, from one of our first tours. His face had changed since then. Since he'd discovered rock stars didn't have a hard time getting booze or drugs or women.

"Your *bandmate?*" Graham gritted out the last word, his lip curled in disgust.

I silenced the call and shot him a scowl. Graham didn't get to be rude about Nix or Jonas. "My *best friend.*"

Graham stiffened, maybe because that title had once belonged to him.

My phone dinged with a voicemail moments later. Knowing Nixon, it was some sort of song meant to cheer me up. Probably a dorky jingle he'd have made up on the spot. The words would rhyme and be epically cheesy.

Curiosity won out. I needed a laugh, that and the tension between Graham and me was nearly unbearable, so I opened my phone and went to the voicemail, hitting play.

QUINN, Quinn, Quinn.
   Quinn, Quinn, Quinn.
   I'm in Ha-wa-ii.
   It's warm outside, the beach is hot.
   But not as hot as me. Hey!
   Quinn, Quinn, Quinn.
   Quinn, Quinn, Quinn.
   Quinn Montgomery.

I'm making bad decisions. Call me back.
Then you can lecture me. Hey!

"JINGLE BELLS." That bastard knew it would be stuck in my head for the rest of the day.

I giggled. "He leaves messages like that to cheer me up."

Graham grunted, unimpressed.

Why was he still sitting here? Clearly, this wasn't comfortable for him—for both of us. So why not leave?

He seemed to hate it when I spoke so maybe if I continued talking, it would chase him away, and he could go hate me somewhere else.

"There was one time when I was sick with the flu and I was sure that I was dying, Nixon left me a two-minute voicemail set to 'Silent Night.'" I still had it saved on my phone. "He always picks Christmas carols for his jingles."

"You and Nan loved your carols," Graham said quietly, his fingers skimming over the piano keys.

"Yeah." Nan would have loved Nixon's messages. Like me, she would have voted in favor of any politician who would have campaigned for year-round Christmas carols.

"Does, uh, Nixon"—Graham swallowed hard at the name—"write songs for your band? Because that was . . ."

"Awful?" I laughed. "No. Sometimes he'll contribute a line or two, but mostly Jonas writes the lyrics. Nix and I write the music."

Graham kept his eyes forward, his frame relaxing from its rigid posture. His fingers kept trailing across the keys. Up and down. Left and right.

He had great hands. His fingers were long and his palms wide. Those hands, a man's hands, would drive a woman wild. If it was my skin he were tracing, not the keys, I'd—

Whoa. Don't go there. Opening the mental door to Graham, or sex with Graham, would be spectacularly reckless.

"Do you still play on Sundays?" I asked to get my mind off those hands.

"Twice a month."

Nan had made it her mission to keep me apprised of everyone's life here in Bozeman. She'd give me regular updates on Walker, since I only spoke to my brother every three or four months. She'd make sure I knew how Brooklyn was doing, since my sister and I rarely talked. And Nan would tell me about Mom, Dad and each of her great-grand-children.

But the one person Nan had seldom spoken about was Graham.

She'd told me about his son, and I think she must have felt my heart break through the phone that day. Updates afterward had been purely coincidental, like when she'd told me how Walker and Graham had started a business together. Nan had been so proud of them both.

Had Graham turned a blind eye to my life, like I'd turned a deaf ear to his?

It was odd not to know him. It was hard to realize that Graham was now a stranger.

Nine years was a long time to forget someone, except I hadn't really forgotten Graham. I remembered every word of our fight. I remembered how it had crushed me when he'd taken my father's side. I remembered the devastation on his face when he'd dropped me at the airport and I walked away.

I had to walk away.

At eighteen, I'd known without a shred of doubt that if I didn't get out of Bozeman, I'd stay forever. I'd stay to be smothered and miserable. A part of my soul would have died here, in this very room, with Graham at my side and my family smiling on.

I refused to apologize for chasing my dreams.

How I'd left, how I'd ended us, hadn't been right, but I'd had to walk away.

"How did you meet?" Graham's question caught me off guard and my gaze swung to his profile.

He had such a straight nose and long, sooty eyelashes. How many times had I traced that nose with my fingertip? How many times had I ran the pad of my thumb over those lashes? The beard on his face changed so much of his appearance, but so many features were the same. Graham's golden eyes shifted my way, reminding me that he'd asked a question.

"Nixon and Jonas? We met at a bar." I lowered my voice, not ashamed of this story but knowing that this was not the place where it would be widely appreciated. Because bars were not an appropriate place for a pastor's daughter to frequent. "College was . . . different than I'd anticipated."

I'd been offered a scholarship for the music program at the University of Washington. My high school band teacher, the one who'd given me my first pair of drumsticks, had gone there himself and he'd made it seem so exciting. College was supposed to have been my adventure.

But one month into my freshman year, I knew school wasn't the right path for me. Only two of my classes had been within the music department. The others were for math, biology and English. I'd hated every moment, which my grades reflected.

So I quit. I forfeited my scholarship and moved off campus.

It was the best decision of my life.

"I moved out of the dorms and into this hole of an apartment. My roommates were these two other girls, sophomores I'd met through a music class. Another girl who was supposed to live with them decided to leave Seattle, so they were short on rent. I moved into the spare room and found a job as a cocktail waitress at a bar three blocks away. Jonas was already working there. Nix started a month after me."

The three of us had bonded as the only employees in the bar under the age of twenty-one. We couldn't mix drinks and work behind the bar, so after our shifts waiting tables, while the other staffers were unwinding with a cocktail, we'd hang out beside the stage.

"The bar was known for its music. On Friday and Saturday nights, the owners would pay to bring in a band, but Thursdays were open mic night. Jonas used to sing a lot. Covers mostly. He'd draw crowds bigger than the paid bands would, and the owners loved it because he was free entertainment."

I would never forget those nights, working and listening to Jonas sing. He had a smooth voice but could pull off raspy and growl when it was needed to convey emotion. His range was incredible and the power in his vocals was unmistakable.

I'd only ever heard one voice that I liked better.

Graham's.

"The three of us were working together one night, about six months after I'd quit school. It was a Wednesday, and the bar was dead. Nix was on stage, messing around on a guitar. One of the bartenders told Jonas to go sing along."

I stood back, watching them toy with a Stone Temple

Pilots song, and wondered why the hell was I watching when what they needed was a drummer.

"I took off my apron, went up on stage and joined in." I grabbed ahold of my dream and had been hanging on with an iron fist ever since. "It grew from there. Soon we were the Friday night band. We were making music like crazy, writing all the time. The girls I was living with got annoyed by my late-night schedule, so I moved out and into Nixon's apartment. Jonas would come over whenever we weren't working and we'd just . . . write music. All night long."

There'd been no expectations other than loving what we wrote. There'd been no studio timeline or pressure to top the charts. Our music had been untainted by fame.

I was still proud of everything we'd written since, but the freedom to create seemed to be slowly diminishing. There were days when I felt like we were being walled into a room, brick by brick.

If the music dried up, if we had nothing to give the label, would they let us out? Or would we die in that room?

"Then what?" Graham asked.

"Luck." That's all fame was—luck and working hard not to screw it up. "We were in the right place at the right time. We got a gig on a Saturday night to play for a private event. It was a sixteenth birthday party for a kid whose dad had more money than he knew what to do with. The parents hired us and chartered a ferry boat to cruise around the sound. One of the guests, a friend of the father's, was Harvey Hammel."

Not many bands were able to get an hour of captive listening time with one of those most successful music producers in the business. Hell, the three of us hadn't known who he was other than a guest of the party who'd lingered close to the stage.

When he'd introduced himself at the end of our set and complimented the one original song we'd snuck into the lineup, Jonas had nearly fainted.

Harvey had seen our potential, or so he'd said. Maybe he had liked how moldable we'd been. How easily we'd all taken instruction and input. Regardless, he'd taken us under his wing. He'd chosen to give us his expertise and experience, making Hush Note the giant we were today.

"After we signed with Harvey, things just took off. He helped us polish our debut album. He got us a deal with the record label. He spent hours and hours with us in the studio, picking songs that would balance the album but still show our range. The first single did well. The second . . . was an explosion."

Harvey deserved a lot of credit for our success, but he was never one to take more credit than was owed. We were talented. Harvey would be the first to tell us that if it hadn't been him, another producer would have snatched us up. Because Jonas and Nixon and me on stage . . . together, we were magic.

Something I doubted Graham wanted to hear.

"Do you still like it?" he asked.

"I love the music. When things click, it's a feeling like no other. The rest has been an interesting ride. We've all changed."

"How?" he asked.

I gave him a sideways glance. What had sparked this sudden interest in Hush Note? For a guy who'd shut off our songs in the truck and hadn't had much to say to me since I'd arrived, why did he want to know?

But I wasn't going to ask. I liked talking to Graham.

Too much.

Because once he'd been my safe place.

"Social media is hard," I said. "That wasn't a thing when we were starting, but it adds a layer of stress. Or I guess I should say it takes away a layer of anonymity, which is stressful. People want to see our lives. They want to know where we vacation and who we spend time with. There's the tabloids and the press. The scandals always make a splash."

"What scandals?"

I lifted a shoulder. "Jonas was a playboy. He's gorgeous and talented. Women flocked and he used to revel in their affections. I mean, Nixon gets around, but Jonas as the front man was always in the spotlight. In the beginning, some chick would get her feelings hurt when he cast her aside and it would inevitably cause drama. He's not like that anymore. He was just searching for the right person."

Kira was everything Jonas had needed in his life. She filled the hole in his heart, and so did their daughter Vivi.

"And Nix?" Graham motioned to my phone.

Nixon, if he didn't change, would shatter my heart.

"Nix is lost. On top of unhealthy relationships with women, he runs away from the past and into the arms of alcohol and drugs."

But the bastard was so goddamn obstinate, he wouldn't admit he needed help. He rarely went to his childhood home in New York, and though I couldn't fault him for that, he'd never confided in me about what had driven him away in the first place. To my knowledge, Jonas didn't know either.

Nix was fighting a war with his demons alone, and they were kicking his ass.

"Hmm." Graham hummed. "And you? What's your scandal?"

You.

My scandal was my solitude. Some speculated the reason I was never photographed with a man was because I was in love with Nixon or Jonas. Every year that passed, every hit that climbed the charts to number one, made my single status became more and more interesting.

The truly desperate tabloids liked to paint Nixon and me as a couple. They'd speculate that our "secret" relationship was tearing Hush Note apart. There was a time when they'd painted all three of us in a love triangle.

But the truth was, there were no romantic relationships in my life.

Maybe because I'd left my heart with the man on this bench.

"There's no scandal with me."

Graham's eyes narrowed, catching me in the lie. Maybe he'd read some of those tabloids. Maybe he thought they were true.

Doubtful. Graham didn't seem like he'd spent much time thinking about me since I'd left.

"The worst people say about me is that I'm the bitch," I told him. "That's normally how I'm portrayed. Maybe there's some truth to it. We get a lot of people around us on a tour and everyone wants to be your friend. The bitch helps scare away those who aren't genuine."

Guarding myself ensured I wouldn't be hurt.

Graham's attention shifted to the piano, his eyebrows coming together like he was thinking over everything I'd told him. "Should we practice tomorrow?"

I nodded. "Meet here at the same time?"

"Sure." He made a move to stand, but I put my hand on his arm.

"Wait."

His eyes locked with mine, sending a jolt through my veins. The heat of his skin seeped into my bones, and I couldn't pull my hand away.

"Why'd you ask?" I whispered. "About the band?" *About me?*

Graham jerked his arm from my touch and stood, taking one long stride away as his eyes turned to granite. "You traded your family—me—for your band. I guess I wanted to know what I was worth. Sounds like a womanizer and a drug addict."

I flinched, his words a slap across the cheek.

His parting shot hit dead center, and he strode out of the sanctuary, keys in hand.

Graham had asked me my story so he could have ammunition. Something to hold against me. My hands balled into fists and I slammed them onto the keys, the sound harsh and angry. A scream burned in my chest, begging to be set free, but I shoved it deep. Then I stood and got the fuck out of this sanctuary where Graham's scent lingered in the air.

One song. We had to get through one song. One funeral. Then I was going back to a life where Graham Hayes was just another painful memory.

Maybe this trip would be good for me after all.

My heart would have some new bruises when I went home to Seattle.

And I'd pour every ounce of this hurt into our next album.

CHAPTER SIX

GRAHAM

"Hi, Quinn!" Colin waved wildly as he ran down the aisle between pews.

She was on stage, at the piano, and her eyes widened as she took him in.

It was the cowardly thing to do, bringing my kid to our practice. But damn it, I couldn't sit on that seat beside her with no one else in the room. With Colin here, I wouldn't be tempted to ask her personal questions. Her life was none of my business and getting involved would only cause trouble.

Yesterday had proven that. I'd asked questions. I'd eaten up every word of her answers. And a part of me had softened toward her. I'd let a fraction of my resentment go, and when she'd touched me, I'd almost caved.

Her lips, soft and pink, had been so alluring. Her nose ring was shamelessly sexy. And her hand on my skin had been thrilling. I'd almost lost my fucking mind and given in to that magnetic pull.

Quinn hadn't deserved my asshole remark. We'd both be better off if she hated me.

Besides, she clearly had something going on with her *best friend* Nixon. I had no interest in competing for her attention. My life was complicated enough as it was. I had my business to run and a son to raise. Rock star drama was not my thing.

"Dad said you guys are playing a church song." Colin plopped down on the bench beside Quinn. His knuckles immediately went to the keys and he rapped out "Chopsticks."

We'd started piano lessons with Ruby about six months ago, but he didn't love them, not like he loved the drums, so I hadn't pushed. When he asked me if he could play football instead, I'd agreed. If he wanted to learn piano someday, Ruby said she'd be happy to teach him. But I'd had a front-row seat to the disaster that could happen when you forced one type of art upon someone passionate about another.

Bradley's insistence that Quinn uphold a certain image, that she'd play certain music, was the reason she'd left town. No way in hell I'd ever risk ruining the relationship with my son over something so trivial.

"Why aren't you playing a Hush Note song?" Colin asked her.

"Um . . . it's complicated."

"Why?" He'd ask over and over until he got a real answer.

"There's going to be a lot of church friends of Nan's here. I don't think most of them like Hush Note music."

"Yeah." Colin shrugged. "They're kind of old. And you don't have Nixon or Jonas. But Dad could sing."

Quinn's gaze lifted, pleading for me to intervene. But my son was right.

What Nan would have wanted was a Hush Note song. "We could take a Hush Note song and sing it as an acoustic."

"No." She frowned. "Let's just stick with 'Amazing Grace.'"

I stepped on stage, nudging Colin out of my seat. "Find a pew, buddy."

"Okay." He jumped off the stage and shuffled to our regular Sunday seats. His was normally right in front of Nan's and as he sat, he glanced over his shoulder, giving her space a long stare.

It was Wednesday. Nearly a week since she'd passed. So far, he hadn't asked me much about her death. We hadn't talked about the funeral because . . . well, no one was talking about it.

Walker had gone into overdrive at the Bridger project, working so hard I'd had to push myself to keep up as we'd framed a bedroom and bathroom today. My parents were avoiding the funeral subject because Ruby was avoiding the funeral subject. When I'd dropped Colin off with her this morning, she'd acted like today was any normal day, not one where she'd be finalizing details with the florist and caterer.

But in the church, Nan's passing was impossible to ignore.

On Saturday, we'd dress in black and pay our respects. We'd say goodbye to a woman who'd not soon be forgotten. A woman my son would remember for years to come.

If all I could do to repay her for the love she'd given Colin and me was convince her granddaughter to play a Hush Note song on Saturday, I'd do my best. Yesterday I'd given up on the song without a fight.

Not today.

"'Torchlight.'" I put my hands on the keys. "Want me to

fumble through this or do you want to play since you actually wrote the song?"

Quinn glared. "I don't want—"

"So I'll play. What key?" It was B-flat. I knew the song and could play the melody in my sleep, but I butchered the opening notes intentionally, baiting Quinn to take over. Maybe what she needed to play was some fire and a shove. I hit three wrong chords in a row. "Oops."

"Move over." Her hands pushed mine off the keys, and her elbow jabbed mine so I'd shift on the bench. "Do you know the lyrics or should I write them down for you?"

"I can manage." I'd played this song a million times, not that I'd tell her it was on my phone.

It was the only Hush Note song I'd ever purchased for myself because it was the one song that was undeniably Quinn. Her boy Jonas had written the lyrics, but she was there, in the pulse of the bass drum and the beat of the snare. She was there in the melody, even if she wasn't playing the guitar or singing the vocals.

On the long nights when I was worn out but couldn't find sleep—the nights when the anger was hard to muster and I'd missed her face—I'd listen to that song and recall the days when she'd been my friend.

That was what I'd always missed the most. Her friendship.

People had told us we were too young to know true love. I'd believed them as a teenager. A part of me believed them now. Was it really possible to find your soul mate at sixteen?

Whether it had been real or we'd only thought it was real, I wasn't sure. But there was no mistaking the raw emotion in "Torchlight." That song had been written by a woman whose heart had been broken by her love.

Broken by me.

But the pain in this song came through loud and clear.

I'd been wrecked because Quinn had abandoned me.

Maybe she'd been destroyed because in a way, I'd abandoned her too.

Quinn played the opening notes, changing the fast-paced rhythm to something slower and more subtle. Tingles broke across my forearms. My pulse raced. There was hardly a whisper of air in my lungs when Quinn began singing.

I'd meant to join in, but all I could do was sit and watch her croon to the rafters.

YOU ARE THE DARK. *You were the bright.*
Your voice was hope. Your eyes are fear.
You are the torchlight.
Here to incinerate my soul.

THE FINAL NOTE echoed in the room, fading until the only sound was my pounding heart. What could I say? That was perfect? That was fucking agony? She didn't need me here to sing that song for Nan. And the truth was, I wasn't sure I had the strength to do it. To sing with Quinn.

Two small hands began clapping.

My eyes turned to Colin who was standing on the honey-colored pew, clapping with a huge grin on his face. That smile was wider than any I'd seen this week, since before Nan.

I cleared my throat. "That was . . . good. Let's do it again. I'll come in this time now that I know where you're taking it."

I wasn't sure how, but I'd find the strength to survive this song. For Colin. Because if I sang beside one of his idols, maybe Saturday wouldn't be quite so hard.

"All right." Quinn's fingers stayed glued to the keys, like now that she'd touched them, she was afraid to let go.

She sang the opening and I stayed quiet because it would be more powerful alone. Then when she hit the first chorus, I harmonized with her, trying not to overshadow her voice but simply lift it with my own.

Our vocals melded, curling into each other like old lovers. They were timid at first, testing and teasing. But when the thread of control snapped, we went at it with abandon.

I'd forgotten how natural it was to sing with Quinn. I'd forgotten how good we sounded together. It was different now. My voice was lower and deeper. Hers wasn't as innocent and unsure. Maturity had changed us both, but the differences made it all the more interesting. There was a dynamic, sultry and surefire, that hadn't been there in our youth.

My eyes were fixed on her mouth. On the lips that formed each syllable with perfection and grace. Quinn's fingers moved in a fluid dance over the piano and her gaze tilted to meet mine.

Somewhere in the room, my son was watching. There was a tether in my focus always tied to him, but otherwise, the rest of the world faded away.

Quinn drew me in, wrapping me in her music, and reality vanished.

This had always been our thing. As teenagers, we'd drive around town with the windows down and the radio blaring. She'd beat her hands on the dash, playing an invisible drum, while we'd sing along to whatever station she'd picked.

Singing and music had been part of my entire life. Every other Sunday, I was the lead for the church band. Once or twice a month, I played in a friend's band at one of our favorite local bars. It was a fun hobby, but it didn't call to me like it did Quinn.

She was in her element, and I blindly followed her from beginning to end.

I leaned in closer and her arm brushed against mine. A flush crept into her cheeks as she continued to play and a storm brewed in her blue eyes. The electricity between us crackled.

We'd been lovers once, but this was beyond any teenage fantasies. This was sensual. Carnal. I wanted her voice in my bedroom, whispering dirty musings in my ear as her blond hair draped across my bare chest. I wanted those fingers to tickle and torment the lines of my stomach like they did the piano's keys.

Gone was the randy teenager who'd always done his best to make it good for his girl. Now I was a man, and I didn't just want it to be good for Quinn, I wanted to hear her scream.

The song was over. She'd played the last chord while I'd been staring at her mouth. The swell of her breasts heaved as she breathed. The haze around us remained, and even as I blinked, I couldn't bring it into focus.

Until my son began clapping again.

I tore my eyes away and stood from the piano's bench to rake a hand through my hair. *What. The. Fuck.*

What was I doing?

"That. Sounded. Awesome!" Colin let out a whoop and

jumped off the pew. He ran to the stage, bypassing me completely to take up my place beside Quinn. "You're a really good singer. How come you don't sing with the band?"

"Oh, I, uh . . ." Quinn forced a smile. "Jonas is such a good singer, don't you think?"

My son didn't seem to care that she'd dodged his question, but I studied her face. It was the same question I'd had yesterday. Why didn't she sing?

I opened my mouth to repeat Colin's question but clamped it shut. Was it any of my business how they'd decided to run their band? No. I'd already gotten tied up in that enough yesterday, and I wasn't getting anymore involved.

This was not my problem.

"I think we should do that for Saturday," I said.

"Okay." Quinn knew it was good, and she knew Nan would have flipped over that rendition. "Should we practice it again?"

"Tomorrow." There was no way I'd survive another round today. I waved Colin over. "Let's go."

"I'm hungry." He patted his stomach and walked over, pausing to look back at Quinn. "Do you think Dad or Jonas is a better singer?"

"Colin—"

"Your dad." Quinn gave him a genuine smile and complete attention. She wouldn't meet my gaze. "Don't tell Jonas I said that, okay?"

"Cool." Colin beamed, then looked up to me with absolute pride. My heart thumped—hard. There was nothing like seeing pride on your kid's face when they were looking at you. "Bye, Quinn."

"Bye, Colin."

I put my hand on his hair, ruffling it as I steered him toward the door. My feet moved in a straight line, my shoulders square, as I fought the urge to look back.

Quinn hadn't looked back.

So neither would I.

After the funeral, she'd be gone. And I doubted she'd look back then either.

———

"WHAT KIND of pizza should we get?" I read over the menu at Audrey's, my favorite pizza place in Bozeman.

"Pepperoni?" Colin had his elbows on the table, his knees planted in the booth's seat.

He'd been bouncing off the walls when we'd gotten home after the church rehearsal, and even an hour playing catch in the yard hadn't mellowed him out. Ruby had told me he'd been hyper all day.

Mom had invited us over for dinner tonight, but I knew he'd be too wound up to sit through a meal and listen to adults visit. That and I didn't want to be next door to Quinn. So we'd come out for pizza instead.

Most nights, I cooked at home, opting to save our disposable income for home improvements rather than restaurant food. But I hadn't made it to the grocery store this week and there were times when I just didn't want to be cooped up in the kitchen. Our normal routine was out the window anyway this week.

"I'm good with pepperoni." I closed my menu.

"Can we get breadsticks too?"

"Sure." I grinned as he took a long drink of his lemonade. "So how was swim—"

"Quinn!" Colin flew out of his seat and bolted toward the door, weaving past tables before colliding with her legs.

"Fuck," I grumbled into my beer. Was this one of fate's evil jokes? Was she going to be everywhere this week? From the corner of my eye, I watched as my son grabbed her hand and dragged her toward our table.

She waved. "Hi."

"Hey."

"I didn't realize you'd be here. I saw your mom earlier and she said this was a good pizza place."

Ahh. Not fate, but my mother.

I had no doubt that the minute I'd hung up the phone with her she'd marched over to the Montgomery house and *suggested* Quinn try Audrey's before she left town.

"Want to sit with us?" Colin hopped into the booth, shifting toward the window to make extra room.

"I was just going to get mine to go," Quinn answered at the same time I said, "She's busy, bud."

"Please?" Colin clasped his hands together and begged. "Please. Please. Please. Please. Please."

Six pleases. The kid was desperate.

I stifled a groan and motioned to the open space. "Join us."

"Are you sure?"

No. "Yeah."

Colin fist pumped as Quinn slid into the space beside him and the waitress appeared. "You guys ready to order?"

"We'll take a large Hawaiian and an order of breadsticks."

"No, pepperoni," Colin corrected.

"Quinn doesn't like pepperoni." I handed the waitress our menu. "Thanks."

"You remembered," Quinn whispered.

"How'd you know that, Dad?" Colin asked.

"Remember how I told you Quinn and I used to be neighbors?"

"Oh, yeah," he drawled, then focused on Quinn. "What other kinds of food don't you like?"

Strawberries. Sugar snap peas. And the worst offender . .
.

"Bacon," she answered.

"What?" Colin's jaw dropped. "You don't like bacon?"

"Nope. I'm weird, huh?"

"Super weird." He giggled. "I don't like string cheese."

"But you like other cheese, like the kind they put on pizza."

"Yep." He swiped up his lemonade, sucking it down as he inched closer to Quinn. When a bead of condensation dripped from his cup, it fell on her arm and she just brushed it away. "Do you have any pets?"

"No pets. I'm not home very much so I think it would be kind of lonely to be a dog or cat living in my house."

"I want a dog." Colin's big brown eyes drifted my way.

"Not until you're eight."

That was the deal we'd come up with. He could have a dog once he was eight and there was a chance he'd be able to share in the responsibility of a puppy.

"Can you do this?" My son set down his cup, then began rubbing his belly in a circle while patting the top of his head. He'd been working on it for months because Nan had told him that Quinn could do it as a child. Nan swore that was the moment she'd known Quinn would be a great drummer.

And anything Quinn could do, Colin wanted to do too.

"Hmm. I don't know." Quinn lifted her hands, patting her belly and rubbing her head. "Is this right?"

"No." He laughed. "Like this."

"Oh. Right." She corrected the motion and his eyes lit up.

"You're doing it!"

"Good thing you showed me how. I guess I forgot."

"Will you teach me something on the drums?" Colin asked, eyeing the drumsticks Quinn had shoved in her purse.

"No," I answered at the same time Quinn said, "Sure."

Of course, Colin only heard her agree. "Yes!"

It was never going to happen, but I wouldn't tell him that today.

I took another drink of my beer, then turned my attention to the window and the cars streaming by on the street. Watching Colin laugh and smile with a woman . . . it would have been fine if she was anyone else.

Anyone but Quinn.

The last thing I wanted was for him to be hurt when she left. And make no mistake, she was leaving.

I should have ordered the pepperoni. She might have excused herself.

It was only pizza, but I wished I didn't remember her favorite type. I wished I would have forgotten how one corner of her mouth raised higher than the other when she laughed. I wished she'd stop talking to my son, making his whole goddamn day. She was learning things about my son his own mother didn't know.

He couldn't fall for her. I wouldn't allow it.

But if I kicked her out of this booth, he'd hold it against me. This week had been hard enough, and I wouldn't steal this moment from him.

Walker had told me she was leaving Monday. We only had to make it a few more days, then she'd be gone.

I just prayed she wouldn't stay.

For Colin's sake.

And for mine.

CHAPTER SEVEN

QUINN

"How are you holding up?" Jonas asked the second I'd answered his call.

"Fine." I traced a circle in the quilt as I sat on my bed, legs crisscrossed. "How are you? How's Kira and Vivi?"

"They're good. I'm good. Worried about you, though. Why didn't you tell me at the show about your grandmother?"

"I just . . ." I sighed. "I didn't want it to be a thing. I needed to play and forget for an hour."

"I get that." Music was Jonas's outlet too. "Want me to come out for the funeral?"

"No, that's okay." As much as I wouldn't mind a friendly face, I had no idea how my family would react to one of my friends visiting when they were having such a hard time adjusting to my presence. "Thanks, though."

"Change your mind, let me know. I can be out there in a flash."

"Okay. Has Harvey been texting you this week?" Because the man hadn't gone a day without pestering me.

"Feels like every damn hour," Jonas grumbled. "He mentioned something about coming to visit."

"Uh-oh." Harvey's in-person visits usually meant he'd convince us to hole up somewhere until the album was finished. Not something I felt like doing when I simply wanted to go home.

"He wants an update on the album, and I can't give him one, so he's frustrated, which makes me frustrated, which makes Ethan panic, which makes Nix twitchy and you—"

"Mad." I gritted my teeth. "We just finished a tour."

"I know. That's what I told him. But we've always been an album ahead, or at least close. He doesn't want us to lose momentum."

Our philosophy had been to hit it and hit it hard. Who knew how long this ride would last? Since neither Jonas, Nixon nor I had anything pressing waiting for us in Seattle, why not capitalize while we were hot, blow crowds away and make a pile of money doing it?

But change was on the horizon. The brutal schedule we'd kept these past five years wasn't sustainable. We'd been on the road more often than home and that just wasn't going to work. Jonas needed down time with Kira and their daughter.

We'd spaced the shows on the last leg of our tour apart, giving him time to spend with his family. I wasn't sure what the next tour schedule would look like. We had a month off, but what next?

The scariest part was . . . I didn't care.

Something inside me had shifted lately, and I was drained. Weary. Lonely.

Nobody wanted to listen to music written by a mopey woman, including the mopey woman writing it.

"Have you written anything?" I asked.

"I've got three songs I'm toying with. They're close, but I'm not quite ready to send them to you and Nix yet. How about you?"

"I wrote something last month that's edgier than our normal, but I like it. Same as you, it's not quite ready, though. And then I've been messing with something this week, but it's too early. I need . . ." I closed my eyes. "I don't know what I need."

"Space. Time."

"Yeah. I'm tired, Jonas."

Maybe I hadn't realized exactly how tired until I'd come here and stopped for five consecutive minutes. There was no tour bus to meet or concert lineup to follow. There were no dress rehearsals or press events. Here, there was only time to sit and wish the music would come.

Why wouldn't it come?

"I've never had trouble like this before," I confessed.

"Want some advice?"

"Sure," I mumbled. Jonas had gone through a block a while back and had come out of it famously, writing some of our most popular songs. "Sweetness," included.

"Don't worry about it this week. Be there for your family. Take some time for yourself. Step away from it."

"Easier said than done." In a way, I craved this stress. Because if I worried about the album, I wouldn't have to acknowledge the hole in my chest that had been there for a long, long time. A hole that fame and success and money would never be able to fill.

Laughter from outside caught my ear and I stood from the bed, padding across the room to the window.

Mom had set up the sprinkler on the lawn. It was hot

today, the high forecasted to be in the eighties, and the kids were decked out in their swimming gear, even baby Bradley. The little ones were shrieking as they ran through the water's spray.

Colin was the leader with Evan trailing close behind.

It was the picture of a mini-Graham and a mini-Walker.

"Thanks for calling," I told Jonas. "I'll let you know when I get back to Seattle."

"If you change your mind and want me there on Saturday, just say the word."

"I will. Bye." I hung up the phone and set it aside, keeping my eyes on the kids.

Their bright smiles were infectious. I laughed along from behind the glass as Maya squealed and jumped over the sprinkler. She was wearing water wings, unnecessary but adorable, and her blond curls dripped down her back.

My eyes tracked Colin as he leaped over next.

He was quite the kid. Eating dinner with him last night had been utterly entertaining.

At the time, I hadn't noticed the gleam in Eileen Hayes's eyes when she'd suggested I try the pizza place. Looking back, I saw it now, but I'd been too anxious to get out of the house. Anything to avoid the dinnertime parade.

Mom and Dad had been receiving a slew of casseroles and covered dishes from church members the past few days. The visits started at five and lasted until around eight. People from the church would stop by to deliver a meal and pay their respects for Nan, then congregate in the living room and gab. Some faces I'd recognized. Others were new, and Dad hadn't been eager to introduce me so I'd hidden in this room.

When Eileen had suggested pizza at Audrey's, I'd

jumped at the chance, especially when she'd told me it was within walking distance.

The woman was a con artist.

Though, eating dinner with Graham and his son last night had been surprisingly . . . effortless. Not because of Graham—he'd barely spoken a word—but because of Colin.

Damn, that kid could talk and talk.

There hadn't been a moment of awkward silence because there hadn't been any silence period. We'd shared a Hawaiian pizza and talked about whatever topic popped into Colin's head. When we were done, I offered to pay and Graham had scowled, refusing a twenty-dollar bill. He hadn't waved as I left. Colin had bear-hugged me goodbye.

I hadn't spent much time around children, not since my babysitting days had come to an end at seventeen. Maybe I wasn't half bad with kids. Maybe Mom's gift for youngsters had rubbed off. Or maybe Colin made kids seem easy.

My mom laid out a blanket over the grass and sat down with the baby, adjusting the sun hat on his head. Maya ran over and grabbed her hand, trying to drag her up and through the water, but Mom pointed for her to run with the boys.

Maya pouted and turned away.

She probably got sick of being told to play with the boys. I knew that feeling.

Impulse hit and before I could change my mind, I ran to my suitcase and pulled out my swimsuit. I traveled with one in case there was ever a hotel along the tour where I'd want to swim. It was rare because I didn't want to be mobbed by fans, but when my muscles were especially sore and I was tired, I'd risk the hot tub.

I put it on and tied the halter behind my neck, then ventured outside so Maya wasn't the only girl.

I spent an hour running through the sprinkler with Colin, my nephew, and my niece. We laughed. We screamed. We played. And when I went inside to dress, the smile on my face was carefree. A corner of my heart was at peace, because for the first time since I'd walked off our jet, I felt like a part of this family.

Life would return to normal after I left. My father would go back to fussing over his flock. My mother would be busy helping my siblings with their children until she returned to school and taught a new class of kids. She'd call when she had time. I'd text when I remembered. Walker would say how badly he wanted to come see a Hush Note concert, but the timing would never work out. Brooklyn would resent her sister like she had for years.

And Graham would either continue to hate me or forget me entirely.

But maybe those kids would remember me with a smile.

They'd think back to the day their Aunt Quinn played in the sprinkler.

And for now, that was enough.

———

"HI, QUINN."

"Oh." My steps stuttered as I walked into the sanctuary. "Hi, Dad."

I'd expected to find it dark and empty, like it had been the other days this week when I'd come to rehearse with Graham. But the florescent lights were on overhead and Dad was at his pulpit with reading glasses perched on his nose.

He looked older there than he did at home. The brightness of the room brought out the speckles of gray in his sandy brown hair. He was still broad and tall, like Walker, but there was a softness to his body that had come with age.

What day was it? *Thursday.* He must still run through his sermons on Thursday afternoons.

"I'm meeting Graham to practice, but we can find a different spot."

"It's fine." He waved me forward. "I'm wrapping up."

As he jotted down a note on his practice sheet, I crept down the aisle. We hadn't been alone together yet. Mom had been our constant buffer.

"Care to sit?" He took off his glasses and motioned to the front row, joining me on the wooden pew. "I heard you singing yesterday."

I knew we should have stuck with a traditional song. *Damn it, Graham.* I loved "Torchlight," and the way we'd tackled it yesterday had given me goose bumps. But it wasn't Dad's style, and I should have expected him to ambush me. "And?"

"It was nice."

I gave him a sideways glance. *Nice?* Was that code for wild? "Uh, thanks?"

"I liked 'Amazing Grace' too."

And this was when he'd tell me how much more appropriate a hymn would be compared to a rock song. That stubborn streak he'd passed down to me flared. "We're doing 'Torchlight.'"

The power Dad had over what music I played and what music I sang was gone. The more he protested, the more I'd dig in.

"The congregation—"

"I don't care about your congregation," I snapped.

He sighed. "I'm only—"

"Can we not do this?" I stood from the pew. "Not today. Not this week. We had this argument nine years ago, and I doubt anything has changed. So let's not fight."

He stared at me for a long moment and I sensed an argument was on the tip of his tongue, but then he nodded. "All right."

I took my seat again, letting my heart rate calm until it wasn't thudding in my ears. As we sat there, side by side, the silence grew uncomfortable. Dad and I had nothing to talk about.

He could talk to anyone, a stranger, a friend, it didn't matter. Dad had this knack for striking up conversation that never felt fake or forced.

I'd seen him charm a grocery store clerk in the time it took her ring up two gallons of milk and a box of garbage bags. I'd seen him sit and pray for hours with a man whose wife had just been diagnosed with cancer.

He had a gift.

With everyone except his own daughter.

It hadn't always been like this. He hadn't always picked at me. When I was young, our relationship had been wonderful. I'd adored him.

It was when I'd begun developing my own ideals, my own desires and dreams, that the fights had started. They'd never stopped.

First, it was my clothes. I wore low-slung jeans and spaghetti-strapped camisoles whenever I wasn't at school. One summer Sunday, I got dressed and walked to church, thinking nothing of my outfit. It was cute and I was tan and it was hot. When Dad got home that afternoon, he told me if I couldn't dress more reasonably for church, without my bra straps or panties peeking out, I might as well stay home.

I didn't stay home. Even in the winter, I went to church in a cami, freezing my butt off in a pew.

After the clothes, it was the music. There was a kid in my high school band class who had an older brother. They had a garage band and needed a new drummer when theirs quit, so they'd asked me to join. I played with them for months, and it was never an issue because my parents thought it was all kids my age. Until my classmate quit the band and I was the only member under twenty-two. And the only female.

Dad forbid me to participate.

I told everyone, except Graham, that I'd quit.

But I hadn't.

Two days before I was leaving for college, Dad caught me sneaking into the house at two in the morning. I'd been at a house party, playing with the band. It had been our farewell gig.

Dad and Mom were furious and refused to take me to Seattle.

I threatened to go anyway.

Dad promised to disown me.

So Graham drove me to the airport two days later and I used all the money I'd made playing with that band to buy my one-way ticket out.

"How long do you plan on staying?" Dad asked, bringing my thoughts back to the church.

"Getting rid of me already?"

"No. Not at all."

"I'm leaving Monday."

He nodded. "So . . . soon."

Was that relief in his voice? Or regret? My eyes drifted to the piano and its gleaming cherry finish. It had cost me a lot to break free. My home. My siblings. My parents. My boyfriend. But my life would have been miserable if I had stayed in Dad's box. He probably would have loved nothing more than for my music career to have peaked as a music teacher who played with his choir each Sunday.

There was an unspoken rule in our family. Behind closed doors, play what you want. Listen to what you want. Be who you want. But in public, uphold the image.

When I'd decided rock music and the drums were more my speed than the organ and gospels, I'd tarnished his image. I was the rebel daughter and he was the pastor who couldn't keep her under control.

We were the real-life version of *Footloose*.

Had Dad even listened to Hush Note's music? He liked rock and roll. His truck was tuned to the classic station on the radio.

Except it didn't matter what Dad thought.

It only mattered what others would think of Dad.

I had eight million followers on Instagram, but Dad's appearance was under more scrutiny than mine.

The door behind us opened and we both turned to see Graham stride down the aisle.

"Hi, Graham." Dad stood, smiled and shook Graham's hand. "How was work today?"

"Hot." He chuckled. His hair was damp at the ends and even feet away, I could smell the fresh soap. "How's it going?"

"I'm doing . . . okay." Dad's shoulders fell and he turned to look at me. "I'll get out of your way. About the song, I really enjoyed it."

He'd enjoyed "Amazing Grace." My teeth ground together. Would he ever hear *me*? Would he ever accept *me*?

Without a word, I stood and walked to the stage, ignoring whatever Dad said to Graham before leaving the sanctuary.

"Did I walk in on something?" Graham asked, taking a seat on the bench beside me.

"The usual," I muttered. "He's just concerned his parishioners will hold the actions of his sinful daughter against him."

"I don't think that's it. Things have changed."

"Changed?" I huffed. "Nothing has changed. The man hasn't spoken to me in nine years, unless you count a birthday card in the mail. Then he wants to have a heart-to-heart so he can convince me to play his approved song for my grandmother's funeral. Heaven forbid I embarrass him."

If it hadn't been one of Nan's explicit requests, I bet Dad would have disinvited me to play. But he wouldn't go against her. He'd follow her instructions word for word and suffer through three minutes of my singing. Then he'd only have to wait until Monday when I'd be gone.

"He's not embarrassed by you, Quinn."

"Don't," I barked. "Don't defend him."

"I'm not . . ." Graham shook his head. "I was always on your side."

"Were you?"

If he'd been on my side, why had he driven me to the airport and stayed behind?

In my heart, I already knew the answer.

Graham had stayed here, waiting for me to come home, because he'd never believed I'd make my dreams come true. He'd stayed behind because he'd thought I'd return.

He hadn't believed in me.

Like my father.

"Can we just do this?" I splayed my hands on the piano, not waiting for him to agree as I played the first notes.

The song wasn't as good as it had been yesterday. There was an angry edge to my voice. Frustration and impatience clouded Graham's. But we made it to the end of the song and there was no stuttering over the lyrics or harmonization.

"Good enough." I stood and strode off the stage.

I'd lay it all out there on Saturday. I'd hold nothing back as I sang for Nan. But I couldn't practice with Graham any longer. It was too . . . hard. It hurt to be surrounded by his scent and feel the heat from his skin on my own. All I wanted was to bury myself in his arms and get lost in his embrace. After every fight with Dad, Graham had been where I'd found solace.

My willpower was weakening, and if I sat beside him any longer, I'd cave. I'd beg him to hold me, and I knew he absolutely would not.

"Wait up." Graham called when I was halfway down the aisle. "I want to ask you something."

In my hurry to flee, I hadn't noticed him follow, but he was three feet behind me when I turned and glared. "What?"

My tone didn't faze him. If anything, it softened his mesmerizing eyes. "Why don't you sing?"

"Uh, I was just singing." I tossed a hand toward the piano.

"That's not what I mean. Why don't you sing in your band?"

"It's not my job. I play the drums."

He crossed his arms over his chest and the sleeves of his T-shirt strained around his thick biceps. He planted his strong legs wide, standing like an oak tree, sturdy and solid. Unmovable until he got the answer he wanted.

I mirrored his stance and lifted my chin. This wasn't his business. My band wasn't his business. I'd made the mistake of playing him Nixon's "Jingle Bells" message, but I should have kept that part of my life—the present and future—far away from the past.

"Quinn," he warned in that rumbling voice.

Why didn't I sing?

Because of you.

I lived for the music. It was as much a part of me as my heart and lungs and blood. I needed the pulse of the drums racing through my veins. I needed to be swept up in a crescendo and set free in the climax. The music made me feel alive.

But singing, that had always been tied to Graham. When I sang, he'd always been in the crowd. The first time I'd performed at church as a kid, I'd been so nervous. The only way I'd made it through was by staring at him in the front row. He'd mouthed the words with me, start to finish.

When I sang, it was for Graham.

He'd given me that courage and my voice had always been for the boy I'd loved. I could sing for Nan on Saturday because he was there, sitting beside me.

How did I tell him that? How did I confess that I was an award-winning musician who was terrified to sing on her own because his face was missing in the crowd? It would reveal too much. He'd know that, to this day, he meant too much.

So I spun away and marched for the door.

Leaving him and his question behind.

CHAPTER EIGHT

GRAHAM

F*uck.* What a stubborn, infuriating woman.

Was it so hard for her to answer a simple question?

Quinn had always been a singer. How many times had she told me about her plan to study music, then compose and perform? How many nights had I tucked her into my side in the bed of my truck, watching the stars as she whispered her dreams? She'd never wanted to be a teacher, like her mother. She'd wanted the spotlight. Her talent deserved it.

She belonged in a band as successful as Hush Note.

But as the drummer? She didn't even sing backup.

Why had she settled? Why didn't she sing? Damn it, I wanted an answer. I wanted to know why, when she had the skill and the range, she stayed behind Jonas and Nixon. I'd seen enough of their music videos and coverage of their performances on YouTube to know she was hiding.

Two long strides down the aisle and I caught her. I stretched and wrapped a hand around her elbow before she could bolt out the door. "Answer me."

She wrenched her arm out of my grip. "No."

"Why don't you sing?"

Her lips pursed in a thin line and that defiant stare I'd seen countless times fixed on my face. But there was something behind her hard expression. Fear? Insecurity?

"You're scared."

"No." She scoffed. "I'm not scared."

That was a damn lie. "Then why?"

"I have my reasons, and they're none of your business. Not anymore."

"Because of you." I pointed at her nose. "*You* walked away and cut me out of your life. *You* made that choice."

Quinn's lip curled. It was the first real flash of the tenacious, rebellious, spirited girl I'd known my entire life. That lip curl meant she was about to lose the grip on her control.

Good.

She'd been holding back this week. There was no way the Quinn I'd known would have let me bark at her all week without a snappy retort.

I wanted to see some of that fire, make sure it was still there. I wanted to see the spark of the girl I'd fallen in love with all those years ago.

Her eyes blazed and blood rushed to my groin. God, she was something. That nose ring glinted under the lights and I wanted to lick the metal to see if it was cool.

"That's not what happened," she gritted out.

"Really? Because it sure as hell seems like you left everyone in your dust while you hooked up with a couple guys content to let you be their plaything because you're good with a pair of sticks." I leaned in closer, ready to push every button until she told me the truth. "If you stop fucking Jonas and Nixon, will they cut you from the band?"

"Fuck you."

I'd seen the gossip headlines. They were impossible to miss when they were splashed across tabloid covers in the grocery store checkout line.

Hush Note Love Triangle

Who Will Quinn Choose?

Team Jonas vs. Team Nixon

There hadn't been much of that lately, not since Jonas had confirmed he was in a serious relationship. Still, the idea of her with them made my stomach turn. Was that why Nixon called to leave her stupid jingles as messages? Was he in love with her?

Was she in love with him?

The thought of her with another man sent my head into a jealous spin. Did she gasp when he kissed her? Did he know that she was ticklish behind her knees and she loved to have her nipples sucked?

I'd been the one to teach her those things. *Me.*

Quinn's chest heaved and her eyes, lethal and cutting, didn't waver from mine. She'd hardened herself. For what? To keep people out? Did she think a scowl and a snarky attitude was going to work on me? Because I knew her too damn well.

"Why don't you sing?"

"Why do you want to know?"

I closed the gap between us, towering over her and forcing her to tilt her head back to keep my gaze. "You owe me some answers."

"I don't owe you anything," she hissed.

"You do. Tell me why."

"No."

"Tell me." The rise and fall of her chest brushed against mine, but she didn't back away. Her sweet scent surrounded me, and if I didn't step away, there was a good chance I'd lose my head. But my feet wouldn't budge. "Why don't you sing, Quinn?"

She held my stare, her eyes searching mine, but she stayed quiet.

I ran a hand down her arm, my fingers barely skimming the soft skin from shoulder to elbow. A flash of lust crossed her face, and the fury melted away with the sparks zinging up my fingertips.

"Because," she whispered.

"Because why?" *Tell me.*

Her breath rushed out between us and her chin dropped. "Because it reminds me of you. Because it hurts too much."

Maybe deep down I'd suspected that answer, so that's why I'd pushed for it. Maybe I'd known all along Quinn was as attached to me as I was to her. She crossed my mind daily, either in anger or curiosity or longing. Nine years, and damn it, she'd never truly left.

Fuck it. I took her face in my hands and slammed my mouth on hers, swallowing her gasp. My tongue swept inside her mouth and I devoured, pouring my frustration into the kiss.

Quinn's hands slid up my chest and fisted my T-shirt, pulling me closer as her tongue tangled in mine.

She tasted exactly like I remembered, sweet and potent and Quinn. Ambrosia. Her teeth nipped at my bottom lip, something that had always driven me crazy. I sucked on the corner of her top lip because it made her moan.

I lost myself in the memory of a girl and the reality of a woman, both gorgeous and addicting. Quinn was unchanged yet so different, and it was screwing with my head. So I blocked it out and kissed the hell out of her. My arms banded around her, pulling her into my chest as every nerve ending in my body ignited.

We were moving. My feet were shuffling us toward the door, stopping only when we pressed against the glass. The truck was right outside and the backseat—

What the fuck was I doing? I was off Quinn in a flash, stepping away until she was out of reach.

Quinn blinked herself out of the haze, then her eyes widened and a hand flew to her mouth.

"Shit." I wiped my lips dry. "I'm sorry."

She kept her fingers pressed to her lips like they'd protect her from me. "That was a mistake."

"Yeah." A huge, fucking mistake. We couldn't be kissing in the church or anywhere else. Nothing good would come from wanting Quinn. Or . . . surrendering to the want.

She had the power to ruin me all over again, and it wasn't just my heart on the line here. I had to think about Colin.

"I, um . . ." *Don't know what to say.*

Didn't matter. Quinn spun for the door and was gone. The tendrils of her silky hair blew in the breeze as she raced outside and left me standing in the lobby.

"Son of a bitch," I muttered, hanging my head.

It was a lapse in judgment I wouldn't let happen again. I only had to make it three more days and she'd be gone, taking the temptation with her.

We'd sing together on Saturday. There was no reason for me to see her tomorrow—we had the song down. So I only had to see her for the funeral, and I damn sure wouldn't be kissing her then.

I reined in the physical excitement, breathing deep until the blood wasn't pulsing in my ears and my cock wasn't twitching behind my zipper. It had been a long time since I'd had a woman, single dad and all. That, and I hadn't had much of an appetite to date. The last time I'd kissed a woman had been two years ago.

Until today.

Until Quinn.

Maybe I needed to take Walker's advice and get out more. It couldn't be healthy for a man to go this long without a release. But that was something I'd consider next week. Or next year.

Things were good with Colin and me. A woman would only complicate my life.

The air was warm and fresh when I walked outside, scanning the sidewalks for Quinn. They were empty. She was long gone, probably halfway home, which was great since my house was in the opposite— "Damn it."

I had to go get Colin.

From Quinn's house.

———

"MOTHER," I growled.

"Hi!" She smiled as she bustled around the Montgomery kitchen. She was as familiar with this one as she was her own. The same was true for Ruby and ours.

"What are you doing?"

"Ruby and I thought it would be nice to have a *manda-tory* family dinner since we're all in town."

"Sure, you did," I muttered.

This family dinner was nothing more than another excuse to force Quinn upon her family—Ruby's motivation— and to play matchmaker—*thanks, Mom.*

Mom riffled through the fridge and frowned. "Do me a

favor and go over to our house and get some ketchup. I have a spare bottle in the pantry. We're doing burgers, but we're running low here."

"Okay." There was no point fighting this dinner, so I'd go retrieve her ketchup. The sooner we ate, the sooner I could leave. I walked through the kitchen and opened the sliding door, scanning the backyard for my son. He was running behind the playhouse carrying a Nerf gun. "Hey, bud."

"Hi, Dad!" he yelled, then lost interest in me as Evan joined him. The two raced for the fence, firing darts at an invisible bad guy.

I closed the door and retreated through the Montgomery house to trudge over to my parents'. I had just stepped onto the concrete pad in front of the front door when it flew open.

Quinn nearly collided into my chest. There was a bottle of ketchup in her grip. "Oh. Hi."

"Hi." From now until Monday morning, I wasn't trusting a single word from my mother's mouth.

"Your mom sent me over for ketchup."

"Yeah. Me too." I shook my head and let out a long sigh. After our kiss, I'd driven around for thirty minutes before coming over, hoping it would give Quinn some time to walk home and hide in her room as she'd been doing in the mornings.

Except with this *mandatory dinner*, there'd be no eluding her tonight. We couldn't go into that house together, both looking guilty, because my mother the sleuth would sniff it out instantly.

Mom had always seemed to know when Quinn and I had been kissing, even before we'd announced that we were dating. She'd never called me on it, but she'd known.

"Can we talk?" I walked to the edge of the wide concrete

pad, sitting down and looking over the yard. Mom's flower beds were overflowing beside me. Every weekend, she'd throw a floppy hat over her dark hair, pull on some gloves and knee pads, and tend to her flowers for hours. Then she'd sneak over and help Ruby's geraniums.

I breathed in the floral scent as Quinn sat down two feet away. She put the ketchup bottle between us. "I'm sorry about earlier. For the kiss."

She nodded. "Same."

"And I'm sorry for what I said. About you and Nixon and Jonas."

"It's nothing the tabloids haven't said a hundred times."

Is it true? I caught the question right before it came rushing out. Tabloids usually printed garbage but based the garbage on a shred of truth, right? Otherwise they'd get sued. Had I kissed another man's woman? Quinn's love life was none of my business. The less I knew, the better.

"About the singing. I get it. I had to sell my Chevy after you left. After the call, I just . . . couldn't keep driving it around anymore."

Every time I'd glanced at the passenger seat, I'd missed seeing her there. When I'd sit behind the wheel, I'd remember answering her call and how I'd beat my fist on the dash after she'd hung up.

We'd both been raw from a fight when I'd driven her to the airport the day she'd left. Bradley and Ruby had grounded her after discovering she'd been sneaking out to play with her band. I'd hated those asshole bandmates, but she'd loved to play. So I'd gone with her to as many practices as possible when I didn't have football. She hadn't told me about the house party gig, probably because she knew I would have insisted on going along or asked her to skip it.

After Bradley and Ruby found out, they'd gone ballistic, rightly so. Quinn could have been hurt and none of us would have known where to find her. They'd told her Seattle was out. She'd argued and then Bradley had threatened to disown her.

I hadn't been there for the fight, but she'd replayed it for me, word for word, as tears streamed down her face.

I was pissed when she told me she'd snuck out. Mad that she'd kept it a secret. So I told her maybe Seattle wasn't the right choice. I'd asked her to stay, to go to college with me, and after a year in the dorms, we could find a place together.

She'd stared at me in disbelief, then shot off my bed and raced home.

Leaving me to wonder what I'd said.

I realized now how wrong I'd been. What I should have done was support her.

Or gone with her.

Instead, I'd driven her to the airport when her parents had refused and hugged her goodbye.

How much strength had it taken for her to walk away? To go to college without a friend or the support from her parents? I'd been too brokenhearted then to admire her for that choice.

I was too stubborn now to admit it to her face.

Neither of us had talked about breaking up. Why would we? We were young and in love.

But the minute her plane took off, the minute I watched her soar into the sky from the airport parking lot, a knot settled in my gut.

Quinn left Montana and didn't call me for three days. Three days in a row.

I didn't call her either.

Because I knew the next phone call would be the end.

It was.

She called me from Seattle, crying before I'd even answered the phone, and whispered, "Do you think they are right?"

They, meaning everyone. My parents. Her parents. Friends. Strangers.

We were too young to know true love.

"Should we break up?" she'd asked.

My pride had stopped me from doing the right thing and telling her no. "Yeah. Probably."

I'd been a stupid, eighteen-year-old kid. A stupid, broken boy, crying his eyes out in a Chevy truck.

"I liked that truck," Quinn whispered, pulling me into the present.

"Me too." I nodded. "But I would have had to sell it eventually. It wasn't exactly a safe vehicle for a newborn."

"Nan didn't tell me much about Colin. About you and his mother. Where is she?"

"Gone." I ran a hand over my hair, the movement giving me a chance to debate opening this window to the past.

Should I tell her about Dianne? It wasn't an easy subject for me to discuss, but this was Quinn. Talking to her had always been easy. Not even Walker was as easy to confide in and the guy had been my friend since diapers.

"I met Dianne freshman year," I said, leaning my elbows on my thighs. "She lived on my floor in the dorms."

Dianne was the wild, crazy girl at the end of the hall who was always up for a party. I was the recluse who thought house parties were overrated and fraternity parties over-crowded. I studied, occasionally played pool at the student union with a few guys from my floor and met up with Walker once a week.

It was hard to be around him during that time. He reminded me too much of Quinn, but he didn't talk about her and his apartment was always stocked with beer. Besides, he was just as angry with his sister for leaving as I had been. She hadn't called him either.

She just left us.

"Colin is seven so . . ." Quinn trailed off, clearly having done the math.

I'd gotten Dianne pregnant our freshman year.

"I expected you to come home for Thanksgiving, but you didn't. I waited for you to call. To come home. I was going to tell you that I would have left Montana. If Seattle was what you wanted, I would have left."

Shock and anger flashed across her face. "You already knew Seattle was what I wanted. You knew why I had to get out of here. So don't say you waited for me. You could have called me."

"Our last phone call didn't work out so well, did it? Forgive me for being wary of dialing your number. And according to Nan, you were happy. Living your dream. I was here, alone and miserable."

"So you stopped waiting." There was no blame in Quinn's voice, only resignation.

"Dianne and I hooked up one night." A night that had changed my life forever. I'd gone to a house party and spotted her from across the room. We'd guzzled Jack straight from the bottle and started making out. Then we'd hitched a ride back to the dorms and I'd spent the night in her room. "A week before finals, she came to my room and told me she was pregnant."

We'd used a condom, I think. I'd been so drunk, I couldn't remember much from that night. She'd been the first since Quinn, and I'd felt so dirty the next morning that I'd snuck out of Dianne's room and taken two showers.

Quinn sat perfectly still, her back stiff and her arms wrapped around her stomach. The color had drained from her face. If listening to this story was painful, she should have lived it.

"Dianne wanted to get an abortion," I said. "I told her I'd pay for it. Then I came home and told my parents."

I'd broken down and cried in their living room, fearing I'd let them down. Fearing I'd let myself down.

Knowing I'd betrayed my love for Quinn.

"What made her decide not to go through with it? The abortion?"

"I talked her out of it. Because of your dad."

"My dad?"

I nodded. "He came over that day to invite Mom and Dad for dinner. He'd walked into the house, saw three pale faces streaked with tears and sat down at my side."

"Did you get a lecture?"

"No."

Quinn would think that because Bradley had given her countless lectures. She was his daughter. But she didn't see how he was with other people. She didn't see his patience or his kindness. Or maybe she did, but they'd been overshadowed. She expected the worst.

"Really?" She arched an eyebrow.

"Really. He just sat down and put his hand on my shoulder. Didn't say a word. He sat there and listened as my parents and I talked it through. The abortion . . . it made me sick. I screwed up and yeah, having a kid that young

115

wouldn't be easy. But I just felt in my heart that it would be okay. That was my kid. Mine. There was love there, or the beginning of love. My parents offered to help. So did your dad. That was the first thing he said. 'We love babysitting.'"

Quinn's eyes widened. "*My* dad?"

"He's changed too." Losing his daughter had opened Bradley's eyes.

"Hmm." Her eyebrows came together as she thought it over. "So, Dianne?"

"I asked her if she'd consider keeping the baby. I would have supported her either way, but I told her I would be there. That I wanted to be there. She'd failed all of her classes that semester and her parents refused to pay for another year, so her choices were to stay in Bozeman and get a job or move home to Billings. She moved home, decided against the abortion and kept me up on the pregnancy. I visited a couple of times. And then in September, Colin was born."

"Nan told me. She called me."

When I'd held Colin in my arms, the first person I'd wanted to call had been Quinn. He'd been so perfect and tiny. I'd been scared shitless, but I loved him. Instantly. And for a split-second, I'd wanted to share the miracle with Quinn.

That feeling hadn't lasted long once reality came crashing down. I'd held Colin, looked at Dianne, and known that day he wouldn't have a mother.

"Dianne didn't want to hold him. She wasn't happy or excited. She was terrified. Five hours after he was born, she begged me to take him. She told me that she'd made a mistake. She wasn't ready to be a mother."

"So you brought him home."

"Yeah. He slept the whole drive home, then screamed for two months straight." I chuckled. "My parents saved my ass. Yours too. I moved in here and knew school wasn't going to happen. So I got a job and did my best to survive. Dianne signed over all her rights and I haven't heard from her since."

There was no blame in my heart toward her, only gratitude. She'd given me a gift. Colin was the best thing in my life and for that I'd be eternally thankful.

"Do you think she'll ever come back?" she asked.

"Maybe. I don't know. But I won't close that door to her if she does. If she wants to know Colin, I'm not going to get in her way." There'd be rules and I'd set the tone for those visits, but I wouldn't forbid them.

"Does he know about her?"

"Some, but he doesn't ask often and usually we avoid the topic completely. I'm honest if he has questions."

A car drove past, the neighbor across the street waving. The kids were yelling as they played in the Montgomery yard.

"I'm going to take this to your mom." Quinn stood and picked up the ketchup.

"I'll be over in a minute."

She took one step before stopping. A smile tugged at the corner of her mouth, the same corner I'd kissed earlier, and I fought the urge to stand and capture that mouth again. Her smile broadened, though there was pain in her eyes. "Colin is a cool kid. You're a good dad, Graham. I always knew you would be."

She might as well have stabbed me in the chest.

"Thanks," I said, watching as she walked away.

Fuck me.

When had I never loved that woman?

Maybe that kiss had woken me up. Maybe it had made me realize how goddamn lonely I'd been without her. I had Colin, but there was a corner of my heart that would always belong to Quinn.

I should have followed her nine years ago.

Because now it was too late.

CHAPTER NINE

QUINN

"Hey, Brookie—Brooklyn." *Whoops.* My finger wave was met with a scowl as she closed the front door.

"Where's Mom?" She scanned the living room as she bounced baby Bradley on her hip.

"She had to run to the church with Dad. They're meeting with the caterer for tomorrow."

She blinked. "And she left *you* with the kids?"

"I'm capable of keeping three kids alive for a couple hours." I glanced at Colin, Evan and Maya playing on the floor, perfectly happy and safe under my watch.

Though I doubted Mom would have left me here with the kids if the baby would have been among today's wards. Brooklyn had Fridays off and didn't need a babysitter today.

"Would you like to sit?" I waved to the free space on the couch beside me.

Brooklyn harrumphed but sat.

"How are you?" I asked.

"Fine."

She hadn't been over last night for burgers. Her husband,

Pete, had picked up Bradley and gone home for dinner. Since I'd arrived, Pete had given me a dozen pleasant smiles, but we hadn't braved much conversation. He seemed wary, as if Brooklyn would label him a traitor if he spoke to me.

"Pete seems nice."

She narrowed her eyes and set the baby on the carpet at her feet. He cooed and gnawed on a set of red, blue and yellow plastic keys. "Don't, Quinn."

"Don't what?"

"Don't pretend you care."

"I've always cared."

She scoffed. "You sure have a way of showing it."

Brooklyn was the second runner-up to Dad's silent treatment. The day I'd left, she'd basically stopped speaking to me. She'd been fifteen and busy as the popular girl in high school who'd played fall, winter and spring sports.

When I'd text and hardly get a short reply, I'd assumed it was because she was busy. She had her life happening and her older sister wasn't around to pester her about how long she spent in the bathroom doing her hair and makeup.

Brooklyn and I had never been close. As teenage sisters, we hadn't fought much; we just didn't have anything in common. Where I'd tag along after Walker and Graham, Brooklyn was content doing her own thing with her own friends.

As the years passed and I texted with her less and less often, I'd chalked it up to sisters who'd drifted apart. She and Pete had gotten engaged after college. She hadn't asked me to be her maid of honor, something that had bothered me more than I'd admitted.

But I'd planned to be at her wedding. I'd missed Walker and Mindy's since they'd eloped.

The day Mom had told me about the engagement, I'd emailed her tour dates, something that had been set in stone for a year. In a twelve-week Montana summer, there were four blacked out weekends when we'd be in Europe.

Brooklyn had picked one of the four.

She'd wanted a June wedding and June had been impossible. Was that why she was so angry at me? Or because I only sent flowers after Bradley was born?

I opened my mouth to ask but closed it before speaking. Maybe this was on me to fix, but I never knew how to talk to Brooklyn.

That hadn't changed.

"How's your *band?*" She infused the last word with more disdain than even Graham could conjure.

"They're good."

She rolled her eyes.

"Why ask if you don't want the answer?"

"I'm being polite," she snapped. "I don't care about you or your band."

Colin's head snapped up from the Legos he and Evan were playing with on the floor.

"Do you guys want to put your shoes on and go play outside?" I offered.

"Yeah!" Evan shot up first.

I winked at Colin as he followed. The kid was bright—he knew there was tension between me and my sister—but he simply went with Evan to put on his shoes. Maya was lost in an app on the pink tablet Walker had brought with her this morning, insisting she only get two hours of screen time.

Mom, the wise grandmother, had allotted those two hours to the hours when I would be watching her.

When the sliding door opened and the boys were

outside, I angled myself on the couch to face Brooklyn. "Don't be polite. Say what you have to say."

"You didn't just leave Graham behind when you disappeared to become famous. You left the rest of us too."

Would it matter if I hadn't become famous? Would there be so much resentment toward me if I was a starving musician playing in small bars and surviving from gig to gig?

"I'm not sorry I left, but I am sorry we lost touch." After the fight, after Graham and I had broken up, after navigating the first few days of college feeling helpless and alone, I'd shut out the world.

I'd put up my guard.

The only person who'd shoved her way through had been Nan. Even if there wasn't anything to discuss, even if our conversation lasted three minutes, she'd never stopped calling.

She hadn't let me walk away from her.

Maybe I needed to take her lead and not let Brooklyn push me away either.

"I don't know how to talk to you," I admitted. "I missed a lot of your life. You missed a lot of mine. We're different people than the girls who lived here once. But maybe we could start over and get to know each other now."

"It's too late." She bent and scooped up her son. "You cut us out, Quinn. Don't pretend you aren't going to leave after the funeral and do a repeat performance."

Without another word, she was out the door and marching to her car parked on the street.

I watched her through the window as she loaded Bradley into his car seat and raced away.

A pang of regret hit because she wasn't wrong.

I was leaving Monday and had no intention of returning

soon. I wanted to go home—to Seattle. I wanted to get back to work and write this next album. If I called Brooklyn, I doubted she'd answer.

She seemed happy. That's all that mattered, right?

"Where's Evan?" Maya looked up from her tablet, searching the room for her brother.

"He's outside. Want to go play?" I stood and stretched a hand for her.

She nodded and followed me to her backpack. I helped her into a pair of flip-flops with an elastic strap for the heel and we went outside where I pushed my niece in a swing.

Was I making things worse by being here? Was it worth trying harder?

Or was it better to leave my family to their lives?

And go back to my own.

———

A DAY SPENT PLAYING with kids was more exhausting than any tour schedule Ethan could have dreamed up.

"They'll wear you out, huh?" Walker chuckled as I plopped down in a chair at the patio table.

Mom had come home from her trip to the church, and seeing that the kids were happy and thriving, deemed me childcare for the rest of the day so she could help Dad finalize preparation for the funeral.

I'd been glad to help, preferring a day with smiling kids to a day dreading tomorrow. But damn, I was wiped.

"How does Mom do this every day?" I asked.

"Hell if I know." He sat beside me and watched his kids in the yard. Colin was spending the night with Graham's parents and they'd already stopped over to collect him. "You're good with them."

"Don't sound so surprised," I muttered.

He grinned. "Heard you talked to Brooklyn today."

"She tattled on me already? For the record, I was trying to be nice. But she hates me and that's not going to change."

"She doesn't hate you. But you know how she is about Dad."

"Yeah."

Brooklyn was Dad's girl. She adored him and when it came time to picking sides, she was always on his.

"Dad was pissed when you left," Walker said. "Brooklyn never understood that he wasn't mad at you, he was mad at himself."

"Oh, I think he was mad at me too."

"At first. That fight was bad and you basically told him to shove it when you disappeared. I mean, Christ, Quinn, you had Graham take you to the airport. You didn't leave a note or say goodbye. They didn't even know where you'd gone."

I cringed. "I'll admit, that was bad."

"Yeah. But Dad got over it. He's spent a lot of years regretting how it turned out."

"This is news to me."

"He doesn't know what to do with you. Dad is so good with people, but you, he never figured you out."

"So rather than try, he disowned me instead."

You are not my daughter.

That was one of his statements I'd never forgotten.

I'd held those words tight every time I'd written a song for a year. Every ounce of pain from that sentence had been poured into my music.

"He's changed," Walker said gently.

"So everyone says." But had Dad called? Had he apologized? No. At this point, I didn't even want an apology. I just wanted to be accepted for who I was. "It doesn't matter anymore. Maybe it's been so many years, it's better to forget and move on."

"Well, when you move on"—Walker stood from his chair —"don't forget there are some of us who will always be here for you."

I looked up at my brother. "I'm sorry I didn't call you more often."

"And I'm sorry I never came to one of your shows. Two-way street, Quinn. This is not all on you."

"Thanks."

"What are you doing tonight?" he asked. "If you want to get out of the house, there's a band playing at the Eagles downtown you'll probably like."

"I don't know." A night away from the house, away from the awkward silence that always came when only Mom, Dad and I were home, sounded wonderful. "With Nan's funeral tomorrow, I don't know if I should push it."

"Tell them you're coming over to hang at my place."

"Are you encouraging me to lie to our parents?"

He gave me a sly grin. "Wouldn't be the first time."

Walker had always been the one to cover for Graham and me. On the nights when we needed to spend more time together, on the weekends when we'd go camping in the mountains, Walker would always claim to have been there too. He'd been the third wheel who'd disappear to spend a night with whatever girl he was dating.

"I think I'll do that." I could use a couple of hours out of this house, doing something I loved and getting my mind off what was to come tomorrow.

"Can't wait to hear what you think of the band. They're my favorite."

"Your favorite? Excuse me?"

"Besides Hush Note."

I smiled. "That's better."

He smiled back and I knew, right there in my parents' kitchen, I wasn't going to lose my brother again. I'd do better to stay in his life. To know his children and his wife.

I'd do better.

———

WALKER WAS A GODDAMN LIAR. That rat bastard.

Of course, this band was his favorite.

Graham was the lead singer.

I closed my gaping mouth and blinked from the dark corner table I'd claimed earlier tonight.

After dinner with my parents, I'd made some excuses about wanting to explore Bozeman a bit and that I might be out late. I'd decided not to leverage Walker's fake invitation and go for vague instead.

An Uber brought me downtown, then I snuck into the Eagles with a hood pulled over my head. So far, no one had recognized me and I doubted they would. None of the bar's patrons had paid me a bit of attention, except my waitress who'd just delivered my third vodka tonic.

The dance floor was empty, but I suspected that wouldn't last long. The noise level in the bar had slowly crept up as groups of college-aged kids trickled through the door. When I'd arrived, there'd been plenty of empty tables, and now, nearly all were full. A line of older men and a few women sat at the bar itself, laughing with their bartenders and people-watching the younger generation. The energy in the room was growing with the promise of a fun night. A table of guys doing shots let out a whooping holler when the band had stepped on stage.

Walker was as bad as Eileen with this stunt.

Thankfully, Graham hadn't spotted me yet.

He'd come in twenty minutes later than the other band members and the stage was mostly set up. He shook everyone's hands and gave one guy a back-slapping hug. Then he took out his guitar, stowing the case against the far wall, and maneuvered to the center microphone.

"Hey, guys," he said into the mic. "How are we doing tonight?"

The crowd cheered and a couple guys in cowboy hats whistled. A pretty brunette standing with them blushed as Graham's gaze swung their way.

My lip curled.

She was practically a child. Had the bouncers not checked her I.D.?

Graham strummed a chord on his low-slung guitar and grinned at the lanky guy to his right holding a bass. The keyboard was set up on Graham's left. The drummer sat behind a decent Yamaha kit.

I lifted my glass to take a sip, but then Graham played a guitar riff that made every muscle in my body freeze. "Life is a Highway."

One of my favorite songs. One he'd play for us in his Chevy truck when we were driving around, windows down and music blaring.

The room erupted.

A crush of people swarmed the dance floor. The table

beside mine emptied except for one lady who stayed and sang along.

The entire bar was fixed on Graham. He'd always been an amazing singer, but when had he gotten so good on the guitar? He had them eating out of his hand.

My throat went dry and I gulped my drink, draining it to empty save for the ice and lemon slice.

Graham's voice filled the room and he flashed that sexy, charming smile as he scanned the crowd.

I hovered deeper into my hoodie, hoping he wouldn't see me. Hoping I could just sit here and watch because . . . holy fuck he was hot.

My tongue darted out to my bottom lip, searching for his taste from yesterday's kiss. His voice washed over me and my foot bounced on the floor. There was no stopping my body as it responded, completely at his mercy. A rush of wetness pooled between my legs.

That smile.

My God, no wonder that little girl was blushing over him. Graham was the complete rocker package—confident, talented and gorgeous. Was this how women felt about Jonas and Nixon? Because I was coming out of my skin as his fingers flew over the frets on his guitar and a lock of hair draped on his forehead.

He was wearing a simple black T-shirt, the sleeves stretching over those corded and tanned arms. His jeans were simple and faded but they fit over his bulky thighs, straining as he moved with the music.

My heart was in my throat as he stepped to the mic, crooning through the song's hook, then stepping away to hit a lick on the guitar that was pure rock-and-roll brilliance.

Someone cheered. Loud.

Me. I cheered.

Shit.

Graham smiled again, his eyes flickering toward the source of the noise. He spotted me. He'd snared me and held me captive, not missing a note, a lyric or a beat. As he sang the final chorus, the crowd disappeared between us.

He sang to me and I forgot how to breathe.

By the time the song ended, my panties were drenched. I was seconds away from walking up on that stage and taking a kiss that would put yesterday's to shame.

I was in deep, deep trouble sitting here.

The song ended and the crowd roared as Graham led them right into Lynyrd Skynyrd's "Sweet Home Alabama." Except he swapped out Alabama for Montana.

Tears flooded my eyes and I focused on my empty glass.

He was so good. So, so good.

It hurt to hear. It hurt to feel his gaze on my face. It ripped my heart out to know he wasn't mine.

We'd survived burgers last night. Hearing everything that had happened with Colin's mom hadn't been easy. But Graham was strong. Stronger than any person I'd ever met.

He was a force. A magnet.

Maybe that was why I'd known a long-distance relationship with him would never have worked. His pull was too strong. Eventually, I would have yielded and come home.

I would have stayed forever, forfeiting my dreams to sit at tables like this one, being Graham's cheerleader and number one fan.

The temptation was overpowering.

When had I not loved him?

I shot out of my chair and ducked my head, sidestepping

past people and maneuvering through the crowd. If I sat here and listened for another minute, I'd stay.

I couldn't stay.

My shoulders bumped into people as I squeezed my way through the mass toward the front door. With every step, Graham's voice faded and my heart ached.

If I stayed, if I let myself remember how it was to love him, I'd break. I'd worked so hard to bury these feelings. I'd worked so hard, period. I had a life to get back to. A band. The door loomed and my feet pushed faster, my boots thudding as I jogged past the bouncer and burst outside.

The air, crisp and fresh, filled my lungs and I let a sob escape.

There were reasons, so many reasons, that Graham and I would never work, and it was easier to remember them without his voice ringing in my ears.

I spun away from the bar and began walking down the sidewalk, the urge to cry lessening with every step. Five steps. Ten. The end of the block was getting close, the pull toward Graham weakening with every stride.

I could breathe again. I could think.

Until his voice called my name.

"Quinn."

My feet stopped, but I didn't turn. I faced forward, staring at the street ahead, until a broad chest covered in a black T-shirt filled my vision.

He'd chased me.

He'd chased me when I really needed him to let me go.

Graham tucked a finger under my chin and tipped it up, forcing my eyes to his. "Why are you always running away from me?"

I couldn't answer him. He'd push and push until I did,

but it was the one thing I wouldn't admit. Because if I admitted that I'd been in love with him since I was fourteen, it would destroy us both.

So I didn't let him push.

I shut him up by standing on my toes and pressing my mouth to his.

CHAPTER TEN

GRAHAM

I trapped her.

My arms banded around Quinn's body and I pulled her into my chest, squeezing her tight. There was no fleeing from this kiss, not until I'd had my fill.

Quinn didn't seem in a hurry to break away either. Her grip on my face was as firm as the one I had on her shoulders and waist. Her tongue twisted and tangled with mine, her desperation clear as she let a whimper escape. I met her intensity stroke for stroke, reveling in the feel of her breasts smashed against my chest and the taste of her on my lips.

Standing on stage, singing to her, I'd been drawn to her lips. I'd almost stumbled and screwed up the song, so distracted by her heavy gaze and panting chest. She'd wanted me. I'd seen it from the across the darkened room.

Then she'd run away.

I should have expected it. The woman was always leaving me, and she would again. But this time, I wasn't standing behind and letting her go until I got what I wanted.

I'd waited a long damn time to see her again, and it was my turn to do some taking.

I hefted her up and her arms wound around my shoulders, holding firm as her toes dangled above the sidewalk. Without breaking the kiss, I walked us toward the building at our side and pressed her against the brick façade. The moment her back hit the wall, she wrapped her legs around my hips and let out another whimper.

My hardness rubbed against her core and a shudder rolled down her spine. Our mouths stayed fused, and my head angled to get deeper. What I wanted to take she was giving me freely. Or maybe she was the one stealing from me. I didn't give a shit about the semantics as long as she kept clinging to my body.

We kissed and kissed, not caring about being on Main Street, dry humping against a wall, until a throat cleared at my back.

Son of a bitch. I ripped my mouth from hers, panting and blinking the world into focus. Then I glanced behind me, searching for the source of the noise.

It was Tim, the guy who led the band and our bass player.

"Sorry." He held up a hand. "You comin' back?"

I arched an eyebrow.

"Right. It's cool. I think I saw Kaylee in there. I'll see if she wants to play tonight." He took a step back, his eyes going to Quinn's flushed face. "Uh, hey. Huge fan. I came to your show in Denver two years ago, and it was awesome. That solo you played on 'Silent Riot' was maybe the best drum solo I've—"

"Tim," I barked.

"Oh, shit. Sorry." He spun away, took one step, only to

turn again. "I don't know how long you're here, but if you want to play, I turned my garage into a studio."

Quinn let out a soft laugh. "Thanks."

"Bye, Tim."

He chuckled. "See ya, Graham."

I faced Quinn, expecting to see guilt in her eyes like there had been when we'd kissed at church. She'd shove me away any second now. But there was a smile tugging at her lips, and her arms were holding me as tight as ever.

I waited until the sound of Tim's footsteps disappeared before dropping my mouth to hers again. Taking. Worshiping. This kiss wasn't as frantic and hurried as the one before, but damn, it was hot. It was deep and consuming. It was a prelude to the kiss that would last all night.

Quinn broke away, her arms adjusting to get an even stronger hold on my shoulders. Her fingers toyed with the strands of hair at my neck as she whispered, "Take me home."

"Which home?"

"Yours," she said breathlessly. "Take me to your bed."

Fuck. Yeah. I hauled her off the wall, shifting my hold so one arm was under her ass to keep her from trying to drop her feet on the concrete. There was no way I'd put her down and risk a fraction of space. I had her. Right now, I had Quinn.

Unless she told me, with words, to let her go, I wasn't taking the chance that she'd run.

I walked us around the corner, turning the block to loop around behind the bar. The alley was dark and quiet except for a couple slipping into the Eagles from the rear entrance.

The bar's door opened, and Kaylee's voice drifted into the night.

"Who's that?" Quinn asked, squirming to be set down.

I swatted her ass so she'd stop. "That's Kaylee. There's about ten of us who play in the band. Tim is the constant. So is Clyde, our drummer. Everyone else rotates out so we're not tied to the band every weekend."

Thank God, Kaylee had been here tonight. Even if she wouldn't have been, I would have left with Quinn. But at least this way, Tim wasn't forced to sing since he preferred to play without a microphone in his face.

"Ahh." Quinn wiggled her hips and unhooked her legs from behind my back. I swatted her ass again, earning a frown. "Are you going to let me go?"

"No."

"I can walk."

"You used to like it when I carried you around."

An expression flashed across her face, slightly pained but wistful, like she'd recalled a bittersweet memory.

Maybe she was thinking of the times I'd pick her up in a cradle and carry her from my locker to her algebra class. It used to embarrass her completely and make her laugh hysterically, but she'd never fought me to put her down. She'd only bury her face in my neck and pretend she meant it when she scolded me.

Then there were the times when she'd fall asleep on the couch while we were watching a movie. I'd carry her from my parents' house to her own, leaving her with a kiss on the forehead as I tucked her into bed.

Those times were innocent and fun.

This was about sex, pure and wild.

I dropped a kiss to the corner of her mouth, showing her the difference. I licked her tongue when it darted past her bottom lip.

"Graham," she whispered as her legs lifted to my hips once more.

The lust and hunger in her gaze spurred me faster, and my strides lengthened as we crossed to the corner of the parking lot.

My house was only ten blocks away, the drive would take us minutes, but damn it, I wasn't sure if I'd make it. Not when she dropped her lips to my neck and trailed wet, open-mouthed kisses up and along the line of my jaw.

"If you don't stop now, we'll never make it out of my truck," I warned.

She leaned back, showing me that sly smile. "You used to like it when we didn't make it out of your truck."

I chuckled, the noise pained and rough. "Not tonight."

Not for this.

If all we had was tonight, I wasn't wasting it in a cramped backseat.

I dug the keys from my pocket and clicked the truck's locks as we reached the passenger door. Quinn reluctantly let me go as I set her inside. Then I shut the door and jogged around the hood, making a quick adjustment to my throbbing cock before getting in and racing out of the lot.

We didn't speak on the drive. We didn't touch. But the electricity between us sizzled, spiking the tension and anticipation of what was to come. Would she feel the same? Quinn was a different woman. I was a different man. But would this feel the same? I was torn between wanting to relive the past and needing something entirely new.

I pulled into the garage, but before I could get out, Quinn had her seat belt unbuckled and she was leaning across the console, her lips seeking mine. The kiss was blinding and short. A tease. Our breaths were ragged when we broke apart and I dropped my head to hers, taking one second to compose myself before I lost all control.

She giggled. "We fogged up the windows."

"If I recall correctly, we both used to like doing that."

"Among other things," she whispered, her lips finding the sensitive spot beside my ear.

"Out," I ordered, shoving my door open. My heart raced and my cock throbbed as I took her hand and led her inside.

We walked straight through the kitchen and living room, my pace forcing her to skip to keep up. I took us straight to my bedroom, not bothering to close the door, as I swept her into my arms and dropped us both on the mattress.

"What do you want?" I asked, covering her with my body.

"Don't be gentle. Don't hold back. Not tonight."

I nodded, staring into the eyes I saw in my dreams.

There was so much familiar about her, but the heat and the boldness in her touch, was not the Quinn from the past. She was a woman, confident and sure. There was no hesitancy in her touch as she slid a hand between us and palmed my erection through my jeans.

She'd done this. She'd been with other men since me. Men who'd helped her experiment and learn. Was Nixon one of them? Did she—

Stop. I gritted my teeth, forcing the image of her with anyone else away. She was here. Quinn was in my bed. If she wanted hard and no-holds-barred sex from me, then that's what she'd get.

I slammed my mouth on hers and my fingers dug into her flesh, kneading her curves through her jeans. I slipped a hand underneath the hem of her hoodie, letting the callouses on my fingers drag across her smooth skin. When my palm found her breast, I tore the cup of her bra away and pinched her nipple.

"Yes," she moaned, her back arching off the bed.

These clothes were getting in my goddamn way.

I leaned back and ripped the hoodie off her body, and her hair fanned out in blond streams on my charcoal bedding. Her bra came off next, easily unclasped and stripped from her arms. I stood from the bed and toed off my boots while she sat up and dove for the button on my jeans.

Quinn yanked them down, along with my boxer briefs, until I sprang free. Then she leaned in and her tongue darted out to lick the glistening drop at the tip of my cock.

"Fuck." I swallowed hard, sucking in a sharp breath. No way I was going to last. It had been a long time since I'd been with a woman. If this first round went fast, I'd make it up to Quinn on the second and third. Because there was no chance in hell this was only happening once tonight. I reached behind my neck and pulled off my T-shirt, tossing it to the floor.

"What do you want?" Quinn's nails raked across my abs, dipping into the valleys between the ridges.

I captured her wrist and dropped to my knees. "You."

One at a time, I unlaced her boots and tugged them from her feet. She wasn't wearing socks. She hated socks. With one hand in the center of her bare chest, I slowly pushed her into the bed and went for her jeans, dragging them down her legs. Then I took a long look at her wearing only a black lace thong.

My mouth watered.

Quinn had curves around her hips that hadn't been there before. Her arms were stronger, the muscles toned and lean.

She'd transformed from a beautiful young woman to a fantasy.

And I'd missed it.

I'd fucking missed it because I'd been so sure she'd come home.

I'd been the blind fool who'd let her walk away.

"What?" She sat up and leaned on her elbows. "What's wrong?"

"Nothing." I blinked the regret away and shook my head. "You're stunning."

"Not so bad yourself." She licked her lips and crooked a finger. It was another bold gesture, something she wouldn't have done at eighteen.

My Quinn had been a timid lover, shy, who'd let me be in control most of the time. We'd been tentative, the way teenagers often were, fumbling as we'd practiced the motions.

Her daring streak had only begun to show in the months before she'd left. Mine too.

We'd been each other's firsts. We'd lost our virginity in my Chevy truck, under a sky full of stars on a warm summer night. I would have been content to live my life having Quinn and only Quinn.

That wasn't the case anymore. Now we were both experienced and confident in the bedroom.

I fucking hated it.

"Graham." Quinn's voice called me back to the room. "Where did you go?"

"Just remembering." *Just wishing things would be different.*

She sat up and took my hand, lacing her fingers through

mine, something she'd done a thousand times. "Do you still want to do this?"

"Yes." There was no hesitation in my answer.

We'd changed. We'd had other lovers. But Quinn was still Quinn, and she was in my bed. I'd savor and soak up tonight because it wasn't likely to happen again.

I kissed her, sucking and nibbling, as I shoved off my jeans and she wiggled out of her panties. Then I was on her, skin to skin, as she hooked those lean legs around me and her wet center brushed against my arousal.

"Are you wet for me?"

She moaned and nodded, closing her eyes as I kissed along the arch of her throat.

The heat from her pussy, the scent of her, drove me mad. Nothing new there.

I'd lost my mind over this woman years ago.

"Hurry." She palmed my ass, pulling me closer. Her nipples rubbed against the hard plane of my chest.

I broke away from her luscious mouth and stretched for the nightstand to get a condom. When I looked back, her eyebrows were knitted together, and her gaze was locked on the foil packet in my hand.

Was that how I'd looked thinking about her other lovers? Because Quinn's thoughts were transparent. She was wondering why I had a stash of condoms in my drawer. She was realizing I'd had others.

I smoothed a lock of hair away from her cheek and her eyes snapped to mine. "Don't go there. It doesn't matter."

"Too late," she whispered. "It hurts."

I traced my thumb across her cheek. "Yeah, baby. It does."

You were supposed to let go when your first love ended.

You were supposed to look at the past and smile at the memory.

You weren't supposed to hold it so close that it wound into your very existence, making every moment impossible to forget.

"Make it stop," she pleaded.

I ripped open the condom and rolled it on. She wrapped her arms around my shoulders and clung to me as I eased my hips into the cradle of hers, positioning at her entrance and pausing only long enough to lock our gazes as I thrust inside.

The feel of her wet heat sheathing me was blinding. The worry and the pain fell away as I slid deep, connecting us in something both new and old.

"Fuck, I missed this. You."

She hummed her agreement and tilted up her hips, urging me to move.

I pulled out only to slam inside with a fast drive that made her cry out and squeeze her eyes shut. The desperation we'd felt on the sidewalk outside the Eagles returned with raging force and I set a hard rhythm, shaking the bed with every move.

We kissed rough as I pounded inside her. Our breathing was ragged, our words and sounds incoherent. We fucked until her limbs were quaking and she cried out, her orgasm taking over and pulsing around my cock.

I gritted my teeth, holding back as she clenched, but the pleasure built in my lower spine, tingles washed up and down my limbs, and there was no fighting my release. With a roar, I let go.

She took my weight when I collapsed on top of her, boneless. Our bodies were slick with sweat and I reveled in her closeness as our breathing slowed and we returned to reality. She felt so warm in my hold that I hated to lose her, but the condom needed to be dealt with.

I kissed her temple and slid out, going to the bathroom to clean up. When I returned to the bedroom, I found her sitting on the end of the bed. Her panties were on and she was hooking her bra.

"Don't."

Her lashes lifted. "I should go."

"Don't." It was a plea.

"Okay." She nodded, then flung her bra to the floor and scooted up to the pillows.

A weight fell from my shoulders as I crossed the room, then turned down the covers before climbing in. I tucked her back into my chest, covered us up, and held her tight.

"Seeing you on stage tonight was incredible. You were amazing." She found my hand, threading our fingers together. "Do you play often?"

"Once a month or so." My parents would watch Colin and I'd have a night to do something fun. I'd offered to cancel tonight, with Nan's service tomorrow, but Dad had urged me to go. They'd wanted some time with Colin too. This week, we'd all been reminded that life was short.

"Would you ever want to do it professionally?" Quinn asked.

"No. I like my job. I'm good at building and creating something with my hands. It's hard work, but it pays the bills."

"But—"

"That was your dream, never mine. I can't see myself living on the road. I'd never do that to Colin. I want roots. I want stability. I want a home like the one I had as a kid. For him. For me."

She didn't move. She didn't speak.

"You can understand that, right?"

"Yeah." She nodded. "Of course."

I tucked her closer and closed my eyes. "Stay tonight."

"Sure." She nodded and blew out a deep breath. "Good night, Graham."

I breathed in her hair and yawned. "Night, Quinn."

———

MY ARM STRETCHED toward the other side of the bed, and it was met with cold sheets and an empty pillow.

She left.

I sat up and threw my legs over the edge, letting my head fall for a moment. There was no need to look around the room for signs of Quinn. Her clothes would be gone. Her boots no longer tangled with mine. All I had left was the scent of her on my sheets that I'd wash later today.

It would do me no good to keep her smell in this room.

I stood and made my way to the bathroom, turning on the shower.

I'd asked her to stay and she'd left. It was so goddamn familiar and pathetic, my stomach turned.

But there wasn't time to dwell on it today. I'd have to wait until later to regret last night.

Because I had to get ready for Nan's funeral.

CHAPTER ELEVEN

QUINN

"Good morning."

Mom and Dad looked up from the table, each holding a glass of ice water.

"You look nice," Mom said. "Is that the dress that arrived here yesterday?"

"Yes. Ethan, our tour manager, sent it over."

I hadn't had a black dress in my luggage. That thought hadn't even crossed my mind until two days ago. I'd planned on hitting the mall, but in true Ethan form, he'd been three steps ahead, coming to my rescue. He'd texted me before I'd even been able to plan my shopping trip and told me a dress and shoes would be arriving by a courier.

Ethan worked for our general manager, Ben, and was technically only required to oversee the tours, but he always went above and beyond.

The dress was demure and black, fitted but not tight with cap sleeves and a jewel neckline. There was a pleat at the hips, giving me the illusion of curves and hiding the pockets I'd already stuffed with folded tissues.

The heels were peep-toe pumps, patent leather with red Louboutin soles. The gorgeous shoes would be wasted in my wardrobe since I preferred boots, but Ethan appreciated nice clothes and made sure that when it mattered we were always decked out in the finest.

Today, it mattered.

I clicked across the tiled kitchen floor, my heels making a cheerful clip that didn't seem appropriate for a day of mourning. I filled a mug with the coffee Mom had made special for me, then joined my parents at the table, taking care with my steps this time to muffle the noise.

"Is there anything I can do today?" I asked.

Dad shook his head. "No, I think we're all set, but thank you. And thank you for singing. I'm glad we can honor her last wishes today."

Her last wishes. My God, I missed her. I'd woken up this morning, buried my face in my pillow and cried. Why hadn't I come back sooner? Why hadn't I spent more time with Nan?

Even while I'd been off living my busy life, she'd been so ingrained in my world. I hadn't missed her because she'd been with me, every step of the way. But I should have come home. I should have hugged her more and held her hand. I should have sung to her in person and played the early drafts of my music for her.

But I'd been scared. A coward.

"She was so proud of you." Mom's hand stretched across the table, covering mine. "We all are."

My eyes flicked to Dad. He simply nodded.

"I should have come to see her. To see everyone."

"She understood," he said quietly. "She was the most understanding person in the world. Like this funeral. I've been to hundreds in my life, but I've never planned one. She wouldn't let me help plan Dad's. She took care of it all on her own. And you should have seen the list the lawyer gave us with her will. She practically planned her own too. What she wanted for the service. The type of flowers. The music. I think she knew I'd be struggling."

The lump in my throat grew ten sizes as his eyes flooded with tears. "I'm sorry, Dad."

"Did you know she used to grade my sermons?"

"She did?"

He nodded. "We leave notebook paper in the pews so kids have something to draw on besides the hymnals and Bibles. Every week she'd take a slip, give me a grade, then drop it into the offering. It was very hard last week knowing there'd be no report card in the offering plate."

The lump in my throat burned. "Did she ever give you an F?"

"A B- was the lowest she went and that was because I was referencing Leviticus. She wasn't particularly fond of that book. She called it dull and far too long."

"That is so . . . Nan." She'd had strong opinions but delivered them in a way that, whether you agreed with them or not, you couldn't help but adore.

"Yes, it was. I drew the lucky straw when it came to parents." He forced a smile, blinking the tears away. "I feel blessed that I was able to live by them for so long."

Dad had grown up in Bozeman. This was where Nan and my grandfather had grown up too. The Montgomerys went back four generations in Montana and not many moved away—and stayed away.

Except for me.

My father had gone to college in Bozeman, where he'd

met Mom. After working for a year, he'd decided to become a reverend. He moved his family—Walker had been two months old—to Colorado, where he got his master's in divinity from a seminary school. I had been born in Idaho, where Dad had been a reverend at a small church. Then the stars aligned and he'd been able to take over at the church where he'd grown up. Nan's church.

His church.

They moved us here three days before my first birthday.

Dad was going on twenty-six years at this church. He'd always said that it could be harmful for a pastor to become too engrained and too permanent. That he'd look elsewhere when his pastoral tenure became too long. Mostly, he'd wanted to make sure us kids could graduate from Bozeman High.

Yet here he was.

Would he stay until retirement? I couldn't imagine Mom and Dad not living in this house, not serving this community.

"Are you all set to sing with Graham?" Mom asked, sipping her water.

Graham.

I dropped my gaze, not wanting them to see the flush that crept into my cheeks.

What the actual fuck had I been thinking last night? I had sex. Sex with Graham.

The two of us had always had an incredible passion for each other, even as awkward teenagers, but last night had been . . . *wow*. My core throbbed and ached.

What a goddamn tangled mess. Resisting Graham last night had been impossible. There'd been so much heat and unbridled lust in his kiss. There'd been so much tenderness in his touch. With him inside me, everything had just felt right.

Then he'd reminded me that our lives were traveling in opposite directions. He had a son. I understood his need for a simple life.

Mine was anything but simple.

And I couldn't stay.

I'd waited until he'd fallen asleep, until the rise and fall of his chest had become slow and deep, then I'd swiped up my clothes and snuck out, dressing in his living room as I'd waited for an Uber to take me home.

How would I face him today? How would I sing beside him?

"Quinn?"

"Oh, sorry, Mom." I hadn't answered her question. "Yes, I think we're set."

"What are you singing?"

"'Torchlight.' It's one of the band's songs." I had no idea if my mother listened to my music.

We sat in silence, none of us having anything happy to say on a day like this, until Dad stood from the table and took his empty glass to the sink.

Mom cast his back a sorrowful look as he walked out of the kitchen and headed down the hall toward his office. She stood, ready to follow. "We're going to leave in about an hour."

"Okay." I nodded, then I was alone.

When I got home to Seattle, I wanted to be alone. I wanted days spent by myself in my music room, interacting with others only when I needed to order takeout.

But not today. Today, I didn't want to be alone, where the silence was punishing and the solitude miserable.

I'd lost my grandmother. I'd missed the chance to say goodbye.

I didn't like myself today. I didn't want to be alone with *me*.

The ache in my heart forced me up from the chair and my heels clicked furiously as I rushed for the front door. "Mom," I called through the house. "I'm going to go to the church early and practice."

"Oh. Okay," she called back from Dad's office.

My walk to the church was brisk, the air having not yet warmed from the rising sun. I shivered and wrapped my arms around my waist as goose bumps broke across my forearms and calves.

Even though the walk was short, my feet ached by the time I made it to the church. When I stepped inside the door, the smell of coffee and sugar cookies wafted from the reception area. The lights were on in the sanctuary.

I poked my head in, seeing two women bustling around the stage, shifting flower arrangements and photos.

"I know Bradley wanted people to be able to walk up and look at pictures, but I'm afraid we're going to need the front row open for seating," one of the women said.

"I think so too," the other said. "Even with the folding chairs, this is going to be packed. Remind me to crank up the air."

One of the women glanced over her shoulder and spotted me. She dropped her chin, peering at me over a pair of clear-framed glasses. "I'm sorry, dear. We aren't quite ready yet. The service doesn't start until ten."

"Oh, I'm—"

"Quinn." The other woman, who'd had her back to me, turned and I recognized her instantly. *Ugh.*

149

"Hi, Susan." I waved to the church's office coordinator and forced a polite smile. She'd been here nearly as long as Dad, though her hair had grayed twice as much since I'd seen her last. It was nearly white, a sharp contrast to her black pantsuit.

"This is Bradley's *other* daughter." Susan sent her friend a look, who turned away, muttering, "Oh."

Nice. This damn church.

It wasn't the building or the messages Dad preached that I hated so much. It was the people like Susan who felt justified to judge. It wasn't the entire congregation. Most who'd gone here were kind and warm and caring.

But Susan was everything wrong with this place. She had this idea in her head of how people should act. Specifically, how a pastor's daughter should act.

Fucking Susan. Good to see she hadn't changed.

I marched down the aisle, not caring when she gave me a scowl. This was my grandmother's funeral. This was about my family today, and she could stuff it.

Stepping on stage, I walked to the piano and hefted the pot of lilies and roses off the top.

"Those are for the piano." Susan huffed, her gaze zeroing in on my nose ring.

"I'm not playing with the lid down," I barked and moved the flowers to the open space at the base of Dad's pulpit.

She took a step, ready to snatch them and put them back, but I leveled my gaze and she inched away.

Bitch.

I walked to the piano and sat down, closing my eyes and pretending the women weren't there. My fingers found the keys and I played, song after song, loud and angry. Grief, rage, pain—every emotion was poured into the music until I finally caught my breath and looked up to see the room was empty.

I'd scared them away.

Ironically, I used to like Susan. She'd always kept Werther's Originals in a glass dish on her desk, and she'd let me have one after piano lessons or on the days when I'd be here with Dad. Then I got older, I became my own person, and she didn't like that person. I didn't fit into her designated hole. I'd worn tight jeans with holes in the knees and my Doc Martens unlaced.

Dad hadn't been the only one who'd disapproved of my church apparel.

The last time I remembered getting one of her hard candies had been before my thirteenth birthday. I was going to sneak in later and toss that bowl in the trash.

No matter how poorly she treated me, Dad had never reprimanded her. He always chose the congregation. Always.

Over his daughter.

Dad didn't want conflict. He'd wanted me to put on a smile and stay quiet. To keep my opinions, my dreams bottled up.

Quinn wants to be a rock star.

Great. How cute. The problem was that dream didn't wither away. I didn't grow out of it.

I chased it with abandon.

"I need to get out of here," I muttered to myself, standing from the piano.

The row of photographs in front of the stage beckoned and I walked closer to take them in. The closest was a framed picture of Nan kneeling in her flower garden. She smiled at a rose bush, a pair of clippers in her hand. Who would take care of those roses now that she was gone?

The next picture was of her and my grandfather at their fortieth wedding anniversary party. It was on an easel beside their wedding photo.

My eyes blurred when I took in the next. It was a picture of Nan and me. We were both wearing headphones, and my tongue was sticking out. My eyes were shut, and my hands were making the rock and roll sign. Nan was smiling at me, her face frozen in laughter.

I had no idea someone had taken a picture that day when we'd been at Nan's house goofing around. It had to have been Graham. I was seventeen in the picture, and those days Graham and I had been inseparable.

My hand covered my heart, rubbing at my sternum, physically trying to push the pain away, as the tears began to fall.

She was gone.

Nan was gone.

And I hadn't been here to say goodbye.

The door opened behind me and a *whoosh* of air ran through the church. I didn't turn to see who'd come in. I didn't want anyone to see my tears, so I stumbled away from the picture. My spiked heel caught on the carpet and I stumbled but managed to keep from falling. When I had my balance, I ran from the sanctuary, disappearing through the side door that would take me to the basement.

The bathroom downstairs was a good place to cry. I'd done it before. So I locked myself inside and let the tears fall into a tuft of toilet paper, hoping my waterproof mascara would hold up for a few more hours.

Footsteps and muffled voices echoed above my head. I

took a deep breath, sucked in the emotions, and approached the mirror to assess the damage. My eyes were red-rimmed and my nose was puffy. My lips were pale and my cheeks splotchy.

"Nice," I muttered, drying my eyes for a final time and sniffling.

The noise above continued as people filed into the church, but I loitered in the bathroom, not wanting to hear condolences or pretend like this wasn't the hardest thing I'd ever done.

But as the minutes ticked on and ten o'clock approached, I knew I couldn't hide for much longer. I tossed the damp tissues away and washed my hands. Twice. Doing everything possible to avoid going upstairs and saying goodbye.

How could Dad deliver a message today? How would he be able to stand?

How was I going to sing?

The noise from above began to dim as people were likely seated and waiting. I gulped, forced my feet to the door, and swung it open.

A pair of golden-brown eyes were waiting on the other side.

"Hey," Graham said, leaning against the wall across from the bathroom. "Thought I'd find you down here."

"I just needed a minute." Or twenty. "You look nice."

His eyes swept me head to toe. "Same to you."

Graham was wearing a charcoal suit, the white shirt underneath starched stiff. His hands were in his pockets making his shoulders look impossibly broad in his suit coat. He looked capable, like he'd hold the weight of today on his back without any trouble.

I envied his strength. Maybe I should have stolen some before sneaking out of his bed last night.

"Um. About last night, I—"

He lifted a hand. "We don't need to talk about it. Not today."

"Okay." Not today, but what he really meant was *not ever.*

"You gonna make it today?"

"I don't know," I admitted.

"I've been thinking about it." He pushed off the wall. "About the song."

"Yeah?"

"I think you should sing it alone."

Alone? My jaw dropped. "What? No. That's not what Nan wanted."

"She wanted you here, Quinn. Not to sing with me, just to sing. I think she thought it would be easier if we did it together, but you and I both know she would have loved it to be only you."

Was this happening? Was he really doing this to me? Now?

"I-I don't . . . but she asked for us to sing together."

"And I'm saying no. You should sing alone."

This was because of last night. Because he'd asked me to stay—last night, nine years ago—and I'd left. He was punishing me.

Fuck him for abandoning me today.

"Fine." I marched past him and down the hallway.

His footsteps followed, but the furious blood rushing in my ears drowned out the noise.

How dare he do this? How dare he switch it up at the last minute? Why wouldn't he have just said he didn't want to sing in the first place? Why practice and go through this entire week only to back out at the eleventh hour?

Was I really so horrible to sit beside for three fucking minutes?

He hadn't seemed to mind being inside me for an hour last night, but he couldn't give me three minutes.

My hands were balled into fists at my sides, my jaw locked tight as I walked upstairs. I was livid with Graham, ready to clutch that fury close so it could propel me through the day, but as I stormed into the sanctuary and spotted two familiar faces hovering above the picture of me and Nan, my anger evaporated.

"What are you doing here?" My eyes flooded.

Jonas's brown hair was tied back neatly, his lean body covered in an Italian black suit. Ethan's doing, no doubt, who stood at his side with his hand outstretched for mine.

"Thought you might need a friend." Jonas put his arm around my shoulders and pulled me close.

There was no stopping the tears as they fell onto his suit.

Ethan's thumb rubbed the back of my hand, and when I pulled my shit together and looked up, his kind smile was waiting. He looked handsome in his dove-gray suit, the light color creating a beautiful contrast to his dark skin. "We love you."

"You good?" Jonas asked as I stepped away and wiped my cheeks dry.

"No. But I'm glad you guys are here."

"Come on." Ethan jerked his chin to the pews. "Show us where to sit."

"Okay." I let go of Ethan's hand and led them to the sections reserved for family. Jonas and Ethan were my family too, and today I wanted to sit between them.

I could feel Graham's gaze on my shoulders as we sat in the row in front of his. I refused to turn and look at his face, but I did risk a glance at Colin, whose mouth was hanging open as he gaped at Jonas.

The room was quiet except for hushed whispers. We sat in silence and I clutched Jonas's hand, squeezing it tight as I sucked in a few deep breaths to get myself under control. Then at ten o'clock on the dot, Dad emerged from a door that led to his office and began the service.

With glistening eyes, he spoke with love and adoration for his mother. He read the obituary that she herself had written, one that made the room chuckle because it was so . . . Nan.

Then after one prayer, Dad found me in the crowd and nodded.

I walked to the stage, my shoulders pinned and my fingers trembling. When Graham didn't stand, Dad looked between the two of us, but just gave him a slight head shake as I sat at the piano.

For Nan.

This was for Nan.

I could do this for Nan.

Except I can't do this.

I forced my fingers to the cold keys. I swallowed the burn in my throat.

I could do this. I would do this.

No tears. I swallowed again. No tears.

Then I made the mistake of looking into the crowd. Mom's chin was quivering. Walker's eyes were red. Brooklyn was crying.

And Colin . . . my heart cracked. Colin's shoulders were shaking as he cried, his face buried in his dad's chest.

My throat was on fire and my hands were shaking. What was I doing up here? I couldn't sing. How could Graham send me up here to do this alone? How could he humiliate me like this? He should be sitting at my side, damn it. He should be here to play when I couldn't. To sing when I couldn't breathe.

If he was up here . . .

If he was up here, I wouldn't sing.

He knew it. He knew I'd lean on him. That's why he sent me up here alone.

My eyes tracked across the faces staring, waiting for me to play, and I found his.

The world disappeared. The pews emptied and the pain faded.

He hadn't sent me up here alone. He'd known the only way for me to sing, for me to honor Nan's wish, was if I could look into the crowd and see his face.

My fingers pressed into the keys and I filled my lungs, the first note coming out with a rasp. Nan would have liked the rasp. She would have liked the softer notes that followed.

The notes I sang to Graham.

The notes I sang for Nan.

CHAPTER TWELVE

GRAHAM

"That was the first funeral I've ever been to with Christmas carols." Jonas chuckled from the seat behind mine.

"Very original," Ethan said. "Now I know where you get your love of carols from."

"Yeah." Quinn gave a soft laugh.

I was eavesdropping.

Quinn, Jonas and a man I heard her call Ethan, her tour manager, were sitting at the table behind mine.

The healthy thing to do would be stand and find another spot for Colin and me to sit, but I couldn't seem to stop listening.

"How you doing?" Jonas asked.

"I'm okay," Quinn murmured. "It was a nice service, wasn't it?"

"You stole the show." Ethan voiced my own thoughts.

Bradley had spoken nice words for his mother and brought a few people to tears, but Quinn's singing—she'd hit everyone in the heart.

That velvet voice held an edge today, like she'd been singing through the tears and heartache. And through it, she'd looked at me.

Maybe I should have explained myself better when I'd found her in the downstairs bathroom. Maybe she wouldn't have been so pissed. But I knew she wouldn't have gone through with it had I been beside her at the piano. She would have let me carry the song.

And she would have regretted it.

Quinn didn't like goodbyes, but she'd managed to say one with that song today.

That was why Nan had asked her to do it, right? Because Nan knew Quinn would feel guilty for not returning to Bozeman. And Nan hadn't wanted that for her girl.

So I'd forced her to sing alone.

Just so she'd sing.

Quinn had held my gaze until about three-quarters of the way through "Torchlight" when her eyes had drifted shut and her voice had peaked. She'd filled the empty corners of the hall, wrapping herself around every person, cloaking them with the music.

Nan would have loved it.

It had been perfect.

"That version of 'Torchlight' was . . . that was incredible, Quinn," Jonas said.

"Thanks."

"You've never mentioned singing something for an album. Why?"

Interesting. So they hadn't shoved her aside, forcing her out of the spotlight. She'd kept her talent a secret from everyone, even her *best friends*.

"You're the singer," Quinn said. "Not me. I'll stick to the instruments."

"If you ever change your mind, a vocal from you on an album would be badass. Think about it."

I didn't need to see her face to know she gave him some uncommitted gesture, blowing off the suggestion. "Speaking of albums, any update on Harvey?"

"He's still thinking about a visit, but I've managed to stall him for a couple of weeks. Has he been texting?"

"Every. Day."

Her voice sounded stressed and irritated. She hadn't let on that she was dealing with pressure from her producer. Though why would she? We weren't friends. Quinn and I didn't talk. We fought.

And last night, we'd fucked.

"Whatever," Jonas mumbled. "We're not worrying about it today. The album will get done."

"How's your stuff coming?" she asked.

"I've got about five songs roughed out and they're in pretty good shape actually, so he's happy about that. Though he says they're a little on the fluffy side. He wants some edgier stuff to add in, balance it out. But . . ."

"You're not in an edgy place," Quinn said.

"Nope. With Kira and Vivi and the bab—uh, house in Maine, things are good."

"Wait a minute. Kira, Vivi and what?" Ethan asked.

Jonas grumbled under his breath. "Baby. Baby on the way. Kira's pregnant."

I turned my attention to Colin as the sound of congratulations and hugs took over their conversation. "How are you doing, buddy?"

"Okay." He kept his eyes on his plate. "Do I have to eat all this?"

"No." I shook my head, seeing he'd eaten half a roll and a couple bites of the cold cuts I'd put on his paper plate. I'd forced myself to eat the sandwich I'd made and some broccoli salad, but I wasn't hungry either.

"How much longer do we have to stay?" Colin looked up to me, his brown eyes sad and pleading for us to leave.

"Not much longer." I ruffled his hair and dropped my arm behind his seat.

He'd had a good time at my parents' place last night and it had been another distraction. But what he needed—what we both needed—was some time alone. As soon as we could, I was sneaking him out of here and taking him home. We'd get out of these suits and be together. He could cry if he needed without worrying that his friends from Sunday school were watching. We could talk it through.

Though I wasn't sure what to say to him.

Today was Colin's first funeral. He was hurt. He was confused. But I didn't want to push him to talk until he'd worked it out in his head. Until he had his questions to ask. That was his style when something weighed heavily on his heart and mind. He needed space alone to process. Like father, like son.

Colin had leaned into my side during the funeral, crying on and off. During Quinn's song, I'd held him tight and muffled his sobs in my suit jacket. He'd clung to me today.

Or maybe I'd clung to him.

The only time he'd had to sit with Mom at the service today was when I'd gone on stage with the other members of the church band to lead the room in Christmas carols—

another one of Nan's requests. I hadn't thought "Silent Night" would be quite as powerful as it was on Christmas Eve, when the entire congregation would hold white candles and we'd dim the lights to sing in the glow. But even in summer, lights on full, it had been quite the ending to her funeral.

Nan would have been damn proud.

She would be so missed. There was a hole she'd left behind that no one would ever fill.

In time, the grief would fade, but right now when the wound was hemorrhaging, I wasn't sure how I'd ever bring myself to delete her number from my contacts. How I'd drive down her street again or eat tomato soup. Nan had made the best tomato soup and nothing I'd ever found outside her small kitchen could compare.

"Dad, can we go now?" Colin leaned his head into my side.

"Yeah."

Bradley and Ruby were mulling around, greeting people and receiving hugs. My mom was clearing plates with a vengeance, refusing to sit down because she didn't want Quinn's parents to lift a finger today.

The caterer had brought in sandwich trays and a plethora of salads, all set up as a buffet in the common area of the church's basement. There was more food here than I'd seen at the annual winter potluck. Carafes of yellow lemonade and red fruit punch brightened the tables. The industrial coffee pot was likely drained given the number of paper cups I spotted in hands around the room.

Walker had told me that in her final requests, Nan had insisted on a low-fuss meal in the church's basement. *Don't rent out a place and spend a bunch of money. Just buy nice flowers.*

And nice they had been. The blooms in the sanctuary were prettier than most I'd seen at weddings.

The basement was packed with tables and every seat full. Small groups hugged the walls as they visited, and even though the air conditioner was running on high, the room was beginning to get stuffy.

There'd be no graveside function today because Nan had been cremated. Her ashes were to be taken to the mountains, to be spread in the fall, her favorite time of year, in the same place where she'd spread her husband's ashes a decade ago.

So this was it. After the reception and the idle chatter that had slowly begun to give me a headache, the day was over, at least for Colin and me. Everyone was preoccupied, the perfect time for us to sneak out and not be missed.

We'd go home and get into some jeans. Maybe we'd play catch for a while outside until dinner. Then I'd order Chinese takeout because Colin loved it.

I collected his plate and stood, holding out his chair, but before I could turn, a body bumped into mine. There was no need to turn to know that body. I'd held it in my arms last night as I'd drifted off to sleep.

Before she'd left.

"Sorry." Quinn met my gaze for only a moment, then seemed to find the lapels of my coat fascinating.

"Close quarters today."

Her eyes scanned the room. "Yeah. I'm surprised everyone fit down here."

"How are you doing?"

"Ready to escape." She dropped her focus to Colin and nudged his elbow. "Hey, Colin. You look nice. I've got some guys I'd like you to meet if you have a second."

He nodded, his gaze darting past her.

"Jonas and Ethan, meet Colin. He's a fan."

"Hey." Ethan twisted in his seat, holding out his hand, shaking Colin's. "I'm Ethan. Hush Note's tour manager."

Wonder filled my son's eyes as Jonas stood and stretched across the table to bump fists. "Hi, Colin. I'm Jonas. Nice to meet you."

"You too." His cheeks flushed and he couldn't stop the smile that stretched across his face.

"How do you guys know each other?" Jonas asked, walking around the end of the table to join us. He looked exactly the same as he did on magazine covers and in music videos, but not as tall as I'd expected, given how much of a giant he was on stage. He was a few inches shorter than my six-foot-three.

"I grew up next door to Colin's dad"—Quinn gestured to me—"Graham."

I shook his hand as he offered it. "Hi."

"Graham. Good to meet you." Jonas looked me up and down, his eyes narrowing before switching to Quinn.

Had she told him about me? That we'd dated as kids?

I shifted Colin into the middle of the huddle, my hands on his shoulders. "Are you in town for long?"

Would they be flying out with Quinn on Monday morning?

"We're taking off before too long," Jonas said. "Just came to pay our respects. I didn't know Nan, but I talked to her on the phone a handful of times over the years whenever she'd call Quinn. She seemed like a special woman."

"That she was."

Ethan stood and put his hand on Quinn's shoulder. "Can I get you anything?"

"No, but thanks." She gave him a sad smile.

"Just your airplane on Monday." He chuckled. "Right?"

"Right," she muttered.

Monday and she'd be gone. I'd been pissed this morning when I'd woken up and she'd been gone, but maybe it was a good thing she hadn't stayed the night. I didn't need that kind of intimacy from Quinn. We'd crossed enough lines with the sex.

"You're leaving?" Colin asked her.

She nodded. "On Monday. I have to get home to Seattle."

"Why?"

"To write our next album," she said. "I have to get back to work."

That might be part of the reason, but mostly she had to get away from here. Away from her family and from me.

"We should go." I nudged Colin forward but he didn't move.

"You said you'd teach me a couple things on my drums before you left."

"Oh. That's right." Quinn's forehead furrowed "We'll do it, um . . ."

"Today?" Colin suggested.

"Make sure she teaches you the good stuff," Jonas said before either Quinn or I could answer.

Colin beamed, and for a day when I didn't think I'd see his smile, I couldn't object.

"I, um . . ." Quinn's eyes hesitantly shifted my way. "Is today all right?"

"Please, Dad?" Colin begged.

How did I say no? "Yeah. Today's great."

So much for an afternoon alone with my son. But if playing the drums with Quinn cheered him up, I guess that was the goal anyway. We'd order Chinese after Quinn left. How long did a drum lesson take? An hour? Maybe two?

"Do you want to go now? Or later?"

She glanced around the room, finding her family.

They were sitting three tables over. Walker and Mindy were helping their kids eat lunch. Brooklyn was feeding the baby a bottle while Pete chatted with Walker. Bradley and Ruby chose that moment to carry over plates of their own and sit in the seats their children had saved for them.

Quinn's family.

Sitting without her.

Did they even glance over as they'd reserved seats? Had they even thought about including her and her friends?

I doubted it was intentional. The Montgomerys weren't like that, but in a way, after nine years, they'd forgotten her. They'd formed new habits.

"We can go now," she said. "Can I have a minute to say goodbye and walk these guys out?"

"No problem." I pointed toward the rear of the building. "We're parked in the back lot. Meet you out there."

I steered Colin through the people, weaving past tables and chairs. Many nodded and said hello, but no one stopped us as we headed for the stairs. We climbed them, going straight for the exit, and the second we were outside, I tugged on my tie. "I hate ties."

"Me too." Colin fought with his, unable to loosen it enough. I'd tied it for him this morning.

"How are you doing, kiddo?" I asked, bending down to undo the tie's knot.

"I'm okay. That was pretty sad."

"Funerals usually are." I lifted the tie off his head. "But it gives us a chance to honor those who've passed. To say our goodbyes."

"I cried." He hung his head.

Colin had been a regular crier as a baby and toddler. I hadn't thought much of it as he'd moved into preschool because what four-year-old didn't cry? But when he'd started kindergarten at five, he'd gotten teased by some of the older kids at school, mostly while they played football or soccer at recess. He was competitive and loved to play, but my boy loved to win.

When he'd lost or made a mistake, he'd get frustrated and cry.

Kids were damn mean, and he'd been labeled a cry baby. His teacher had called me because it had become something of a regular occurrence. So I'd spent a lot of time talking about it and teaching him ways to deal with his frustration without breaking down into tears. We'd also talked a lot about how winning wasn't everything—we were still working on that one.

Though his crying tendency had stopped, I worried we'd gone too far in the other direction. He was nearly afraid to cry.

"There's no shame in crying on a day like today."

He lifted his chin. "You didn't."

"Doesn't mean I'm not hurting in here." I put my hand over my heart. "We're going to miss Nan, aren't we?"

"A lot." His chin quivered.

"Let's talk about her often so we don't forget. Remember how she used to trick us and point to our shirt, ask 'What's that?' then flick our noses when we'd look?"

Colin giggled. "You fell for it every time."

"Every time. Oldest trick in the book, she'd say. But not you. You didn't fall for her tricks."

"Nope." His chest puffed with pride. "I'm not gullib, like you."

"Gullib-*le*."

"Gullible," he repeated.

"Come on." I nodded toward the parking lot and stood. "Let's get buckled in while we wait for Quinn."

He slipped his hand in mine as we walked.

I looked down, taking in his small fingers. When had they gotten so long? His head came to my waist now. The baby fat on his cheeks was only a memory.

I'd been such a wreck as a single dad, just trying to survive, that I hadn't savored enough of those times when he'd fit in the crook of my arm. I imagined most parents felt that way when they looked at their kids and realized time wasn't just moving fast, it was a damn lightning streak.

We got to the truck and Colin climbed in the back, securing himself in his booster while I got in and rolled the windows down, forgoing air conditioning for some fresh air.

It didn't take long for Quinn to walk outside the side door with Jonas and Ethan in tow. She hugged them both, holding tight. Jonas kissed her cheek and said something in her ear that made her nod before they walked toward the street, Ethan's fingers flying over his phone's screen.

She stood there, staring at their backs. Then she looked to the door of the church.

Had she told anyone she was leaving? My guess was no. Would they notice she was gone? Or would it take hours, until everyone else began to leave the building, and they'd remember the woman with the golden voice?

Quinn looked lost. Alone.

It broke my damn heart to see her standing there by herself.

I leaned out the window and whistled, the shrill noise echoing through the lot.

Quinn's eyes snapped to my truck and she jogged from the church, her heels clicking fast as she fled.

I leaned across the seat, stretching for the door handle. It popped open just as she reached the door. She opened it wider and hopped inside.

She wouldn't look at me as she strapped on her seat belt, but she did cast a glance to Colin behind her. Quinn did her best to camouflage the anguish on her face with a tight smile.

"I was thinking of ordering Chinese takeout for dinner." The words were out of my mouth before I could think them through. *So much for a short drum lesson.* But I couldn't send her home to a lonely house. Not today. "Sound good to you guys?"

"Yes." Colin fist pumped.

Quinn nodded, finally lifting her chin to look at me. "Sounds great. Sweet and sour pork?"

My favorite. Hers too.

"Obviously."

CHAPTER THIRTEEN

QUINN

"This is a beautiful home," I told Graham as we pulled into his driveway.

Last night, it had been too dark to notice the details. That and I'd been in a haze, my mind consumed with lust and heat and anticipation. When I'd snuck out, I'd kept my chin down and tiptoed out the front door silently before meeting my Uber.

"We've been fixing it up." Graham shot Colin a smile through the rearview mirror.

"How long have you lived here?"

"Four years. We were in an apartment before, but I was sick of the noise and neighbors. We needed our own space. I needed a decent garage to store tools. So I saved up for a down payment and bought it the year Walker and I started the company."

The house was a single-level rancher surrounded by towering oak trees and a row of paper birch beside the garage. The exterior was painted black, something I wouldn't have suspected would work for a smaller home, but with the white windows, honey-colored wood shutters and matching door, it worked.

It was charming yet masculine, balanced perfectly between classic style and modern flair.

"Want to see my room?" Colin asked, unbuckling as Graham eased into the garage. There was a white trailer parked in the other stall, the Hayes-Montgomery emblem on the side, and tools upon tools in every free space.

"Sure." I stepped out of the truck and followed him inside, taking it all in as I walked.

We entered through a laundry room that must not have ranked high on Graham's update list because the tan linoleum floor had a visible wear pattern leading straight through the center of the room. The brown laminate countertop beside the washer and dryer was chipped.

The kitchen came next and it was much like the laundry room. Clean and tidy but out of date. The cabinets were a yellowing oak and the counters matched the laundry room's. But the stainless appliances were new.

"Come on!" Colin waved me to follow when I hesitated in the living room while glancing out the French doors to the deck beyond.

Graham came in behind me, his keys rattling as he dropped them in the kitchen and shrugged off his suit coat. The starched cotton of his shirt pulled at his broad shoulders, and my mouth went dry.

After last night, I hadn't planned to return to Graham's home. Ever. But here I was, and I couldn't seem to stop thinking about his bedroom. I took a deep breath and instantly regretted it. The smell of his cologne and soap filled my nose.

"Quinn!" Colin shouted from a room and I walked

faster, not letting myself look toward the master down the hallway.

Why had I thought this was a good idea? I'd had sex with Graham last night, in that room. But staying at church hadn't been an option, not today when my heart was too fragile.

Jonas and Ethan were headed to the East Coast, and though they would have stayed if I'd asked, I knew they each had people waiting for them at home. If not for Graham, I would have been alone at the church, lingering while my family flitted around. Someone might as well have tattooed *outcast daughter* on my forehead.

Maybe I should have stayed and forced my way into my family. But I just . . . didn't belong. My fault or their fault, I was struggling to place the blame. It was reality. We'd grown apart.

Then Colin Hayes, and his father, had come to my rescue. Bless that kid.

"Wow." I stepped into his room. "Sweet room."

"Thanks." He plopped down on the bed, grinning as he glanced around.

The walls were painted a light, neutral cream and each seemed to have a different theme. His twin bed was pushed against the wall opposite the closet and above the headboard hung a baseball bat. The shelf above his white desk in the corner was crammed with assembled Lego race cars and monster trucks. A Hush Note poster was tacked up beside the window. It was signed by Jonas, Nix and me.

It was no surprise that Colin was a child with multiple interests. Graham had been that way too.

"Nan gave that to me." He pointed to the poster.

And I'd given it to Nan.

His smile faded along with the light in his eyes, and my

heart squeezed. If there was something I could do today to
take away some of the pain, I was here for it.

"That was from our second tour," I told him. "If you
want, I have some from the other tours too. The first poster is
very rare and they sell for over five-hundred dollars on
eBay."

"Really?" His jaw dropped.

"I'll send them to you once I get home." I kicked off my
shoes, sinking into the thick carpet. The soft, mushroom-
colored fibers squished between my toes, soothing some of
the ache from my heels.

Graham had updated this room with the paint and
carpet. While the living room and dining area had faded oak
hemlock trim, this room had solid white bordering the chocolate doors.

"So where are your drums?" I asked.

"Downstairs." He shot off the bed. "Wanna see?"

"Sure." I spun to follow him and staggered when I saw
Graham leaning against the door frame. I hadn't heard him
behind me because somewhere between here and the
kitchen, he'd toed off his polished dress shoes.

"Want anything to drink before he takes you hostage?"
he asked.

"No, thanks." I smiled, grateful that he was taking it easy
on me. I didn't have the strength to fight an angry Graham
today. "I'm okay."

And surprisingly, I was okay. Here with Graham and
Colin, I was okay.

"Listen, about the song."

I held up a hand. "It's fine."

"You're not pissed?"

"I was at first, but I get why you did it. I wouldn't have

been able to sing with you up there. I would have let you do it on your own."

A wave of relief washed over his face. "You were . . . it was perfect, Quinn. She would have been so proud."

The sting hit my nose, but I forced a smile. "She was the best."

"Quinn!" Colin shouted, drawing our attention.

"I'll be up here if you need anything." He turned away, his hands stuffed in his pockets causing his slacks to pull tighter around his ass.

I ogled. Blatantly. If he turned, he'd catch me, and I didn't have the energy to care. The man was mouthwatering. I'd had my hands on that ass last night, gripping and squeezing as he'd taken me to the edge.

He continued down the hallway, past a bathroom, to his bedroom.

I continued to stare.

"Quinn! Are you coming down?" Colin's shout caused me to flinch.

I scurried toward his voice. "On my way."

Graham's chuckle followed me down the stairs.

Busted.

I hurried down the stairs—a split-level flight with a landing in the middle—and hit the cool, concrete floor after the last step. The chill soothed my aching soles.

Colin was already behind his kit, situated in the corner of a huge, open room. The basement seemed to be nearly the entire width and length of the house. All of it open into this cavernous space.

In one section, two overstuffed leather chairs and a matching couch angled toward an enormous television. The floors were bare except for the biggest area rug I'd ever seen sitting beneath the furniture. The coffee table in the center was empty except for three black remotes.

Canned lights were recessed into the ceiling. The floors added an industrial vibe. The walls were painted the same shade as Colin's room upstairs. This was the rec room. The man area.

"This must be the hangout spot."

"Yep." Colin smiled, waving his sticks. "Ready?"

I arched an eyebrow and crossed the room. "Are you? Scooch."

He jumped off the stool so I could sit and handed over the sticks. I'd left mine at home today because they didn't go with my dress.

Colin's drums were only a pocket kit with a snare, bass, rack and floor toms. He had two cymbals—a high hat and crash. It was smaller in size but similar to a set I'd started out on. I'd been a lot older when I'd become interested in the drums. My first love—thanks to Mom and my lessons beside Graham—had been the piano.

"Guess how many cymbals I have for my tour kit?"

"How many?" Colin stood over my shoulder, soaking up my every move as I began a slow, steady rhythm on the snare.

"Guess?"

"Four."

I shook my head, picking up the tempo. "Eight."

"Wow."

"Okay. I'm going to show you an easy sequence so you can hear it, then you're going to do it."

He nodded, his eyes glued to my hands.

"Let's start with the money beat. It's easy peasy. Eighth notes on the high hat. Bass drum kicks on one and three.

Snare on two and four." I showed him twice, counting it out, and then gave him back his stool.

He played it perfectly the first time and shrugged. "Dad lets me do YouTube videos."

"Ahh. Then let's ramp it up a bit."

Next I went through a common drum fill that he'd hear a lot in pop music, something he could use to play along with the stereo. Because that was the fun of it, right? Playing to a song on the radio. The drums were fun and fancy licks were a blast, but there was nothing better than when it all came together. That was the magic, not someone playing solo in their basement.

When I'd handed over the sticks, he'd shot me a look over his shoulder that said *I got this.*

And I smiled.

Over and over we played, Colin soaking up my every word. He was my first student, and I couldn't have asked for better. He was so eager, his excitement so contagious, it was like going back in time. I'd been like that once.

"Should we take a break?" I asked Colin after glancing at the clock. We'd been down here for three hours, though it felt like minutes.

He grumbled but followed me over to the couches, plopping down.

Graham must have heard us stop because moments later, he appeared at the base of the stairs, two glasses of ice water in hand. "Thirsty?"

"Yesssss." Colin gulped his as I sipped mine. I laughed as he collapsed in the couch, flopping and flailing. "That. Was. Awesome!"

"What do you say to Quinn?" Graham took a seat in the chair farthest from me.

Colin shot up on his knees and threw his arms around my neck.

"Whoa." I wasn't sure where to put my hands as he hugged me, but they sort of just drifted down to his back and wound around his frame.

"Thank you."

"You're welcome." I dropped my cheek to his hair. "It was fun."

He squeezed me tighter, then let me go and went back to his water.

"Where'd you learn to play?" he asked with an ice cube in his mouth, the words coming out jumbled.

"School. I didn't start the drums until I was eleven."

"Sixth grade," Graham added.

"That's right." I'd been just a girl in middle school who'd had to pick an instrument for band.

My teacher, Mr. Black, had suggested I try something other than the keyboard so I wouldn't be bored. The French horn and tuba had held no interest. The other girls had claimed the clarinets and flutes—hello, predictable. So when I'd asked for the drums, he'd raised an eyebrow and booted David Hill out of percussion to the trombone, making a space for me among all the boys.

Mr. Black.

That guy changed my life.

He'd been my favorite teacher, and luckily for me, when I'd moved on to ninth grade and the high school, he'd come along. The previous high school teacher had retired, opening the position.

"Did you know Mr. Black moved away?" Graham asked. "After we graduated, he took a job in Oregon to be closer to his wife's family."

"Yeah. He emails me every few months. He's come to some concerts, and last year when we had a stop in Portland, he brought his whole family." It had been one of the best shows, looking over to see my childhood mentor standing backstage, rocking out with his wife and kids.

A flare of annoyance crossed Graham's face that I'd kept in touch with Mr. Black, and I pulled my lips between my teeth to keep a comment to myself.

Graham could have stayed in contact. Maybe not at first, but years later. They all could have kept in touch. For a woman who lived on the road and had never had an office in her life, I excelled at returning emails.

"Who's Mr. Black?" Colin asked.

"He was my teacher. My favorite teacher. He got me hooked on drums and rock and roll."

Mr. Black had been a classical musician but had loved rock from the sixties and seventies. Jazz was his second love. He'd introduced me to drummers like Keith Moon from The Who and John Bonham from Led Zeppelin.

He'd introduced me to artists who'd taken an influence of jazz and funk and infused it into rock and roll. Drummers who didn't only accent the bass line but focused on the melody to change the flow of a song.

It was how Nixon and I wrote music. I zeroed in on Nixon's guitar riffs, merging the beat with them instead of keeping with Jonas on the bass. I liked my drums to be tight with the lead phrase, something that had all started because Mr. Black had loved John Bonham's style.

I'd developed my own style and idolized my own stars, like Travis Barker from Blink-182. The day I'd met him at Coachella, I'd nearly fainted.

Nixon, the asshole, had made sure to film a video of me crying and fangirling like a damn idiot. He'd posted it on Instagram and to this day, it was my favorite content on his feed.

"I met Travis Barker," I told Graham. He'd been there in high school when I'd played Travis's drum solos over and over and over again, making him listen as I analyzed them to death.

"I saw that."

"You did?" I didn't think he followed me, though with millions of followers and counting, it wasn't a surprise I didn't know who saw my posts.

He nodded, a smile tugging at his mouth. "You *freaked* out."

I giggled, covering my face with my hands. "So embarrassing."

And one of the best moments in the past nine years.

"Who's Travis Barker?" Colin asked.

I blinked. "Only one of the best drummers of the millennium."

He only shrugged and leaped off the couch. "Dad, can I have a snack?"

"A little one. We'll order dinner in a couple hours."

"Okay." He raced toward the stairs but paused before he could disappear. "Want anything, Quinn?"

"No, I'm good. Thanks, though."

His feet flew up the stairs, leaving me alone with his father.

"He's talented, Graham. It comes naturally for him."

"Yeah, it does. I set him up with some YouTube videos and thought it would take him a few weeks to get it down. Two hours later, he hauled me down here to show me how

179

he'd figured them all out. But he goes in spurts. He'll hit it hard for a week then not play for three."

"That's probably normal for kids."

"Not you."

No, not me. The minute Mr. Black had put me behind a kit and showed me the basics, I'd been hungry. I was still hungry.

The drums and the music came instinctively. It was as much a part of my make-up as blood and bone, but I didn't take that gift for granted. Every album I pushed myself to practice and experiment. To do something different and new.

"He's only seven." Graham sighed. "Who knows what he'll want to do? Some days he's hot on the drums. Some days he's all about baseball or football. Others he'll sit down at the dining room table to draw and color for hours. Before school got out, he was obsessed with Pokémon."

I suspected that was normal too. But if he wanted to be in music, Colin had talent. And if there was anything I could do to help him when the time came, I'd do it.

So would Graham.

He wasn't like my parents. He'd support Colin no matter what path he took in life.

"Dad!" Colin shouted. "Can I show Quinn my Pokémon cards?"

Graham chuckled and gave me an evil grin. "Sure."

"Quinn!"

I pushed up from the couch. "Coming."

Colin made the rest of the afternoon pass quickly and without any awkward moments, mostly because he hardly let me out of his sight. We spent hours in his room, up until the time Graham called us for dinner, going through all of

Colin's worldly possessions. Pokémon transitioned to Legos to Hot Wheels to Nerf guns. Then we played games on the floor of his room, me sitting with my legs curled under my seat as we played Old Maid and War.

We ate at the dining room table, cartons spread out for our feast. It was still light outside when I insisted on doing the dishes since Graham had bought dinner.

"Colin, time for you to go take a shower."

"But, Dad—"

"It's seven thirty." There was a ritual in Graham's tone. Seven thirty was code for it's time to start getting ready for bed.

"Okay," the boy mumbled as he trudged to his room.

"I'm going to say goodbye, then get out of your hair," I told Graham.

He nodded, his eyes trained to his backyard from where he sat in the living room. We both knew that without Colin, things would get uncomfortable. We'd be forced to deal with last night. I had no desire to go through that, or worse . . . end up in his bed again.

I found Colin in his room, digging out a pair of pajama shorts and top from a drawer. He still wore a white shirt from Nan's service and a pair of gray pants, but his feet were bare like mine. The only one who'd changed into jeans and a soft T-shirt was Graham.

"Thanks for inviting me over today."

His head whipped my direction, panic in his gaze. "You're leaving?"

"I better get home." To Seattle, before this kid sucked me in for good.

"Oh." He hesitated by the drawer, his eyebrows narrowing. Then he flew across the room, crashing into my waist before I could realize what was happening. It was the second time his embrace had surprised me, but this time, I didn't hesitate to wrap him up, kneeling down to his level.

"Practice lots. Call me if you get stuck."

He nodded, his arms banding tighter.

And I hugged him back, until I felt Graham's presence behind us. He reached over my shoulder and placed a gentle hand on his son's head.

Colin unwound his arms and went to the dresser, picking up his pajamas from where he'd dropped them on the floor. Then he brushed past us for the bathroom, closing himself inside.

When the rush of water came, I let out the breath I'd been holding.

Was that goodbye? It didn't seem like it, but I doubted Graham would want me to keep in touch with his kid after I left. Better to leave it unsaid. Colin—all of us—had said enough goodbyes for the day.

"Thanks for letting me come over," I told Graham, standing and making my way to the front door.

"You're welcome." He stood against the wall, staying five feet away like there was a line drawn between us. A line it wasn't safe for him to cross.

I ordered an Uber, grateful and lucky that there was one three minutes away, and swiped up my shoes from where I'd moved them earlier. "I like Colin. A lot."

"The feeling is mutual."

"I'm glad I got to know him."

He gave me a flat smile, one that said he didn't like how quickly I'd become, or rather, Colin had become used to me in their house.

Because I was leaving.

"Would you care if I kept in touch with him?" I asked.

"I, uh . . ." He sighed. "I don't think that's a good idea."

Damn, that rejection stung, sharp and biting. Graham was only looking out for his son. After all, he knew better than anyone how it felt for me to leave and cut them out entirely. But I wouldn't do that to Colin. I wasn't eighteen and running away from my fears. I wasn't hurting.

Except no matter how many promises I made, Graham had his mind made up.

"Thanks for dinner." I let myself out, pulling the door closed behind me, but then Graham was there, holding it open.

"Take care of yourself, Quinn."

"You too, Graham."

I looked up to him, stalling for a moment as I memorized his face. I'd done the same thing the day he'd driven me to the airport nine years ago. This time, the man's face. I studied the strong line of his jaw covered in that sexy beard that felt delicious against my skin. I stared at the crinkles by his beautiful eyes and how they deepened when he'd smile or look at his son.

Not a day would pass when I wouldn't think of his face and mentally whisper his name.

A car rolled to the curb, the driver waving to make sure he'd found the right spot.

I backed away a step, my feet heavy and hard to pick up.

"Graham, I—" Before my brain could register my body's decision, I was moving. I walked into Graham's space, stood on my bare toes, and pressed a kiss to his cheek. "Thank you. For today. For last night. For this week. I don't know how I would have gotten through it without you. So thank you."

He swallowed, his Adam's apple bobbing. "Welcome."

I stepped away, giving him a finger wave before spinning and tiptoeing to the car at the curb.

"Quinn," he called, making me pause.

"Yeah?"

"You never really answered my question. At least, not enough for me to understand."

"What question?"

"Why don't you sing?"

I gave him a sad smile. "Because of you. I just . . . can't. Like today, I needed you."

"A crutch."

"No." I shook my head. Crutch wasn't the right word. "A muse."

I needed him for the words to come and for them to hit the right notes. To do more than sing the same old song, to make it different and new. It was Graham who inspired me to sing.

"Goodnight, Graham."

He nodded. "Night, Quinn."

A weight came off my shoulders as I rode home. Unexpected, for a day like today.

But that was Graham. And Colin. And in a way . . . Nan.

She'd brought me home, and this week, I'd buried some old ghosts.

I was leaving on Monday, but for the first time all week, my heels didn't feel aflame.

I'd leave.

But maybe this time, I'd look back.

CHAPTER FOURTEEN

QUINN

"How did you sleep?" Mom asked as I filled my morning coffee mug.

"Good. You?"

"Like a rock," she said, tidying up the kitchen. "I was exhausted."

When I'd come home from Graham's last night, she'd been nearly asleep beside Dad on the couch. The TV had been on, volume low, playing a black-and-white classic from AMC—Dad's favorite channel.

Neither of them had mentioned my disappearance from the funeral reception. Either they'd been too tired for conversation or they just hadn't cared.

"Sorry I snuck out early yesterday."

"Oh, it's fine. We had lots of hands to make the work light. Our fridge is packed with leftovers, and I won't have to cook for a week. And that's just a third. I sent trays home with Walker and Brooklyn."

"It was a lovely service."

"That it was." She nodded. "Your song was . . . beautiful. Truly."

My heart warmed. It had been a long time since Mom had complimented my music. Once, I'd lived for her praise as I'd sat at the piano. "Thanks, Mom."

"You have far surpassed anything I could have taught you. I'm sorry I didn't get a chance to meet your friends."

"You were busy." And I hadn't expected anyone to make time to sit with Jonas and Ethan yesterday. "Maybe another time. Maybe you could come to a show."

"That would be exciting."

Not a yes. Not even a maybe. A cheerfully disguised dodge that most would have assumed was agreement, when really it was a no.

"Are they still here? Your friends?" she asked.

"No, Jonas and Ethan"—I stressed their names since she hadn't asked and I didn't like them being categorized as generic friends—"left yesterday. They only flew in for the service."

"Oh." Her forehead furrowed, likely trying to figure out where I'd spent my day if it hadn't been with them. I gave her props for not asking. She was doing her best to remember I was an adult.

"I promised Colin a drum lesson," I told her. "He's a pretty amazing kid."

"You were at Graham's?"

There was an edge to his name. The same wary tone I'd heard daily in high school.

Mom loved me. Mom loved Graham. But Mom had always been nervous and skeptical about the love between Graham and me.

I nodded. "Yeah. They took pity on me and let me stay for Chinese takeout."

"Good. That's good."

It didn't sound good.

"Colin is a natural at the drums."

"He's a natural at nearly everything," she said. "He reminds me of Graham in that way."

"I thought the same thing myself." Would Colin do something with the drums? Would he practice what I'd taught him? I'd told him to call me if he got stuck, but I doubted I'd hear from him. Graham's rejection, though polite, had been absolute.

He didn't want me making calls to Colin, but what if I visited? Would he turn me away if I were here in Bozeman? I wouldn't be able to return often, but every couple of years was possible. I'd fly in to see my parents, siblings, niece and nephews. Then I'd get to hang with Colin too.

"I was thinking, what if I came home for Christmas? Would that be all right?"

Mom blinked. "Really? Of course! We'd love to have you."

I might have to bring Nixon along. We normally spent our holidays together—Nixon, Jonas and me. There were many Christmases and Thanksgivings where we'd been on the road, either at a show or on our way to one. The few times we'd been on break, we'd had a quiet gathering in Seattle.

Now that Jonas had a family of his own, we'd have to change tradition.

"Is Dad gone already?" I asked.

"You know how he is on Sunday mornings."

Yes, I did. Because while a lot had changed, some things never would. Dad had likely woken up at four to be at the church before dawn. He'd practice his sermon one last time before settling into his office for coffee. Then he'd bustle around, talking to anyone who needed a few extra words this week.

Dad thrived on Sunday mornings. They were when he performed. I expected today, like last Sunday, would be hard without Nan. But the entire church would be there to lift him up, like he'd lifted them so many times before.

"It's so lovely out this morning, I was going to walk over," Mom said. "Is that okay with you?"

"Oh, uh . . ." I hadn't planned on going to church. My time there this week had been more than enough.

"Please? It would mean a lot to me if you were there today."

Shit. "Okay, sure. I just need to put on some makeup and dry my hair."

"We've got time."

After eating a bowl of cereal, I hustled upstairs to finish getting ready. The vacuum flipped on as I was in the middle of my makeup. Mom had probably already dusted the main floor.

While Dad had been at church, cleaning had been our ritual. We'd dress for church, then clean our bedrooms and around the house. The chore board in the kitchen was long gone, and oddly, I missed seeing it beside the fridge.

This house wasn't the church's parsonage. My parents had decided to buy their own home when Dad had taken his position here, wanting that separation from the church. There was a security knowing that if he decided to retire, he wouldn't have to leave his home.

But even though this wasn't church property, it didn't

stop people from visiting often, especially on Sundays. So Mom always kept it clean in preparation for unexpected visitors.

She was waiting by the door when I came downstairs, the smell of lemon polish and window cleaner hanging in the air.

"Ready?" she asked.

"Ready." Or not. I slid on my sunglasses as she opened the door. My drumsticks were tucked securely into my jeans pocket.

The walk to church was fresh and unrushed. The air was warm and clean. I filled my lungs, savoring the smell I'd miss after tomorrow. There was a comfort in the sunshine and green-grass scent of a Montana summer. I'd been ignoring the comfort of this place all week. I'd turned a blind eye to the peace here.

But the truth was, it was nice to be home, even with all that had changed.

"I missed it here," I told Mom. "More than I'd let myself admit."

"Are you happy, Quinn? Your life is so exciting. You're always on the move. Do you enjoy it?"

"Most days. It's not as exciting as it looks. I mean, the shows are amazing. There's nothing like it. The energy and the noise. But the days in between are mostly quiet. We travel. We work on songs while we're on the road."

She smiled. "All I see is the fun. It does look wild."

"See? Where?"

"Instagram. Duh."

I giggled. "Duh."

My mother was on Instagram, another follower I'd missed in the explosion.

"I think we will try to make it to a show," she said. "Your dad's due for a vacation."

"What?" I nearly tripped over my own feet. "You think he'd come?"

"I think your dad loves you very much." She took my hand, giving it a reassuring squeeze. "And he's had a lot of time to think about how things went so terribly wrong."

"Then why—"

"Ruby!" a woman called from across the street as she pushed a stroller.

"Morning." Mom waved back, pausing on the sidewalk as the woman came over, then made introductions. She was a member of the church and on her way to service.

My question would have to wait. Or not get answered at all.

If Dad had changed so much, why hadn't he talked to me in nine years?

We made it to church and Mom was mobbed, like it had been when we'd been kids. This was normally the time when we'd find our friends, race around the basement and burn off excess energy before being regulated to a pew and expected to sit still for an hour.

I found a seat, nearly in the same place as I'd sat yesterday for the funeral. But instead of a dress and heels, today I'd gone for a pair of faded jeans, no holes, and a simple white T-shirt. My boots were on my bedroom floor and I'd traded them for my Chucks.

My fingers found their way to my necklace, fidgeting with it as I glanced around the sanctuary. The necklace was a long golden chain with a pendant of drumsticks. Nan had bought it for me last year on my birthday. It had probably cost twenty bucks from Target, but it was my favorite piece.

Jewelry companies sent me pieces all the time in the hopes I'd wear their jewels and get caught on camera. But nine times out of ten, I reached for this necklace.

I dug my phone from my pocket and opened the camera. Then I snapped a series of selfies from different angles, capturing the necklace and an asymmetrical angle of my face.

The photo was the first I'd posted on Instagram since arriving in Bozeman. With my nose buried so no one would interrupt or see my glassy eyes, I wrote the caption.

Nan. Necklace giver. Music lover. Unwavering believer. Always in my heart.

I hit save and closed my phone, taking a deep breath as I shoved away the urge to cry. The moment I looked up, I noticed the room had filled quickly.

"Good morning." A couple with an infant greeted me as they made their way to the seats across the aisle.

I received a lot of nods and smiles from faces I recognized from Nan's service. The dull rumble of conversation grew louder as the empty seats dwindled. With ten minutes until it was time to start, the spaces beside me filled up with my family.

Clearly, people knew to save this row.

"Morning," Walker said as I slid down toward the end, making room.

"Hi." I waved to his wife and kids, then leaned forward. "Morning, Brookie."

"Hey, Quinnie." She caught the slip and froze. For one moment, she'd forgotten to be mad at me and had used my old nickname.

I leaned back in my seat, dropping my chin to hide my smug grin in the fall of my hair.

Mom took her place at the other end of the row, the two of us bookending our family, as Dad emerged and walked to the pulpit. The bustle of the congregation settled as he placed his Bible and papers on the top.

"Slide over."

My head whipped to the voice as a man's body shoved mine over a few inches.

Nixon.

"What are you doing here?" I whispered.

He leaned down to whisper. "Came to rescue you."

I took him in, the black button-up and dark-wash jeans—nice jeans without holes. His Chucks were next to new without a single scuff. "You do know that the memorial service was yesterday, right? This is just church."

"I know. But you had Jonas and Ethan yesterday. I thought maybe you could use someone today too."

My heart. I looped my arm through his and dropped my head to his shoulder. "Thanks."

Nixon knew all about the fight I'd had with my parents. He knew about my issues with Dad's job and how Dad had pandered to the emotions in this building, even when it had broken his oldest daughter's heart.

"Good morning and welcome," Dad spoke and the room listened.

I stayed close to Nixon's side, having missed him this week. The man was a huge pain in the ass, and I worried about him more than ever before, but he was a good guy. He was just dealing with some personal stuff.

We all had our secrets.

Jonas's had been Kira. When that secret had come out, it had only meant good things.

Dad continued his welcome messages, then nodded to

someone in the crowd. The same woman who'd been with Susan yesterday, arranging photos for Nan's service, came on stage and sat at the piano. She must be the music director. Trailing behind her, five people emerged from the congregation.

Since the service yesterday, they'd set up the stage differently. I'd been distracted earlier with my selfie and keeping my head down, but they had a legitimate setup for a band. A whole band? They even had a drum set tucked behind the piano. What had happened to the choir and their maroon robes?

The questions vanished from my mind as a tall, gorgeous man with a sexy beard, rock-hard ass and chiseled arms strode on stage and took the lead microphone.

Graham carried the same guitar he'd had at the Eagles the other night. He made no introduction as he started playing, the others joining in immediately. A woman played bass and a man sat at the drums while the other two members sat on stools with mics of their own.

I expected the congregation to stand, to sing along to a traditional hymn, but butts remained in seats as Graham and the band performed.

Goose bumps broke out on my forearms. My heart jumped into my throat. At the bar, I'd been drawn into the sex appeal of Graham on stage, and while he was absolutely intoxicating up there, the atmosphere and faith music brought out the majesty of his voice. There was no hint of a growl or a rasp as he sang today, only a voice so clear and pure it left me reeling.

Did these people even know how lucky they were to hear him? Did he have any idea how good he was?

He finished the song too soon and the clapping started.

When had we ever clapped in church? It took me by yet another surprise, but not as much as the smile on Dad's face as he cheered, returning to his own microphone. "They get better and better each week, don't they?"

Lord, have I died and entered an alternate universe?

The service went on and I sat in my seat dumbfounded. There were more songs, this time the congregation standing to sing along. Dad delivered his sermon and then Graham took the stage once more, finishing with yet another song that left me speechless.

There was more clapping before Dad adjourned. People in the rear rows filtered out first as others swamped the stage, clustering around Graham still wearing his guitar and a grin.

"You've got some drool on your chin." Nixon swiped his thumb over the corner of my mouth.

"Stop." I swatted him away.

"You couldn't take your eyes off him. What's the story?"

"Not now," I hissed, elbowing him in the gut as I motioned to Walker. "Let me introduce you to my family."

A string of hellos and handshakes ensued, people leaning across people to greet Nixon. I'd hoped by the time the pleasantries were over, we could escape our row and I'd get to avoid Nixon's inquisition about Graham.

No such luck.

We were stuck because the line to leave the sanctuary was moving slower than a three-legged turtle.

On the other side of the aisle, I spotted Graham's parents. There was no sign of Colin, but in the summers, kids didn't have to sit through the beginning of the service. It had been a bonus. They were excused immediately to Sunday School—meaning the outside playground. During the school year, things were more regimented but summers here were all about fun.

My eyes drifted to Graham. He was in the same place as before, surrounded by people talking, but he stood unmoving. His guitar was in one hand, balanced on the floor, and his eyes were on Nixon's arm.

The arm Nixon had thrown over my shoulders after we'd finished introductions.

One of mine was wound behind his back in a casual sideways hug.

There was no reading Graham's expression. It was cold, devoid of all emotion, like the man who'd met me at the airport one week ago.

My arm dropped from Nixon and I shimmied my shoulders, shaking out of his hold. There'd been nothing to the hug. Only unity and support. I willed Graham to lift his eyes and meet my gaze so I could silently tell him there was nothing but friendship here, but Susan—I really did hate that woman—walked up and grabbed his attention.

"What?" Nix's forehead furrowed as he lifted his arm to sniff his pit. "Do I smell?"

"No, it's . . . never mind. When did you get here?"

"Nice try." He jerked his thumb over his shoulder. "It's the guy, huh? You're hung up on him. Is now the time you'll tell me the story while we wait for the line to move an inch an hour?"

"There's not much to tell."

"I'm not a religious guy, but I think lying in church is frowned upon." He tapped his chin. "Let me guess. High school sweethearts?"

"Something like that."

"What's his name?"

I curled my lip, wishing he'd stayed in Hawaii. Jonas and Ethan hadn't been nearly as nosy during their visit. "Graham."

"Graham," Nixon repeated. "Well, I have to say. He's good. That was unlike any church service I've been to before. Kinda cool actually."

"A first for me too," I muttered. "You should hear Graham sing something with an edge."

"He's almost as good as Jonas." Nixon pinned me with a stare. "And if you ever tell him I said that, I'll tell him you were the one who was messing around on his acoustic and dented it."

"Blackmail? Really?"

He shrugged. "Whatever works, babe."

I rolled my eyes.

"So the ex-boyfriend can sing." Nixon rubbed his hands together. "But is Graham a better guitar player than I am?"

"Nope." I crossed my fingers beside my leg.

He grinned, but it fell when he noticed my hand. "You suck."

"I'm just kidding." I giggled. "He's good but you're better."

"Whatever."

"Did you miss me?"

"A little." His arm came around me again and I leaned into his side.

It was another innocent hug, one-hundred-percent platonic, but at that exact moment, Graham looked over again.

Damn it.

I shoved Nixon aside.

"Hmm." Nixon hummed as Graham strode toward the

rear exit, guitar in hand. "I should have stayed in Montana. I have a feeling I missed an interesting week."

"Interesting is one way to put it, but it's over now."

Nixon was here, presumably with the airplane. Tomorrow was Monday.

It was time to go home.

"So are you all set for tomorrow?" he asked.

"Yeah. What time do you want to fly out?"

"Not too early. I flew in late last night. Getting here this morning nearly killed me. Why does church start so early?"

I laughed. "It's nine."

"Exactly."

"Let's leave around noon." That would give us plenty of time to make it to Seattle and settle in. My couch was calling and I wanted to get takeout from my favorite sushi place and curl up with a book.

Home.

My other home.

Would it feel strange to be in my apartment after a week in Montana?

"Are you going to say goodbye?" Nixon asked.

"To who? My parents? Uh, yeah. I'm staying with them."

"No, dummy. To Graham."

"Oh." I stared at the door where he'd disappeared. "Uh . . . I don't know."

We'd parted ways last night without issue. Wasn't that enough?

Was there a goodbye to say?

Or would it be better if I played it like last time and simply walked away?

CHAPTER FIFTEEN

GRAHAM

"Let's go, Colin!" I hollered from the edge of the church's playground.

"Five more—"

"No. It's time to go."

His shoulders fell as he shuffled down the bridge between the monkey bars and stairs leading to the slide. The other kids screamed and laughed around him. He gave Evan a weak wave goodbye as his lower lip jutted out over his chin.

No matter how long he played, he wanted five more minutes. He'd be the last kid standing and still want five more minutes.

But I needed to get out of here.

Seeing Quinn cuddled up with Nixon was unbearable.

I knew they had something going on. I fucking knew it. There was a reason that tabloids speculated.

The pictures of them together over the years had been of them touching. Hugging. Laughing. There'd been one of them holding hands about a year ago that had bothered me so much that I'd decided to unfollow Quinn.

It was too much to witness on social media.

It was definitely too much to see in my own church.

One more day.

She'd be gone tomorrow. Life would return to normal. Now that she'd come back, I'd have a better chance at moving on.

All these years, the hours I'd spent thinking about her . . . it was time to put it away.

I could send her off and be grateful that she'd made a positive impression on my kid. As she'd played with Colin yesterday afternoon, I'd watched and listened in. When I'd caught her sitting on the floor of Colin's room, reading him a book, the sight had damn near brought me to my knees.

Because I'd let myself for one desperate, hopeful second wonder how incredible it would be if that was permanent. I'd imagined Quinn filling the hole as Colin's mother.

But he didn't need a mother. Definitely not one who lived her life on the road, had no qualms about ignoring her family and was okay with playing two men.

She'd had sex with me.

Me.

And there she'd been, cuddled up to Nixon.

Had she gone to him after leaving my house last night? *Fuck me.* Jealousy was a nasty bitch.

"Do we have to go?" Colin asked, his eyes pleading as he reached my side.

"Yeah. You can play longer next week." I put my hand on his shoulder and guided him toward the parking lot. I'd ditched my guitar in the storage area in the church's basement. The keys were in my hand and we were out of here. I hadn't even bothered to say goodbye to my parents. "Should we do something special today? Just the two of us?"

"Like what?" he asked as I opened the rear door to my pickup.

"Hop in and get buckled. Then we'll talk about it."

There was a steady stream of people leaving the church now and we melded right in with traffic. "Want to hike the M? We could pack a picnic lunch."

"Peanut butter and jelly?" The pout on his face disappeared. "Can we get some Doritos too?"

"You got it."

The M was the collegiate letter from Montana State and an enormous setup of white rocks on a mountainside that could be seen from everywhere in the Gallatin Valley. It was an easy hike for me, more challenging for Colin, and if I had to, I'd let him ride on my shoulders for a stretch. Some physical activity might improve my mood—and the air clear my head. At this point, I'd do anything to stop thinking about how easily Quinn had fit into Nixon's side.

I drove straight home and made two peanut butter and jelly sandwiches while Colin changed out of his church clothes. I swapped out my dark-wash jeans and white button-up for a pair of cargo shorts and a T-shirt. Then we spent the rest of the morning hiking up a dirt trail, smiling and waving at the people we passed on the way. Colin and I reached the top, sat on a bench and devoured our sandwiches.

The distraction helped but only marginally. Quinn's face lurked in the not-so-dark corners of my mind, and the trail itself didn't exactly help. That was the problem with Bozeman. There weren't many places I could go that I hadn't been with Quinn. The two of us had hiked this route a dozen times as teenagers.

Things would get better once she left.

Tomorrow. I only had to make it until tomorrow, and there was no reason to see her before then.

"What should we do next?" I asked Colin before taking a drink from a water bottle. The last place I wanted to go was home, where her sweet perfume still lingered on my sheets and in the air. I hadn't gotten around to washing those sheets after all. "How about fishing?"

I'd never taken Quinn fishing.

"Yes!" His smile beamed.

"Let's do it." I clapped and stowed our gear.

Colin and I hiked down the mountain, swung by the house for fishing poles and went to a local pond where they stocked fish for kids. I would have preferred the solitude of the river, but I'd wanted to guarantee Colin a catch. He'd reeled in and released twelve before we'd called it a day.

After fishing, we went for ice cream. After ice cream, we went to the hardware store, a place Colin loved nearly as much as his father because there was always someone selling puppies in the parking lot on the weekends. We went out for cheeseburgers and fries, not Audrey's because Quinn had now ruined my favorite place and I couldn't stomach Chinese either.

I spent the entire day with my son, savoring his smile and his laugh.

I spent the entire day trying not to think about Quinn.

There were only a handful of minutes where I'd actually succeeded.

It was getting close to seven and I still wasn't ready to go home, but Monday morning and a busy week loomed on the horizon, so I conceded defeat and came home to get Colin into the shower.

"That was a fun day." He yawned as I tucked him into bed.

"It was fun."

"Can we do that every Sunday?"

"Yeah, why not." We'd do hiking and fishing in the summers. We'd ski, snowmobile or snowshoe in the winter.

"Yes." He fist pumped under his quilt.

"Sleep well, bud." I dropped a kiss to his forehead. "Love you."

"Love you too, Daddy."

Daddy. My kid could slice me open with one word.

The times he called me Daddy were getting fewer and further between these days. But when he'd slip one in on the rare occasion, my heart would melt.

I kissed him one more time and picked up the book we'd read—or he'd read. I'd made him read tonight for some summer reading practice. With the book returned to its shelf, I eased from his room. His eyes were closed before I shut off his light and carefully closed the door.

The dim house was lit only by the fading sun streaming through the windows. It always seemed too quiet this time of night, after Colin was in bed and his chatter was noticeably absent. I went to the kitchen and filled a glass with water, drinking it as I leaned against the counter.

What I needed was a project to tackle for a few hours each evening. Remodeling the kitchen would be a pain in the ass but starting it this summer would be better than waiting until fall. I could cook on the grill for dinner and wheel the fridge into the living room. We could survive for a month or two, right?

Tomorrow, I'd get up early and run some numbers. If cabinets were in the budget, I'd get measurements taken and new ones ordered. While I was at it, the floors should be replaced too. My goal was to extend the hardwood I'd run in the hallway by the bedrooms through the entire house. If I was going to bring it into the kitchen, I might as well lay it in the living and dining rooms too.

A project, something guaranteed to distract me, sent a jolt of excitement through my veins.

When I'd been house shopping, I'd told my real estate agent to find me the oldest, shittiest place on a nice street in a decent school district. It had taken him six months, but when this house had come on the market, we'd pounced. It was the only one on the block that hadn't been remodeled in the past fifteen years. I'd had to go ten thousand above asking with a quick close to buy it.

I'd spent the past four years making updates and improvements when there was a bit of extra money to spend. The finishes were as nice as those I'd put in a Hayes-Montgomery house, and I'd worked room by room, starting with Colin's. He'd spent a lot of nights in my bed, sleeping on my chest while his room was being fixed up.

I missed those days too, when he'd stick his head in my neck and sleep sideways but somehow manage to contort his feet into my ribs at the same time.

Why put off for tomorrow what I could do tonight? There was nothing waiting in my bedroom but thoughts of Quinn.

I swiped my laptop from the kitchen counter and fired it up, taking it to the dining room table along with a beer from the fridge. The numbers came together, and I mentally decided to pull the trigger. It was dark outside, but there was no reason not to start on measurements.

Just as I'd pushed away from the table, a flash of headlights in the front window caught my eye.

My stomach knotted. "Keep driving."

The car slowed.

I knew before the back door opened that it was Quinn. She climbed out, said something to the driver and away he went.

"Son of a bitch." The beer bottle got fisted and slammed to my lips, the liquid sliding down my throat in long gulps.

What was she doing here? Wasn't she supposed to be leaving?

Didn't she have Nixon to keep her bed warm tonight?

She spotted me through the glass as she walked, her stride stuttering a step. If she could sense my glare, it didn't turn her away, and I grumbled as she lightly rapped on the door.

I strode to the door, flipped the deadbolt with a *clunk* that mimicked the feel of my sinking heart and I took in her unsmiling face.

"Hey." She looked nervous and the normally rosy color of her cheeks was missing.

"What's up?" My tone was short and clipped. I doubted it would scare her away, nothing I'd done this week had alienated her, but it was worth a last-ditch effort.

"I, um . . . I wanted to say goodbye."

"Colin's asleep already."

"I figured."

Then she'd come to say goodbye to me. "Can we not do this? I'm not interested in Nixon's leftovers. If you need a man's bed tonight, go to his."

Her mouth parted and she blinked, but the shock lasted a nanosecond before she fixed me with a death glare that only Quinn Montgomery could summon.

Shiiiiiit. I was an asshole.

"Don't you dare speak to me like I'm a whore, Graham Hayes. Don't you fucking dare."

"I—oh, hell. I'm sorry." What was wrong with me? My mother would have slapped me across the face for that remark. I ran a hand over my hair and pushed the door open wider. "Come in."

She crossed her arms over her chest. Her feet didn't move.

"Please?"

"Fine." She stepped past me, careful not to touch.

Quinn had turned me inside out and I wasn't myself. I didn't speak to women this way. Ever. It had to be because of the sex. I'd become a jealous and insensitive prick because she'd climbed into my bed.

"Want a beer? I'm having another one." Maybe two.

"Sure." She sat in a chair in the living room while I went to the fridge, returning with opened bottles. "Thanks."

I sat on the couch, the seat farthest from her, and drained half my beer. "What time are you leaving tomorrow?"

"Around noon."

I nodded, keeping my gaze on the floor because I didn't trust what might come out of my mouth.

Quinn took a swig of her beer, looking anywhere but at me, until the silence droned on and she caved first. "Walker said the house you guys are working on is coming along. He said it's going to be massive."

"It's for a rich guy with money to burn. You probably know how that feels." I cringed the second the words were out of my mouth. I didn't fault her for her money and wasn't exactly sure why I'd decided to throw it in her face.

"This was a bad idea." She set her beer aside and stood.

"I'm going to go."

"Damn it. No. Sorry. I'm in a shit mood."

"Am I the reason?"

"Partly," I admitted.

"And the other part?"

"Nixon."

"Nixon?" She sat down on the edge of the chair, ready to race for the door if I screwed up one more time. "What did he do?"

"He had his hands all over you," I grumbled. "In church."

"It was a hug." The corner of her mouth twitched. "And you're jealous."

"Yep." I tipped the beer bottle to my lips. There was no use denying it. My skin was probably green.

"Well, there's no reason. Nixon and I are friends. Nothing more."

"That's not how it looks to the outside world."

"Photographs are deceiving. There's news and then there's celebrity news. I'm not sure if either are really true. So why don't you ask me the question on your mind instead of sulking in your chair."

I swallowed. Braced. "Are you sleeping with him?"

"No. Never."

The knot in my stomach loosened. "All these years, I'd see pictures and wonder if he was the reason you didn't come home. I wondered if you were keeping your relationship a secret."

"I haven't been in an actual relationship with anyone in a . . . a long time."

"How long? Specifically."

Her shoulders fell. "Nine years."

The same was true for me. There'd been a few casual hookups but nothing with a commitment.

It would be easy to pin the blame on Colin. He'd been my go-to excuse for declining dates. But the truth was, I just wasn't interested in falling in love again. If it had been love.

"Was it real?" I whispered. "Was it love?"

"I thought so."

So did I. "Do you think if we would have tuned everyone out, if we would have just ignored them, things would have been different? That maybe we would have come out of that fight together?"

"I don't know." She sunk deeper into the chair. "Maybe."

"Or maybe they were right. Maybe we were too young. Maybe us splitting up was inevitable."

"I am sorry, Graham." Her voice cracked. "I'm sorry for hurting you. For leaving like I did."

"I'm sorry too."

That apology was nearly a decade in the making and the words were heavy on my tongue. But then a piece of my chest loosened, like the last thread of a fraying rope clinging to the past finally broke free.

"I used to think about that day a lot," I told her. "The fight. And I wondered what I could have said that would have made things different."

"That you'd come with me."

"I almost did. But . . ." Those doubts had gotten louder after she'd left. My friends had taunted me to play the field, get some experience. Adults, even my parents, hadn't seemed to understand that my heart had been broken. Sure, they'd been sympathetic for a few weeks, but they'd expected me to bounce back and move on with life. Date other girls.

Except I hadn't wanted other girls.

"The truth is, I thought you'd come back."

"I figured." She dropped her eyes to her lap. "You thought I wouldn't make it and give up."

"What? No. I thought you'd come back to visit. Then, you didn't. But I always knew you'd make it."

Her chin lifted. "You did?"

"Any idiot who listens to you play piano or the drums or sing would know you were meant for greatness. I just never expected you to forget us."

"I didn't forget, Graham. It was just . . . easier. Cowardly. Things got so crazy and so hard, I needed easy."

"I get that." In her position, at that age, I might have done the same.

She picked up her beer, sipping it as I finished my own. "You followed me? On Instagram?"

"Yeah." Or, I used to, but I kept that to myself.

"Why?"

Why follow the woman who'd broken my heart? Because there wasn't a moment in my life when I'd hated Quinn Montgomery, no matter how hard I'd tried. Even when she'd been eight and had broken the Lego pirate ship I'd spent two weeks building.

"I was a coward too. Following you, being one of many, was easier than asking Nan for your number. I didn't want to miss it when you stretched your wings. And, Quinn . . . you soared. I'm so damn proud of you."

I didn't want her to leave here and not know that.

A smile tugged at the corner of her mouth. "I'm glad we had this chance to clear the air. I'm just sorry it didn't happen a long time ago."

"Same here."

She stood, setting her bottle aside. "I'd better get going.

Let you get back to work."

I followed her to the door, holding it as she stepped into the night. "I'll wait until your Uber gets here."

"Thanks." She took out her phone and her fingers flew over the screen. "Five minutes."

I leaned against the door, breathing in the night air and glancing to the stars glimmering in the inky black sky. "Remember when we used to lie in the back of my truck and count stars?"

"You'd count one, then I'd count one. I think the highest we ever got was—"

"Two hundred seventy-one."

She laughed. "We'd get bored and start making out."

I stepped away from the door, turning my head to the heavens so I wouldn't stare at her lips. "One."

She moved closer. "Two."

"Three." I dropped my gaze and found hers waiting.

"Four," she whispered.

Five came when my lips brushed against hers, slow and soft at first, teasing and testing. But then her arms wound around my shoulders and all rational thought disappeared. A surge of heat washed over my body and her taste consumed my senses. I pressed into her, my cock throbbing into her hip, and held on for the ride.

God, this woman could kiss. She could drive me wild with just a lick of her tongue and her fingers in my hair.

Quinn's Uber pulled up, breaking us apart. Quinn's cheeks were flushed, her lips wet.

"Don't go." My hand clamped on hers. I sounded a lot like my eighteen-year-old self, but *fuck it*, this was my last chance. She was leaving tomorrow, and I wanted one more night. "Stay."

CHAPTER SIXTEEN

QUINN

After a breathless *yes* and a hastened apology to my Uber driver—definitely earning myself a one-star rating—Graham carried me inside.

He swept us through the house, his lips never leaving my neck as he closed us inside his dark bedroom. His hands molded to my curves, and he laid me on his bed with an unhurried kiss that curled my toes.

"Graham." I tugged at his shirt.

"Slow. This time"—he ran his cheek along my jaw, his beard deliciously scraping my skin—"we go slow."

I moaned in protest, my eyelids growing heavy when his lips began a lazy descent. His rough fingers pulled at the collar of my tee, pulling it aside to reveal a sliver of flesh by my collarbone. He worshiped the spot with his tongue, his lips, nibbling and sucking until I quivered beneath him.

The blinding throb between my legs was unbearable. I snapped my eyes open and shoved Graham up, pushing and clawing at his clothes until his shirt was bunched at his ribs.

His response was to stand at the foot of the bed, wearing a smirk and all his damn clothes.

"Graham," I warned.

He chuckled, reached behind his head and off came the shirt.

I let him strip my tee and tug at the button on my jeans. He cupped my jaw, holding it in his grip as his lips came to mine. He used the hard kiss to push me to the bed, the soft mattress enveloping me as his hard chest covered mine.

Graham arched his hips, and his arousal pressed into my wet center. "I'm going to ruin you."

"Yes," I hissed as he palmed my ass through my panties. *Ruin me. Destroy me.* Graham could do whatever he wanted with me as long as his body was touching mine.

My moans came in a steady stream as I clawed at the bare skin of his back, my nails short but enough to leave a mark. He nipped at my lower lip when they dug deep. Then he growled against my neck, and the vibration ran straight to my clit.

If he kept at it, I was going to come, just like this. Just from his kiss.

But I wanted him inside me, the two of us joined at the climax. I stretched for his jeans, sliding my hand beneath the waistband. When my fingers wrapped around his shaft, he thrust into my grip.

His eyes, those beautiful golden swirls, lifted to meet mine. "You are . . ."

I cupped his stubbled cheek with my free hand, prompting when he didn't finish. "What?"

"Stunning. Sexy." He turned his cheek, putting a kiss on my wrist. "Mine. For tonight, you're mine."

Slow became frenzied as we shed the last of our clothes

and he hauled me deeper into the bed. His cock rubbed against my folds, his hips swirling as the root found my clit.

I shuddered and my legs trembled. I panted into his ear, whispering his name and begging for more. "Inside. Please."

"Not yet."

"Please." I tilted my hips, searching. "I need you."

He reached a hand for the nightstand, but I caught his forearm and shook my head.

"Are you sure?"

I nodded. "I want to feel you. Nothing else. I'm on birth control and it's been . . . a long time."

"Same here."

My teeth found the lobe of his ear. "Then what are you waiting for?"

With a single thrust, he buried deep.

I cried out and his hand clamped over my mouth, both of us stilling as we listened. I'd forgotten Colin was sleeping down the hallway. When the quiet returned, we both let out the breaths we'd been holding, and the intensity peaked.

Graham's eyes flared, sliding impossibly deeper, before he began to move in gliding, punishing strokes.

"Quinn." My name in his voice was sweet music. "You feel so damn good."

I hummed in agreement, relaxing into the feel of his strength above me. The stretch, the sensation of being filled by Graham, consumed me and I squeezed my eyes shut, committing every move to memory.

This was not something I wanted to forget. I'd made that mistake before.

His pace quickened, his cock hit hard and true, as my hands roamed, grabbing with desperation for more. Our kisses were wet and chaste, neither of us patient enough to let our lips lock.

I was on the edge, so close, but I fought my release.

Graham growled, his hips moving faster. "Come on, baby."

"More. Not yet."

He pulled free and got to his knees. My eyes flew open in time to see the world spin. He gripped me by my hips and twisted me in the bed so I was on my stomach. His large hands yanked at my thighs, pulling me to my knees.

Then he slammed home.

I cried out, and his hand clamped over my mouth once more, smothering my whimpers and moans as my back arched. His free hand ran up and down my spine, and as his fingers rounded the curve of my ass, his lips dropped to my shoulder.

The man was everywhere. There were too many touches to concentrate on just one, and the sensations overwhelmed me. My entire body shook as he rammed into me, over and over. The sound of our flesh slapping drowned out our heavy breaths.

I didn't want it to be over yet, but fighting my orgasm was impossible. When he reached around my front and found my clit with his finger, I broke.

My chest fell forward, my cries muted by the pillow, as wave after wave of pleasure crashed over my body. Tingles rushed from my toes and fingertips to my center where I pulsed in the longest, hardest orgasm of my life.

Tears leaked from the corners of my eyes, joy seeping from my body.

"Fuck," Graham groaned, right before he buried deep, holding me to him as he came. The heat of his release dripped down my leg as he pulled out and collapsed on the mattress, pinning me beneath him.

My vision was blurry when I dared to crack my eyelids. My heart was pounding faster than if I'd just performed for a sold-out arena. I was drenched and sated and in Graham's arms.

I never wanted to leave.

His arms never loosened as he pulled my back to his chest. "Don't go."

No, not this time. "What about Colin?"

"We'll wake up early and we'll tell him you came over to say goodbye. We just won't tell him *when* you came over."

"Okay." I smiled, curling into his front as he turned us on our sides.

Staying the night, sleeping in his bed, was foolish and impulsive and . . . I didn't care. This was our last night, and when I went home tomorrow, I wanted to know I hadn't wasted a single second of this trip.

This man had my heart. Completely. He'd had it in his hold since I was sixteen. How could I have doubted that? How could I have thought he hadn't believed in me?

This, his faith, was as real as anything in my life.

And now I was leaving. It was time for me to go.

I squeezed my eyes shut, staying in this moment and pushing away what was to come. The airplane and reality were for tomorrow. Tonight, I'd live in the dream.

Graham woke me up twice to make love to me.

And when morning dawned, I slipped out of his bed and out of his home, unable to say goodbye.

"MORNING, QUINN."

My cheeks flamed as I tiptoed into the kitchen. I'd hoped Mom and Dad would still be asleep at five thirty in the morning. No such luck. Mom was standing beside the coffeepot as it sputtered. "Morning, Mom."

"Where did you sneak off to last night?" she asked, though she had to know the answer.

"Graham's."

"I figured." She nodded and lifted a mug from the cupboard. "Coffee?"

"Yes, please." I sat at the table, feeling like I was a teenager again who needed to explain her relationship in an attempt to make her mother understand. "I went over to say goodbye."

She brought me my coffee and sat across from me, not saying a word.

"I chickened out," I blurted. "I wasn't sure how to say goodbye, so I just . . . didn't. I snuck out before he woke up."

"If I know Graham, which I do, it was probably better that way," she said. "He's careful with who he brings into his life. And with you, well, you two were always complicated."

Complicated. What she really meant was reckless.

I brushed it aside, ready to change topics. "Thanks for everything, Mom. I know this week has been hard, but I'm glad you called me to come home."

"And I'm glad you did. Christmas, right?"

I nodded. "Christmas. Though I'll probably bring Nixon along too. If that's okay."

"The more the merrier." She smiled. "He's a charmer, isn't he?"

"You have no idea." I giggled.

Nixon spent the day with us yesterday after church.

215

DEVNEY PERRY

While Walker and Brooklyn went home with their families, Nix and I took my parents to lunch at a local restaurant. We chose to sit at one of the outdoor tables shaded by a pergola overflowing with hanging flower baskets.

When the waitress brought over menus and Nixon immediately ordered a beer, I feared conversation might be awkward. But Nix had a gift for taking uncomfortable situations and making them the ones you'd remember for years.

We talked for hours. Well, Nixon talked and the rest of us had listened.

He told story after story about life with the band. About our favorite shows and life on a tour bus—the PG-rated parts. He answered Dad's questions about our recording process and the studio in Seattle. Occasionally, Nix would glance at me to fill in the gaps.

And in a way, it was better that Nixon told them about life with the band from his perspective.

He was a neutral party and the way he described it made our lifestyle sound simple. As the wild one in our bunch, he'd ironically made it seem tame.

After lunch, we spent a couple of hours downtown, exploring and enjoying the sunshine, before my parents returned home and left Nixon and me to spend some time alone. The two of us found a bar with good popcorn and country music playing in the background. By the time Nixon was drunk—I stayed sober because I'd seen that glint in his eye, the one that said he was going to go until he passed out— it was nearly dark.

I helped him into a cab and took him to the motel, situating him in his room before leaving to go home.

Except I hadn't gone home.

I'd gone to Graham's.

"Can we take you to the airport?" Mom asked.

"I think Nix is coming over to pick me up. Then we'll go."

"Do you want some breakfast?"

"That would be great." I'd only had the bar's popcorn for dinner, and after a long, blissful night with Graham, I was starved. "Cereal is fine."

"Let me spoil you on your last morning. Are huckleberry pancakes still your favorite?"

My stomach growled. "Yes."

"Then that's what we'll have."

"Are the kids coming today?" I asked as she took out ingredients from her pantry. *Please, say no.* I didn't want to have to hide in my room until Graham was gone.

"No, they have Vacation Bible School this week."

Phew. "One of my favorites."

"They actually run it two weeks in a row now. It runs the week of the Fourth since so many daycares close and parents were having trouble finding care. Your dad already left to pop over for their six a.m. kickoff meeting. Kids start to show up at seven. The new children's director is fantastic but she's . . . intense."

"At six in the morning? Sounds like it."

"She's taken a lot of work off your dad's plate though. Susan's too."

I scrunched up my nose at her name but didn't let Mom see.

"Do you think he'll be back before lunch?" I asked.

"He promised he would be home by nine thirty. Ten at the latest."

Unless Dad, like me, wanted to avoid a goodbye.

I drank more coffee as Mom whipped up our pancakes,

then we ate together. As she started the dishes, I went upstairs to shower and pack my suitcase. When I hauled it downstairs, along with my backpack, I found her in the living room, reading a book.

It was ten thirty.

Dad wasn't coming home.

Maybe it was for the best. The last thing I wanted was for us to fight before I left. Again. But the gnawing ache in my stomach wouldn't go away.

I'd missed my chance to say goodbye to Nan and hug her one last time.

Graham and I'd had our own kind of farewell. Mom would be here when Nix arrived.

But Dad . . . he wasn't going to get out of this. My stubborn streak flared. "I'm going to go to the church and say goodbye to Dad."

She frowned at the clock. "I'm sorry. You know how it goes. Sometimes he gets caught up."

"Yeah, I know. Be back in a few."

I hurried outside and to the church, my irritation growing with each step. The shouts and laughter of children greeted me before the building came into view, and I took a calming breath.

We didn't need to fight. I was only going to say goodbye.

I approached the church and spotted a large VBS banner above the main door. Stations of games dotted the green grass of the front lawn. When I pushed through the side door, I expected to be assaulted by noise, but the kids must have all been outside or on an adventure because it was nearly silent.

A laugh caught my ear and I headed down the hallway toward the offices.

Susan was at her desk, laughing with the woman sitting

across from her, and her smile disappeared when she spotted me. "Oh. Hello."

I didn't bother with a greeting. "Is my dad here?"

"He's in his office."

I strode past her without another glance and found Dad behind his desk, his nose in a book. I knocked on his open door. "Hi, Dad."

"Quinn." His gaze snapped to me as he stood, then to the clock. "Shoot, it's after ten. I lost track of time."

"It's fine. I just wanted to come say goodbye."

"Do you have a minute to sit?" He gestured to the chair across from his desk.

The room was the same as I remembered, though I fit in the chair better than I had as a child balancing a coloring book on my knees. Shelves hugged the walls, each teaming with books and trinkets he'd collected over the years or received as gifts. The scent of sandalwood and citrus air freshener made me feel like a girl again.

"What are you reading?" I asked.

"I learn something every time I read this." He lifted the book, flashing me the cover. *Dante's Inferno.* "So you're getting ready to leave?"

"Soon."

"It was good to have you home, staying in your room. Even under the circumstances."

"I miss her already."

"Me too." He sighed. "Me too. The truth is, I started reading this because it's always been an escape. My Mondays will never be the same without Nan."

"Same here—wait. Your Mondays?"

"Oh, I, uh . . ." He placed a bookmark in his book and closed it. "I used to talk to her every Monday."

"So did I. She called me every Monday without fail."

"I know." He gave me a sad smile. "Because I asked her to. She'd call you. Then she'd call me."

My jaw dropped. "You?"

"Don't get me wrong. She called because she wanted to talk to you too. But early on, after you left, I wasn't sure what to say. After the fight, I just . . . I didn't want to make it worse. You two always had a special bond, and I thought if she kept tabs on you, she could relay information. Then a year went by. Two. She liked talking to you and I didn't know, still don't know how to make things right."

Wow. This was . . . wow.

My mind raced as I thought over every call and the questions Nan would ask. One of her regular questions was if I'd met anyone. If I was drinking enough water. And if I was taking time to read.

Those last two questions, they'd been Dad's.

And I'd been blind not to see it until now.

"It's Monday."

He nodded. "It is."

"Maybe today we can start again. And next week, you can call me."

"I'd like that. Quite a lot."

"Okay." I stood from the chair and walked to the door.

"Quinn?"

I turned. "Yeah?"

"The song you played on Saturday was lovely. I've never been prouder."

Tears flooded my eyes and I blinked them away. "Thanks, Dad."

"What I said to you during the fight, I regret it. I want you to know I'm so very sorry. I'm about nine years late in saying that, but I . . . I'm very proud to be your dad. You have accomplished more than I would have dreamed."

Shit, he was going to make me cry. "Thank you. And I'm sorry too."

"No. Don't." He stood from his chair and crossed the room. "Please, don't apologize. The fault is mine. I'm ashamed of what I said and how long it's taken me to admit I was wrong. I shouldn't have forced my beliefs on you."

"Huh?" The apology was welcome, but beliefs? What was he talking about?

"I do my best to keep an open mind but with you kids, I wasn't—"

"It was never about the faith. The beliefs or the message. It was about the church."

His forehead furrowed. "The church?"

"You are a shepherd, guiding your congregation, your family, down a path. If everyone walks in the same direction, it works. It's harmony. But when someone wants to go a different way, specifically your daughter, things fall apart."

"And things fell apart, didn't they?"

"Epically," I teased. "I wasn't a rebel, Dad. I was a good kid who got good grades and liked tank tops. I wanted to play in a rock band and have a boyfriend. These aren't sins."

"I know that."

"But there were some who didn't. And you stayed on the path, in the middle, when you were supposed to say screw everyone else and stand up for me."

He hung his head. "I didn't know you felt that way. I didn't realize . . . it was never my intention to stifle you. This is not an excuse, but I wanted to keep the peace. It's taken me twenty-something years to realize peace is overrated. But back then, the last thing I wanted were complaints to the church's board. If they would have fired me, we would have had to move. Or I would have had to quit. Until you kids were out of high school, I didn't want to take that risk."

At twenty-seven, I could appreciate the logic of his actions whereas they'd only hurt at eighteen. Because those people, the ones like Susan, vocal and judgmental, would have been the ones to complain. They would have had his job and forced Dad to another church and community.

Dad placed his hands on my shoulders. "What I said that night—that I was disappointed in you and that you were disgracing our house—I regretted it the second the words came out. Forgive me."

He'd always preached that forgiveness was the purest form of love.

And I truly loved my father, no matter what had come between us.

"I forgive you."

He pulled me into his chest, hugging me tight. "I love you, Quinn."

"I love you too, Dad."

We stood there, holding on to each other, until a throat cleared behind us. I let Dad go, swiping my eyes, and turned to see a beautiful woman with a short black bob lingering in the hallway.

"Sorry to interrupt."

"No problem." Dad grinned at me. "Chau Tran, meet my daughter, Quinn. Chau is our children's director and the drill sergeant this week."

"Nice to meet you." I shook her hand.

"Nice to meet you too. I was at the service on Saturday and heard you sing. You brought me to tears. My wife and I are huge Hush Note fans too."

"Thank you. If you ever come to a show, just get word to me and I'll get you guys some backstage passes."

Her eyes widened. "Seriously? We were already talking about a trip to your show in San Francisco this fall."

We weren't doing a full tour this fall, but we'd organized a couple of concerts along the West Coast since we'd spent so much time on the East Coast this summer. "Just get my email address from Dad as it gets closer and let me know if you decide to come. I'll hook you guys up."

"This is amazing." She beamed. "Thank you."

Susan appeared behind Chau, tapping the younger woman on the shoulder. "They're calling for you downstairs."

"Oh." Chau pulled a walkie-talkie off her belt and checked the volume. "Damn. I turned it to mute."

"Language," Susan scolded.

Chau just rolled her eyes. "I'd better get back. Nice to meet you, Quinn. And thanks again."

"You too." I waved with a smile that morphed into a scowl when Susan turned her back.

Dad blew out a frustrated sigh and dropped his voice. "I'm letting Susan go next week. It's going to be a shitshow."

My mouth fell open. First, that he was actually firing Susan. Second, that he'd cursed. Third, that he'd brought in a lesbian to direct the children's program.

Maybe what everyone had told me was right. Things were changing.

"I like Chau," I said.

"She's been a breath of fresh air in this stuffy office. It's been long overdue," he said. "Your mother mentioned something about Christmas."

"I was thinking about coming home."

223

"You're always welcome." He put his arm around my shoulder and walked with me down the hallway to the exit.

"I warned her that means Nixon will likely tag along too."

"Good. Bring him along. And if you ever need someone to talk to about his addictions, I'm here."

Dad had always been observant. "How did you know?"

He shrugged. "A hunch. Am I wrong?"

"No. I worry about him. We all do."

"Want to talk about it?"

"How about we save that for next Monday?"

"I'll call you."

I had no doubt that he would.

How crazy is this? I'd walked here angry, but when I searched for a lingering shred, there was nothing. Poof. It was just gone. He'd call me on Monday, and we'd fumble into a new type of father-daughter relationship. Maybe Nan had patched more holes than I'd ever given her credit for.

"See you soon, Dad." I hugged him once more.

"Safe travels, sweetheart." He held the door open for me, waving as I walked down the stairs to the sidewalk.

Kids were playfully shouting on the front lawn. There was a giant parachute stretched out between little bodies arranged in a circle and they were tossing a ball in the air with the fabric.

I searched the group for Colin but didn't see him. Maya was in the ring, giggling with the others, but she didn't spot me as I passed.

My heart felt lighter as I walked home, even with my departure looming. Because I'd be back. This would always be home.

A text dinged in my pocket and I pulled out my phone,

seeing Harvey's daily text. But instead of cringing, I simply cleared the notification and put it away.

It was time to be in Seattle and return to work. I was ready to go home, to my space and my bed and my city. I was ready to create again. This week hadn't been planned and there had been a few excruciating moments, but the break had given me a chance to clear my head.

And my heart.

Would Graham move on now that we'd made amends? Would I?

The knot in my stomach signaled a resounding *no*.

My God, I was going to miss him. The idea of not seeing him every day, not being here to see his smile . . . my heart was breaking.

He was mine.

I wouldn't move on from him. No one would ever replace Graham.

He'd ignited something in me this week. He'd brought to life a slew of emotions that I'd been suppressing for years. It was time to let them breathe.

I'd spent my entire adult life downplaying or denying my love for Graham. So for a while, I'd embrace it. I'd carry him in my heart as I continued on with life.

And when it was time, I'd let go.

Though, I couldn't imagine a day when I wouldn't love Graham.

Mom was waiting for me on the front stoop when I turned the corner of our block. "You just missed Nixon."

"What?" I scanned the street, looking for a car. "Where'd he go?"

She handed me a piece of paper folded in half. There

was a smile on her face, one more mischievous than happy. "He left this for you."

I flipped open the paper and scanned his sloppy scrawl. Once. Twice. Then I crumpled the page in my fist.

"That son of a bitch stole my airplane."

CHAPTER SEVENTEEN

GRAHAM

"How was church camp, bud?"

"Good," Colin said, buckling his seat belt and shaking a white water bottle that I hadn't sent him with this morning. "I won this."

"Yeah? Nice." I glanced at the floor. I'd sent him with a backpack, right? "Where's your bag?"

"Uh . . ." He slammed a palm against his forehead. "I forgot it inside. Sorry."

"It's okay." I rolled down his window and shut off the engine. "Sit tight. I'll go get it."

If I let him go retrieve it, he'd get distracted by friends and probably forget the reason I'd sent him in the first place.

"Be right back." I winked at him as I got out and jogged to the church, scanning the crowded common room for an adult as I walked inside. "Hey, Chau."

"Hi, Graham. How's it going?"

"Good. Colin forgot his backpack. Any ideas where his group keeps theirs?"

"They are in the music room downstairs."

"Thanks." I waved and went downstairs, finding Colin's bag on the floor. I swiped it up and kept my chin tucked on the way outside, avoiding eye contact with other parents who might want to chat. It had been a long-ass day and I was ready to get home.

Walker and I had pushed hard at the Bridger project and finished framing out the house today. It was a tall hurdle to leap and with it behind us, all the other tasks would begin falling into place. We had an inspector coming by tomorrow. Later this week, we'd get plywood and house wrap up on the exterior walls so the place would begin to resemble a home. Then subcontractors would show to get started on HVAC, electrical and plumbing.

The next few weeks would be busy, and I prayed it might keep my mind off Quinn.

Quinn, the woman who'd stayed in my bed all night, then disappeared this morning without a word.

So much for her goodbye.

I'd spent the day mulling it over and still couldn't decide if I was mad that she'd snuck out at five thirty this morning or glad that she hadn't woken me before leaving.

Considering I'd been in a relatively good mood today, probably the latter.

I didn't want a difficult goodbye, and I suspected she didn't either. Which was why I'd let her go, feigning sleep as she'd collected her clothes and tiptoed out the door.

Quinn would be in Seattle by now, home and back to her rich life.

It was strange to know she was gone from Bozeman and not feel angry. Angry at her. At myself.

She wasn't the girl who'd walked away from me at the

airport and never looked back. She was Quinn. Destined for fame. Living her dream.

This time, she was gone, and I was happy for her.

But that didn't mean I wasn't going to miss her. Damn, would I miss her.

But I wanted her to live that great life.

Even if it meant she was away from me.

"Here you go." I tossed Colin's backpack beside his booster seat and climbed in the truck. "Let's go home."

The moment we walked into the house from the garage, Colin went right for the fridge. "Can I have a snack?"

"How about we do an early dinner?" Lunch had been a long time ago and my stomach rumbled. I stepped up behind Colin, both of us surveying the contents of the fridge. A trip to the grocery store was overdue. "What do we have? Leftover Chinese? Or burgers?"

"Burgers."

I ruffled his hair. "You got it."

This was good. This was normal. After last week, with the rehearsals and the added family dinners, we needed normal.

I went to the back deck and fired up the grill. Colin came racing out behind me with a baseball and two gloves, mine and his.

"Grounders or pop flies?" I asked.

"Pitches."

I chuckled. My son loved playing catch. He loved pitching the ball, but he dreaded the last ten minutes when I'd force him to practice fielding.

Too tired to argue, I threw the ball until the grill was plenty warm enough, then I went inside and prepped our burgers. When they were done, we opted to eat outside on the deck, me inhaling two burgers as Colin devoured one.

"I'm going to clean up these dishes, then take a shower." The stink from a sweaty day was potent.

"Okay." He stayed in his chair, his eyes drifting to the yard, which made me pause. Colin was a kid who usually bolted to play the second he was dismissed from the dinner table. He worried his bottom lip between his teeth as he stared at nothing.

"What's up, bud? Got something on your mind?"

"Simone asked me who my mom was today."

My stomach dropped. My head spun and I fought to keep my breathing steady. The topic of Dianne in my son's company flipped the panic switch. "And what did you say?"

"I told her I didn't have a mom. And she said everyone has a mom. And I told her that I know everyone has a mom, and that I *know* I have a mom. But I don't have a *mom* mom, like a real mom."

"Whoa. Slow down." His chest was heaving. "Take a breath."

He obeyed. "How come?"

It wasn't the first time Colin had asked me about his mother, but it was the first time he seemed able to comprehend the answer and pick it apart. To dig deeper. He'd been too young for our other conversations and had accepted my simple explanation.

Every family was different.

This time, he'd want the full story. My son was growing up and wanted to understand why he was different.

"Being a mother is the hardest job in the world." My throat was rough and my voice hoarse.

I'd practiced this. I'd thought about what to say when the

day came, but no matter how many times I'd run it through in my mind, it was still the hardest conversation I'd ever had with my son.

And we'd only just begun.

"Your mother was—is—a smart person. And she was smart enough to know that she wouldn't have done a good job as your mom. That you'd be happier living with me."

He thought about my words, his face set in firm concentration. "She didn't want me?"

The answer was yes.

How did I tell him the truth? That his mother didn't want to be a mother?

Honestly. I'd promised myself that when he asked, I'd answer with honesty.

"No, bud. She didn't want to be a mom. And that has nothing to do with you. Nothing at all. Does that make sense?"

He shrugged.

"But I wanted to be a dad. And I feel darn lucky that I got you as my kid."

Colin stayed quiet, his gaze fixed firmly on his plate and the few potato chips he'd left behind.

"Are you good with that? You and me? The two of us?"

He nodded.

"I love you, son. I know it's not fair, having only me when other kids have both a mom and a dad."

"Do you think you'll ever get married?"

That question, I hadn't expected. "I, uh . . . I don't know. Maybe someday. Maybe not."

"What about Quinn? Would you marry her someday?"

"No." I stretched my hand across the table, covering his. "Quinn is just a friend. Your friend."

"You don't like her?"

"Yes, I like her. But she lives in Seattle."

"And she's famous." His eyes got wide, like Quinn's fame meant she was out of my league.

I chuckled. "And she's famous."

Colin blew out a deep breath, sinking heavily into the chair as the wheels in his mind whirled.

He'd gotten so big these past few years, so independent. I didn't have to run his bath every night. He picked out his own clothes and brushed his own teeth.

He was my greatest source of pride. This boy—this talented, kind and funny boy—who was feeling lost today because he didn't have a mother.

"When people ask about your mother, is it hard to tell them you don't have one?"

He shrugged. "I guess."

"What would make it easier?"

"I don't know," he muttered.

It was not fun to be a kid who was different. Not at this or any age.

"I know I've told you this before, but every family is different. Some have a mom and dad. Some just a mom. Some just a dad. Some have two moms or two dads. All that matters is there is love in a family. We have love. Lots of it. If you ever want to talk, I'm here. You know that, right?"

"Yeah, Dad."

"Do you have any questions about her?" I'd do my best to answer even though I didn't have a lot to go on.

He nodded and slipped his hand free, dropping it to his lap. "What's her name?"

"Dianne." I wished I could tell him that she'd given him

something—his nose or his eyes—but Colin was me entirely. "Any others?"

He shook his head. "Can I go practice my drums?"

"Sure. I'm going to hop in the shower."

He stood, picking up his plate. I followed with my own to the kitchen sink, watching with a twisting heart as he dumped the rest of the crumbs in the trash and loaded the plate into the dishwasher.

Stop. Stop growing.

Colin took off, racing toward the basement, only pausing on the top stair as the doorbell chimed.

"Can I?" He knew to ask before opening the door, but I wasn't expecting anyone.

"No. Hold up." I crossed the room, joining him by the door that I'd eventually replace because I wanted one with a window, then flipped the deadbolt.

To Quinn.

My heart swelled. There she was, not gone but standing at my front door wearing jeans, a tank top and a smile that stole my breath.

"Quinn!" Colin flew at her, wrapping his arms around her waist.

The hug surprised us both, but she recovered first, ruffling his hair and putting an arm around his shoulders. "Hey."

"I thought you were leaving," he said.

"Want to hear something crazy?"

He nodded. "What?"

"Nixon stole my airplane. He just stole it." She threw her hands in the air. "He left me stranded here, so I thought I'd come over and see if we could jam for a while."

"Yes. Yes! We are so gonna jam." He took her hand and dragged her inside.

She smiled as she passed, the light glimmering off the nose ring I'd kissed last night, but she didn't stop or say a word. She just followed my son to the basement, where I heard the bass drum thumping not thirty seconds later.

God, I could kiss her. Not just for coming here, with some stupid excuse about an airplane, but for putting that smile on my son's face after a not-so-pleasant conversation.

I laughed to myself, closing the door. Then instead of a shower, I crept down half the flight of stairs to sit on the landing and listen to Quinn teach Colin some different techniques on the snare.

They spent an hour down there, long enough that my ass fell asleep. But still, I didn't move. I listened, hearing the joy in my son's voice and the affection in Quinn's.

She'd make a good mom.

I shoved that thought down deep, mostly because it was impossible. Quinn didn't need to be Colin's mother. It was a sacrifice I wouldn't ask her to make. But friend was good.

When they finally called it quits, I didn't bother hurrying up the stairs. I sat on the landing and let them catch me eavesdropping.

Colin rounded the corner first, his hand slapping over his heart as he giggled. "You scared me, Dad."

"Did you have fun?"

"Yeah." He nodded wildly as Quinn joined him, placing her hands on his shoulders.

"Colin will be able to play with you on stage at church soon."

"Maybe." I grinned, shoving up to stand. "But first, a shower. Tomorrow is another early morning."

"No," he grumbled. "Is it seven thirty already?"

"Pretty close. What do you say to Quinn?"

He didn't just thank her. He threw his arms around her once more for a hug that made my chest tighten. "That was so extra."

Extra? Hell, I was getting old.

"Way to rock, kid." She let him go and gave him a fist bump.

"Can we do it again? Since you're stuck here?"

Quinn glanced up to me, silently asking permission. When I nodded, she smiled. "I'd like that."

Colin let out a whoop, then flew up the stairs, leaving us both with a smile.

"Want something to drink?" I asked, leading the way to the kitchen. "How about a beer?"

"Sure." She leaned against the counter as I took out two amber bottles, twisting the top off hers before handing it over.

"You can't afford a plane ticket, huh?" I asked, tipping the bottle to my lips.

She scrunched up her nose. "Commercial? Eww."

"Snob."

"It's true." She giggled. "I don't splurge on much other than drums and that airplane."

"I suppose there are worse vices for rock stars."

Something flashed in her eyes. Understanding. Agreement. "Yes, there are."

"So you're here." My heart was skipping every other beat. "For how long?"

"Another week. Nixon went somewhere for the Fourth. He was good enough to leave a note with Mom before disappearing, saying he'd be back on Saturday."

"You don't seem too upset."

Her stormy eyes locked on mine as she licked her lip. "I'm not."

The air in the kitchen grew hot and thick. The undertones of sex filled the air.

She hadn't only come to see Colin.

She'd come for me.

I crossed the room and set my beer on the counter at her side. Then I slid hers from her grip, setting it down too. The water in the bathroom was running so we had a few minutes.

Minutes I intended to use wisely.

"You left this morning."

Her breath caught as I leaned in closer.

"Why?"

"I don't know how to tell you goodbye," she whispered.

Me neither.

I slammed my mouth down on hers, swallowing her gasp. My tongue dove past her lips, tangling with hers as she looped her arms around my neck. The taste of Quinn and hops broke on my tongue and I pressed in deeper, molding us nearly into one.

I angled her head to one side, taking our kiss to the next level. Her hands gripped my ass, pulling my arousal into her belly.

The water in the bathroom shut off and I took one last lick, then stepped away. I wiped my mouth dry as she did the same, then adjusted my erection behind my zipper. With my beer in hand, I retreated one step at a time so that when the bathroom door flew open, a billow of steam following Colin's wet head, I wasn't in any danger of dry humping Quinn against my kitchen counter.

That would come later.

Because she was here.

"Do I have to go to bed?" Colin asked with pleading eyes as he spotted Quinn.

"Not yet. How about this? I need to take my own shower. Why don't you and Quinn play a quiet game in your room or read a book? Then I'll come in and say good night."

I wasn't giving her the option to leave. She'd come here and she was going to spend the night.

The entire night.

My shower was cold and only long enough to rinse away the stink before I got out and toweled off. I pulled on a pair of briefs and a pair of navy sweats, then I walked out of my bedroom with a few lingering droplets of water dripping off my bare chest to find Quinn and Colin in his room.

He was in bed, tucked beneath the blue blankets. Quinn was above the covers, her legs, clad in a pair of those tight jeans, stretched out beside him as he read her his favorite book.

The tightness in my chest returned. No matter how many breaths I dragged through my nose, my lungs wouldn't hold the air.

Colin had asked me about his mother tonight. And here he was, sitting beside a woman who might have been his mother in another life. Their picture was . . . flawless.

Neither of them noticed me as I stood in the doorway, hidden behind a corner and spying once more.

"Great job reading." Quinn took the book from his hand and set it aside. Then she looked up and over, spotting me beside the door.

Her eyes raked down my naked chest. Her throat bobbed as she gulped.

I grinned and entered the room, her eyes dropping to the

trail of hair that disappeared beneath the waistband of my sweats. "Say good night, Colin."

"Good night, Colin," she parroted, making him laugh.

She giggled with him and kissed the top of his head before sliding off the bed to make room for me.

I tucked the blanket under his chin as he snuggled deeper into the pillow, a smile still on his face. "Sweet dreams, bud. I love you."

"Love you too."

Quinn stood in the hallway as I shut his door. Then she followed me to my bedroom.

Our beers in the kitchen were forgotten. So was the full dishwasher I'd forgotten to run and the grill that should be covered in case of rain.

But I shut us inside my bedroom and ignored everything beyond the door when her hands snaked up my spine.

I spun, her fingers splaying on my chest, and caught her wrists, trapping them on my skin. "No sneaking out. Not tonight. Not in the morning."

"What about Colin?"

"We'll get up early. You can be gone before he wakes up, but if you leave me alone in this bed, I'm going to spank your ass tomorrow night."

She inched closer, not denying the fact that she'd be here tomorrow. And the next night. Quinn and I had a week. She could hang with her family during the day. Chill with Colin in the evenings. But at night until morning, she was mine.

"Understood?" I warned.

"Understood." A sly grin spread across her face as she worked her hand free to pinch my nipple. "I'll just have to do something else to earn that spanking."

CHAPTER EIGHTEEN

QUINN

"A re you coming too?" Brooklyn looked me up and down as she stood by Mom at the front door.

"Yep. I just need to grab my shoes." I sprinted upstairs and swiped my boots off the floor, sitting on the edge of the bed to tie them up.

Did I want to help clean out my late grandmother's house? Not really. But I wouldn't make Mom and Brooklyn do it alone while I sat around and watched Netflix.

With my sunglasses in hand, a hair tie on my wrist and my drumsticks in my pocket, I joined them downstairs. "Ready."

Brooklyn's minivan was parked at the curb. She'd taken the day off work to do this with Mom and the baby was with a sitter. Both of them wore dingy jeans, T-shirts and tennis shoes, likely expecting to do some heavy-duty cleaning and purging.

"Do you have the list, Mom?" Brooklyn's eyes flickered to me through the rearview mirror as she drove, but otherwise, she pretended like I didn't exist.

She probably hadn't expected me to help out today, but when Mom invited me this morning, I'd immediately agreed.

"It's in my purse," Mom said. "All thirty-one pages."

Nan had been busy cataloging her belongings. When Mom had shown me the list earlier, I'd laughed, thinking it was a joke. But no. Nan hadn't wanted there to be any squabbles over her possessions, so she'd taken the liberty to divvy them out herself.

In detail.

Color coded.

Goddamn, I missed her.

"I think today we should try to tackle the house and save the garage for later." Mom blew out a deep breath. "The house I know will be organized. But the garage . . . Nan didn't go in there much after she stopped driving. I think it's a lot of your grandfather's things that were too hard for her to deal with."

"Would you like me to go through it?" I offered.

"No, let's leave it. I think your dad wants to help with it too. And Walker."

We pulled into Nan's driveway and all three of us stared at the front door.

Okay, maybe I should have stayed home with Netflix. How was I going to make it through the door, knowing Nan wouldn't be there to greet me with a hug?

Mom braved her car door first, her movements slower and heavier than they'd been minutes ago. Brooklyn seemed to struggle with shutting off the car. If she decided to drive away and pretend that Nan was still here, she would get no complaints from the backseat.

"Come on, girls." Mom opened the van's sliding door and I had no choice but to step outside. My boots sunk into the thick grass of Nan's lawn that needed a mow. "This is part of life."

Dealing with death.

I didn't want to go inside and riffle through Nan's private things, but I'd do it. Nan had put a lot of time and effort into her affairs and requests, and like singing at her service, the least I could do was honor her wishes.

I took another step but stopped when Brooklyn snapped her fingers and opened the van's rear hatch. "Quinn. Boxes. I'm not carrying them by myself."

If my stage crew knew Brooklyn, they'd never call me a bitch again.

With a bundle of flat, cardboard boxes tucked under each arm, I trudged toward the house behind my sister. Mom led the way, carrying a plastic sack of packing tape and scissors on one arm so the other was free to open the door.

The smell of lavender, fabric softener and vanilla filled my nose. Tears prickled at the corners of my eyes and I ducked my chin as I blinked them away.

"So . . ." Mom sighed, hesitating for a moment, before straightening her shoulders and walking into the house.

The lights were off, but the window blinds were up and the curtains open, so sunlight flooded the living room. It looked exactly the same as it had when I was a little girl. Nan's floral-print sofa clashing beautifully with my grandfather's lime-green plaid armchair. The bookshelf in the corner didn't actually have books but a plethora of knickknacks she'd dust weekly. The coffee table was a dainty wooden piece dotted with lace doilies she used as coasters.

A neatly organized stack of magazines rested on the coffee table. The top issue was one I recognized immediately. It was *Rolling Stone*, and Hush Note was on the cover.

"How do you want to divide things up?" Brooklyn asked.

"Why don't you start in here," Mom suggested. "I'll take the kitchen. I'd like to get the refrigerator emptied and the dry goods to the food bank today. Quinn, how about you go through the office?"

"Okay." I waited as she set her supplies aside and pulled out the list from her purse. The office section was ten pages long. Armed with a sharpie, boxes and packing tape, I headed through the house to the office.

Familiar frames hung on the hallway walls, though the pictures inside had changed. Instead of photos of my siblings and me, most were of Nan's great grandchildren. School photos. Family shots. There was even one of Graham and Colin.

The door to the office was closed and I pushed through gingerly, nervous to disrupt the air. Conscious that I was about to ruin the room's serenity. Dust particles caught the light from the far window as they floated.

I walked to the desk and sat in Nan's chair, my shoulders slumping. Mom and Dad's wedding photo was positioned on one corner. Nan and Grandpa's from decades prior was on the other. In between were Walker and Mindy's beside Brooklyn and Pete's.

Four wedding photos.

If I ever married, mine wouldn't join them.

"Ugh." I hung my head. Where did I start? It felt wrong to poke around, but the sound of opening kitchen cabinets and items being tossed into a box echoed down the hallway.

Brooklyn would love nothing more than to scold me if I didn't get through this room, so I opened a drawer and found a row of neatly stacked pens. I checked the list, scanning each page. No mention of pens.

Drawer by drawer I worked, separating items to donate or to trash. Anything noted on the list was set aside for the intended person. A ruler, stapler, ball of rubber bands and a stray paperclip were headed to charity. Nan's half-used notebook could have been trashed, but I decided to keep it myself.

Her neat and tidy handwriting made my heart squeeze and I traced the words with a finger. Every page was a to-do list. Nan hadn't had a planner, just a spiral notebook with the date listed in the upper-right corners. Items on the page were listed beside a checkbox, all including a checkmark.

Except for the last page.

Grocery Store and *Prune Rosebush* were unchecked because she'd died the night before.

The sting in my nose returned and I changed my mind, placing the notebook in the trash pile.

I filled three boxes by the time I was through with the desk and the bookshelves. Another five by the time I was done with the closet and filing cabinet. The room looked bare without the framed photos or books. The boxes on the desk were sad.

There was only one item left on the list as I dove into the final drawer of the file cabinet.

Letters (file cabinet, bottom drawer) — Quinn

Besides a handful of books, it was the only thing on the office list with my name beside it. I found them bundled together with two rubber bands. The corners of the envelopes were tattered, and the paper had faded to cream from white.

I unstrapped the bands, taking out the first one and turning it over.

It was addressed to Nan with her maiden name. The

return was a government base in Germany. They had to have been from my grandfather. Why would she want me to have them? Wouldn't Dad want them instead?

The pages inside slid out easily and I unfolded them with care, scanning the words. As I'd suspected, it was a letter from my grandfather. The beginning was pleasantries, the mention of the weather and how he missed her. It was dated 1943.

He'd written this to her while he'd been at war. They hadn't been married yet, but he wrote to her like they were. The letter wasn't overly sweet, but more of a matter-of-fact report about what he was doing. He asked her questions about her friends and if she'd finished her needlepoint.

It was cute. Endearing. I suspected the others would be too. So why had she set them aside for me?

I flipped the last page over to see if there was more written on the backside after Grandpa had signed his name, and my heart dropped.

There was a poem on the back.

No, not a poem.

Lyrics.

He'd written her a song. There was a line of hand-drawn music at the bottom with notes penciled in place. I hummed the short chorus and wished there was more. It was beautiful but incomplete.

I dove for another letter, extracted the pages from the envelope but skipped the actual contents. Just like with the first, the lyrics were on the back of the last page. He'd changed some of the first. He'd penciled in more of the chorus.

My grandfather had spent his time at war writing my

grandmother songs. How many had he finished? Why hadn't we heard them before?

I was giddy to keep going, but Mom's voice startled me.

"How's it coming in here?" She stood by the door with a trash bag in her hand.

"Good. I'm done in here."

"Great. Would you mind helping me tackle her bedroom?"

"Not at all." I folded up the two letters and rebound them with the pile. Then I set them aside to go through later.

Mom and I spent the better part of an hour folding and sorting Nan's clothes. Her cedar chest was earmarked for Dad as it had a lot of Grandpa's things. Though all of Nan's jewelry had been divided between members of our family, none of her clothes had been included in the list.

"Would you mind if I took this?" I clutched an oatmeal cardigan in my hands, hoping Mom would say yes.

"Take it." Mom smiled. "I'm going to go check to see if there are any that Brooklyn wants too."

She breezed out of the room as I brought the sweater to my nose, breathing it in. It smelled like Nan. Like sugar cookies and Downy and warm hugs. I'd seen her wear it a hundred times and the thought of sending it to Goodwill was unbearable.

Brooklyn followed Mom into the room, her eyes filling with tears as she took in the contents of Nan's closet strewn across the bed. She reached for a cardigan, bulky and cable knit, in a dusky blue color and hugged it to her chest.

She breathed it in. When she looked up, my sister made my whole day. She smiled at me. "You can have this one if you'd rather have the blue."

"No, that's okay. I like this one."

"Thanks for helping us today. I think she would be glad that it's us. The three of us."

Mom walked over and put her arm around my shoulders. She took Brooklyn's hand. "I think she would have liked it too."

We let the moment sink deep, then got back to work. Brooklyn stayed in the bedroom to help box up Nan's night-stand belongings while I tackled the clothes and Mom dealt with the abundance of shoes.

By the time lunch rolled around, the minivan was teaming with boxes for charity and I was starved. Our lunch break was a roll through the McDonald's drive-through. Then we went back to Nan's and kept on working. Before we called it quits for the day, we'd taken two more trips to Goodwill.

Brooklyn dropped us off at home, her van empty except for the items Nan had designated hers. She was also getting a dresser and a bureau, but those Pete would help collect.

"Who gets that awful plaid chair of Grandpa's?" I asked Mom as we stood on the sidewalk, waving goodbye to my sister.

"Graham."

"No way." I laughed. "He hated that chair. Remember he called it the lime puke chair?"

"I think it's perfect. He teased her about it, but he always sat in it. And he'll never get rid of it."

"No, he won't." Graham would keep that chair, exactly as it was, until it either fell apart or it was time to pass it down to Colin.

"Maybe instead of taking an Uber to Graham's, you could borrow Dad's truck and deliver the chair yourself."

My cheeks flamed. I was twenty-seven years old, but it

was still embarrassing that my mother knew I'd gone to Graham's and had done more than sleep in his bed.

"Is it smart? This thing with Graham?" she asked.

"Probably not," I admitted.

"You two . . . you never could stay away from each other. Even on the nights you and Walker would both lie to me, I always knew you were with Graham."

"You did?"

"I might not have said anything, but I knew. I assumed as long as you were with Graham, you were safe. It was the times when you weren't with him that always made me nervous."

"I was just playing in a band, Mom."

"With a group of twenty-one-year-old men who I didn't know. Put yourself in my shoes. You'd freak too."

I thought about Colin and how I'd feel if he snuck out of the house to be left unsupervised with, well . . . Nixon. *Yeah. I'd freak.*

"If you trusted me with Graham, why were you always pushing me to spend time with other people?"

My senior year, she'd been constantly harping on me to go out with my friends. To spend one weekend without my boyfriend. The few times I'd doubted Graham's love, it had been because she'd planted the seed.

"You were leaving," she said. "You two were getting so serious and I just . . . I wanted you to get some distance. Some perspective. You were so young. Too young for that kind of love."

"No, we weren't, Mom."

"You were eighteen."

"And I loved him."

She studied my face, the conviction behind my words.

Then a wash of apology crossed her face, like for the first time, she was actually hearing me. She was actually believing.

"It was never fleeting." I pressed a hand to my heart. "It's always been him."

"But you're leaving?"

I nodded. "Yes, I am. We're on different paths."

"You always were." And there, in her words, I heard the warning.

Mom had worried once that we were too young and I'd get my heart broken. She hadn't been wrong. Now she worried our life circumstances would keep us apart.

Again, she wasn't wrong.

Graham had built a good life for himself and his son. He wouldn't sacrifice his normalcy for me.

I wouldn't ask.

"Well, I'm wiped." Mom brushed a lock of hair out of her face. "I'm going to take a thirty-minute power nap before running to the grocery store."

"I could use a little down time myself." I picked up the box at my feet, a handful of items from Nan's that she'd left to me, then took it inside. With Mom heading to her room, I went upstairs to my own, but not to nap.

Instead, I dove into the letters.

I took my time, reading each, not just the lyrics. My grandfather had signed them all, *Love Always*. The song had been included in every letter, but when I reached the end of the stack, it was still incomplete. And the letters stopped after the war ended.

At least the ones from my grandfather to my grandmother.

There was one more letter, the envelope newer, with my

name written on the front in familiar script. A lump formed in my throat as I took out the single page.

YOUR GRANDFATHER never finished the song.
  Do me a favor, finish it for him and for me.
  Love Always,
  Nan

TEARS DRIPPED down my cheeks as I read the words again and again. It took me a few moments to blink them away, then I shuffled through the stack of letters again for the first.

Finish the song.

I hummed the first bar a couple of times, but there was no rush in my pulse. No connection to the melody. I hummed it again. Then again.

Still nothing.

It was plain. Simple.

Boring.

I moved to the second letter, seeing that he'd tweaked the lyrics, and only the rhythm of the chorus. The same was true for the third, fourth and fifth. But on the sixth, I saw he'd changed the notes. It was an entirely new bar.

Scrambling off the bed, I whipped out my sticks and sat cross-legged on the floor. I hummed the new bar again, this time tapping out a beat on the carpet. It only took one time through the notes for goose bumps to break out across my forearms. The nape of my neck tingled.

This song would be bold. It would be enduring, like my grandparents' love. It would have a tender undercurrent with the bass, but the melody needed something dynamic.

There was a zing beneath my skin. The euphoria that only came when new song burst from my soul.

Nixon wouldn't need to help me write a song for Nan, after all.

I practiced and practiced, honing that bar until it grew into the chorus. Then I added a hook. When Mom hollered it was time for dinner, I forced myself off the floor. My legs had fallen asleep from the hours seated, but I hadn't noticed.

The song rang in my ears as I ate with my parents and as I borrowed Mom's car to drive to Graham's house.

I sang it for him and Colin. My grandfather's lyrics and his song that I'd embellished.

For the first time in months, I was energized for the new album. The floodgates were open, and I was ready to unleash, to drown in the music. This was beginning. This song.

The one we'd call, "Love Always."

CHAPTER NINETEEN

GRAHAM

"Oh, shit. Run!" The spark on the fuse jumped an inch. I shoved my hand in Quinn's stomach and pushed her away before the thing exploded.

She bolted for the lawn, tripping over her own feet and tumbling on the grass as she laughed hysterically.

"Take cover!" I tackled Colin—carefully—whose laughter was drowned out by the boom of the firework cannon.

He scrambled to his feet, jumping and shouting as the flare shot into the night sky. It burst with a loud pop into sparks of golden light, crackling as they streamed above us.

Collective *oohs* and *aahs* sounded from the audience seated in camping chairs in the driveway.

Like we'd done for as long as I could remember, we were celebrating Independence Day at my parents' house. We'd spent the evening grilling burgers and hot dogs, eating and visiting in the backyard, while we'd waited for nighttime to fall.

Then as twilight approached, Walker, along with Bradley, Dad and me, came outside to prepare for the show.

We'd let the kids throw snap pops and twirl sparklers. Then we'd set up a row of chairs, brought out blankets to ward off the chill and moved on to the pyrotechnics.

Walker and I had worked for a couple of hours this morning at the Bridger project before calling it a day. Then we'd headed to a local firework stand. The two of us had been stockpiling fireworks for weeks, but that hadn't stopped us from dropping another three hundred dollars, each.

No way we weren't kicking Judd Franklin's ass this year in the street's unofficial contest.

My mom and Ruby were snuggled in chairs. Brooklyn cuddled her son beside Pete while Mindy held Maya, who'd miraculously fallen asleep. And the rest of us took turns lighting fuses and goofing around.

"Can I light the next one?" Colin asked, bouncing around me and tugging on my jeans.

"It's my turn." Quinn swiped the lighter from my grip and smiled at my son. "But you can help."

I stayed seated on the lawn, close to Walker, who had Evan on his lap, and watched as they approached the row of cannons. Walker and I had set it up strategically so the big bang was at the end.

Quinn took Colin's hand, shielding him with her shoulder, before she clicked the lighter on and touched it to the fuse.

"Go! Go! Go!" She made a show of diving for the lawn, our safety zone, and held Colin tight as the spark inched close to the base of the cannon.

Boom.

"Bees! Yes." Quinn threw her arms in the air. "My favorite."

They buzzed around above us, zipping through the air, until they burned out.

"What do you normally do for the Fourth?" I asked Quinn when she sat down beside me. Walker and Evan were up next.

She leaned back on her elbows, blond hair dangling to the grass, and smiled up at the sky. "If we're not on the road, I usually stay home and do nothing. You can't see the fireworks from my apartment. Though, normally, we're traveling. There's always a gig for the holiday weekend."

"Anything memorable?"

"A couple of years ago, we had a performance at this amphitheater outside of Boise on the Fourth. They did fireworks during the last song of our final set. It was really amazing. Ethan told me that they spent fifty grand on fireworks. But this is better. I missed this."

"It's hard to beat."

The street wasn't officially blocked off, but everyone knew not to drive this way until the noise had stopped. No traffic meant we could set up in the road and have lots of space to play.

The tradition was, we'd do our own show of fireworks, competing with the neighbors, until it was time for the city's show. Then we'd burrow into our chairs and watch. From Mom and Dad's driveway, we had a great view of the fireworks set off at the fairgrounds.

Our row in the street was dwindling and I checked the time. There was only fifteen minutes before the big show.

"Should we do the finale?" Walker asked as Dad tossed me his lighter.

"Can I help?" the boys asked in unison.

"Not this time, guys." I stood beside Walker. "This is for the men."

Colin plopped down on the grass beside Quinn as Evan raced over to sit in his red mini chair beside Mom.

"Ready?" Walker asked.

I grinned. "How much money do you think Judd Franklin spent this year?"

Walker wagged his eyebrows and clicked his lighter. "Not enough."

We loved the Franklins. They'd been our neighbors for decades. But once a year, we went to war. Last year, Judd had gone to the reservation to buy his fireworks, and though we didn't have an official judging system, we'd all known he'd won. But Judd had gotten reprimanded when word of his illegal fireworks had spread and this year he'd bought local too.

"Three and three?" Walker asked, pointing to the six large canisters we'd staged away from the others.

"Sounds good. Let's go for seven seconds apart."

Walker shot an arrogant smirk across the street. My wave was equally as cocky. Then we lined up by our fireworks and began touching flame to fuse. By the time they were lit, the first was nearly ready to explode. We jogged to the lawn and I collapsed beside Colin and Quinn.

"Here we go." I looked at her profile. "Don't blink."

She smiled, and the light in her eyes danced as a pink starburst filled the sky.

And that was how I watched the finale. Not with my eyes aimed above, but at her face. I watched as the blue and green and red lights bounced against her skin. I watched the sparkles from the glitter in her eyes.

Two more days.

She'd been coming over each night after dinner. She'd play drums with Colin for a while, then hang out until he was asleep in bed. Then she'd come to mine. Each morning, she'd leave around five, and though we'd had the night together, it wasn't enough.

Two more days.

Then she'd be gone.

"We definitely won this year, huh, Dad?" Colin asked, forcing my eyes away from Quinn's face.

I held up my hand for a high-five. "Totally."

"Nice show, neighbors." Judd waved from across the street.

"Same to you, Judd," Bradley called back with a smugness to his voice.

Quinn giggled. "Dad is rarely competitive, except when it comes to this."

Bradley had chipped in a hundred fifty bucks to our fireworks budget. Dad had matched it too.

"I'm going to get a snack." Colin popped up and ran to his chair beside Evan's, digging into the cooler that Mom had packed for the grandkids. He pulled out a juice box and a bag of Cheetos Puffs. We didn't do healthy food with fireworks.

I stood from the lawn and held out a hand to help Quinn up. "Want to stick around for the main show? Or do you want to sneak out?"

"Sneak out," she answered, no hesitation. "Like old times. What about Colin?"

"He's spending the night with Mom and Dad."

"Where's your truck?"

"In the alley."

"All planned out."

I winked. "Like old times."

No one asked where we were going or what we were doing when we said our early goodbyes—a welcome change to the interrogation we'd gotten in high school whenever we'd left alone. I hugged Colin, who was so distracted with his snack that he barely noticed my good night.

"Don't worry." Mom kissed my cheek. "We've got him."

"Thanks, Mom. See you in the morning."

When I glanced around, Quinn had already disappeared. I gave the group one last wave, ready to go find her, but Ruby's stare gave me pause.

There was worry on her face. The expression familiar to a lot I'd seen in high school.

But Quinn and I weren't *too young* now. We'd had our fair share of experiences, the ones she'd wanted us to have. Apart.

So why the concern?

Ruby blinked and the look was gone. She gave me a smile before I turned and jogged around the side of the house, crossing through the yard to the alley.

Quinn was shrugging on a jacket as she stood by my truck. "So where are we going?"

I hit the locks and opened her door. "You'll see."

Fifteen minutes later, after I'd driven through town, I pulled off the highway and onto a gravel road that led toward the mountain foothills.

Quinn smiled. "Story Hills."

I nodded. "It's changed some over the years."

"Hasn't everything?"

"True."

Quinn and I had spent a lot of weekends finding places

256

to disappear, and Story Hills had been a favorite. It was no more than a parking lot and trailhead to the mountains, but at night it was usually empty, and the cops hadn't once chased us away.

I steered us through twists and turns, bouncing along the bumpy road until we reached the parking lot. It was empty, as expected, because from here, you couldn't see the fireworks in town. But we'd come here for a different set of lights.

Without needing to explain, I parked and reached into the backseat to get the blankets I'd stashed earlier. Quinn was already out her door and climbing into the truck bed.

"Here." I handed her the blankets to spread out, then hopped up to join her.

She laid down on her back, her legs crossed at her ankles and her hands folded on her stomach as she looked up to the stars.

I eased down beside her, our arms brushing. "One."

"Two."

The stars were bright this far from town and there was the faint glow of the Milky Way's creamy haze. "Three."

She relaxed on a sigh, leaning closer so her cheek touched my shoulder. "Four."

"Five."

"Six," she whispered.

"Seven." My hand stretched to take hers.

"What are we doing?"

"Counting stars."

She squeezed my hand. "You know what I mean."

"Yeah," I muttered. I knew and didn't want to have this conversation. She'd been right earlier in the week, to go without a goodbye. I didn't want one.

Quinn shifted so our eyes met. "Do you hate me for leaving?"

"No. I hate that I knew you had to go and that I handled it so badly. But that's on me. Not you."

"I didn't handle it well either."

"Doesn't matter now." With my free hand, I cupped her cheek. "I'm glad we had this time. To put it behind us."

"Me too. What happens after I leave Saturday?"

You come back. "You tell me?"

Instead of an answer, she turned her head to the stars again. "Eight."

"Nine."

We counted until we reached fifty-six. "What's it like being on tour?"

"Stressful," she said. "Tiring. At least, it has been lately. We're under a lot of pressure to write our next album and it's sucking the joy out of the travel."

"Can you take a break?"

"We're on one now. It's been good. That song I'm working on from Nan's letters has been . . . it's been the most fun creating I've had in a while. It was overdue. We've been so caught up in the touring these past few years, I think we forgot why we started this in the first place. But the shows. They're addictive."

"How so?"

"The lights. The crowds. The intensity." Her free hand floated into the air, dancing above us as she spoke. "It's a rush. It's a high. You go up there, and no matter how tired you are from taking a red-eye across the country or not sleeping because you're stuck on a tour bus, you get this energy. It feeds you and makes you forget about everything else. For one magical hour, it all makes sense again. So you put up with the in-between."

"And you live hour to hour."

"Exactly."

In my own way, I could relate. Playing at the bar was a blast. Amp that up to a larger scale, I could totally see how it would become a drug of its own.

And she'd leave here to keep living those hours.

"Fifty-seven," I said.

"Fifty-eight."

We reached one hundred eleven before she stopped counting again. "You asked me last week if we were real. As kids."

"Yeah," I drawled, having no clue where she was going with this.

"We were real, Graham. We are real."

I shifted, rolling up on my side to look down at her face. "What are you saying?"

"I'm saying that I never stopped loving you. I doubt I ever will."

The sadness in her eyes broke my heart as I spoke her next word. "But . . ."

"But it's not you," she said. "You said it yourself that night after the Eagles. My lifestyle would make you crazy. The schedule is grueling and there's no such thing as routine. If we tried to make it work, you'd end up resenting me. I'd end up hating the music. And Colin would suffer the most."

I loved her for considering my son in the equation.

"I don't want to give it up," she whispered. "The magic hours. I don't want to quit."

"And I wouldn't ask you to." I closed my eyes, taking a moment for the pain to fade.

Colin and I couldn't follow her around the world. We couldn't hop on and off buses and airplanes for months in the year. I wouldn't subject myself to that kind of chaos, let alone my son. He needed to be here, in Bozeman with our family. In school. In our home.

There was no practical way to merge our lives together. The give and take, the sacrifices, would end up destroying us both.

"Where does that leave us?" I asked. "Do we end this now? Tonight?"

Her chin quivered as she nodded. "If I wake up in your bed one more time, I won't want to leave."

And I wouldn't let her go.

"I loved you too. It's taken me this week to see it, but you were right. It was real. Every minute."

"Maybe it was destiny. We were always meant to walk different paths. Before, we were too young to understand it. But now . . ."

Now we could walk away without anger or frustration or words left unsaid.

Her hand came to my cheek. "Graham, I wish—"

I cut her off with a kiss, stealing whatever words she was about to say that would only make it harder for me to let her go.

And I would.

I'd let her go.

She belonged on that stage. She'd earned those magic hours.

Quinn hadn't said she *wouldn't* give it up. She'd said she didn't want to quit. There'd been a hesitancy in her voice, in her words, like if I'd asked, she'd cave.

So I kissed her before my resolve weakened. Before I broke my promise and begged.

My tongue darted into her mouth, my hands roamed her gentle curves. And when she came apart in my arms later, both of us panting and sweaty, I memorized the warmth from her lips in the cool night air and the way the moonlight turned her hair silver.

The drive home was silent, every mile toward her house agonizing.

When I pulled onto the block, I noticed that most of the firework debris had been cleaned away. The Franklins had already pulled their trash can to the curb for tomorrow's pickup.

I parked in front of her house and moved to shut off the truck, but her hand shot out, stopping me before I could shift into park.

"No, don't," she pleaded. "Don't get out."

"Why?"

"Because I can't do it." A tear dripped down her cheek. "I can't say goodbye. So just let me walk away."

Like she'd done at the airport nine years ago.

That was why she'd walked away.

"Will you tell Colin goodbye for me?"

I nodded, unable to speak.

Then she leaned across the console and pressed her lips to mine, the taste of her salty tears falling onto my lips.

I held her to me, savoring one last kiss before she ripped herself away and yanked at the door handle.

She flew up the sidewalk and vanished behind the door.

My throat burned as I stared up at her bedroom window, waiting to see if she'd appear in the glass and wave. The room stayed dark. So I pulled my foot off the brake and drove home. When I walked inside my dark house, the sense of loneliness nearly brought me to my knees.

Was this how it would be? Was this my life? Living for my son. Using his activities to keep me busy. Using work to distract me from the fact that there was a hole in my chest.

I'd been doing it for years, so why not a few decades more.

My body flew into action and I began ripping open the kitchen cabinet doors. I emptied the upper cupboards first, hauling plates and bowls and glasses to the dining room table. Then I cleared out the lower. Things I used regularly were stacked beside my dishes. The other items that my mother had given me over the years—two slow cookers and a bread machine—went downstairs for storage.

The first swing of my sledgehammer was around two in the morning. By four, I'd filled the bed of my truck with cabinets to donate to Habitat for Humanity. By five, I'd made an impressive pile of junk in my driveway.

As dawn approached, I stood in the kitchen, staring at the demolition.

Fuck.

Why hadn't I begged Quinn to stay?

CHAPTER TWENTY

QUINN

"Ha! Look at that." Dad shifted a box aside and peeled away a tarp to wheel out a tricycle that was buried in the disaster that was Nan's garage.

Mom had called it. The house had been Nan's domain, organized and easy to sort through, but this garage might take months.

"Was that yours?" I asked Dad, abandoning a box I'd just opened.

"Can you believe they saved this?" He crouched to run his hand over the handlebars. It was dirty, but the red trike was free of rust and nearly unscratched. "I remember pedaling this around the driveway. I used to have a wagon too, but—" Dad pulled at the tarp, feeling through the cluttered mess.

Brown boxes coated with a layer of dust were stacked to the ceiling. Tarps covered some items while others were left clustered together. There was a clear aisle that circled Nan's Subaru Outback like a walking trail through a dense forest. But otherwise, the space was packed.

Nan had told me all about the car, the first she'd ever bought brand-new. She'd only driven it for two months before deciding, even with shiny new wheels, driving wasn't for her anymore. Traffic was *horrendous*, she'd explained on a Monday call.

So the Subaru had been safely parked away a few years ago, and any free storage space she'd since filled up with forgotten keepsakes. They were probably items from the house she hadn't wanted to organize.

Or maybe she'd known that this would be like a treasure hunt for Dad.

"Found it." He grinned as he unearthed a wagon, steering it into the aisle beside the trike.

"Keep pile?" I asked.

"Definitely." He carried the wagon as I steered the tricycle through the maze to the yard where we'd been making piles. Or should have been making piles. So far, everything we'd come across was a keeper.

"Is that all for donation?" Mom asked as she came through the front door, a garbage bag in hand.

Dad and I shared a look. "Uh . . ."

"Oh, no." Mom wagged a finger. "I know that look, Bradley."

"What?" He feigned innocence. "These are great finds."

Her mouth pursed in a thin line and I fought a smile. Mom would huff about this, but she'd let him take all of this home and turn their own garage into a slightly more orga- nized version of Nan's.

"Here." Mom walked up to me and took a spare garbage bag that she'd stuffed in her jeans pocket. "Sneak some stuff into the donation pile when he's not looking."

"Okay, Mom." I giggled. When she turned away, I caught Dad's eyes and mouthed, "Never."

He beamed.

It had been nine years coming, but the rift between me and my father was beginning to heal.

Dad and I returned to the garage, working in separate corners. I did my best to take away the obvious trash. Dad had no interest in keeping yard rakes and shovels and Nan's gardening tools so those went into the charity pile. The photos and scrapbooks she'd put in clear tubs were immediately loaded in his truck to take home. The crates of bottles she'd kept Dad wanted to try to sell online.

"How did this get here?" Dad took the lid off a gray plastic tote.

"What is it?"

He waved me over. "See for yourself."

My mouth dropped when I looked into the tub. It was my stuff. The decor I'd had in my room as a teenager. The books and CDs I'd left behind.

"This must have gotten mixed up with some of Nan's other things because I thought this was at home in the crawl space."

At least they hadn't thrown it away.

I lifted out a poster, rolled into a tube, and slipped off the rubber band and unrolled the paper. "Aww. My Neil Peart poster."

The famous drummer from Rush had died recently. I'd been lucky enough to meet him once and as I'd shaken his hand, I'd remembered this poster, wishing I'd had it along for him to sign.

"Here." Dad handed me the tote.

"Thanks." I set it on the concrete floor and kneeled

down, taking a few moments to pick through it all. Another poster was rolled up inside and as I opened it, I cringed. This band had been my favorite and the poster had been tacked to my ceiling.

Then I'd met them about five years ago. Hush Note was growing, but we weren't at the level where we were now. We'd been newcomers, opening acts with a few hits. Every member of that band had made me feel like a pretender. A leech.

Assholes. "I can't believe I liked you."

Rip. I smiled as the paper tore easily. I crunched it up in a tight ball, both halves destined for Mom's trash bag. Then I replaced the lid to the tub and hefted it from the floor, planning on taking it home to dig through later.

"Your mom wants to take Graham his chair today," Dad said as I walked past.

"Oh." I stumbled but regained my footing. "Okay."

"Would you like to come along?"

I didn't answer as I walked outside, squinting in the bright sunlight.

Since Graham had dropped me off last night, he'd constantly been on my mind. Sleeping alone in my bed had been miserable and lonely. But ending it had been the right decision.

He didn't want my lifestyle and I couldn't blame him. What would my fame do to Colin? Neither of them needed that kind of attention. They didn't need to worry about the creeps on social media sending them inappropriate messages or the tabloids publishing a picture with a misleading caption.

And my focus needed to be on the band and this next album. Harvey didn't want us to lose any momentum and he was right. If we lost our focus, we'd never make it to the next level.

I was finally, *finally* writing music again. The letters Nan had given me were the inspiration I'd been missing. My grandfather's song was finished and I was in the middle of three others.

They were good. They were fresh, different from the music on our last album. One of them had a bite, a darker edge we hadn't done before. My grandfather's song was sweet and soulful. The other two were classic Hush Note and I had no doubts that Jonas's lyrics would fit in seamlessly.

Those songs would appease our die-hard fans and the label, because they were what people had come to love about our music. But the others were a stretch and would show the world our versatility.

They'd ink us on the map. Permanently.

I had an obligation to Jonas and Nixon. I had an obligation to Hush Note, and that meant staying in Montana was impossible. It was time to return to work.

And this was my dream, right? This life was what I'd been chasing. Just because Graham and I had found each other again didn't mean I could just give it up.

No matter how badly I wanted Graham.

The idea of leaving tomorrow was excruciating. Spending one night away from him had been terrible. I'd cried for an hour, then tossed and turned through the night. It felt like I was eighteen and losing him all over again.

Maybe after a few months apart, it wouldn't hurt as badly. Maybe when I came home for Christmas, we could navigate to something like friendship.

But not today. Today it hurt. So today, Dad would have

to deliver the chair alone.

"I think it would be better if you took the chair to Graham's later," I told him as I returned to the garage. "Without me."

"Okay." He was gracious enough not to ask why.

We worked for hours, organizing and sorting, until the piles on the lawn were more equally divided. Dad and I loaded up the items to donate and made our first trip to Goodwill. The manager came out personally to give his thanks before we waved goodbye with the promise to return with more.

"It's hard to let go, isn't it?" Dad asked, glancing in the rearview mirror.

"I'm sorry you lost her."

"Me too." He reached across the cab and put his hand on my shoulder. "But it's not forever. We'll see her on the other side."

"It still hurts saying goodbye."

"Yes, it does. But I've always thought goodbyes were a part of the healing process. Until you acknowledge something is in the past, you can't look to the future."

Was that why I couldn't bring myself to say goodbye to Graham? Because I didn't want to see a future without him?

Graham was no longer the boy from my youth. He was a man—a good man. The man I'd always known he would become.

He was responsible and an amazing father, which was insanely sexy. And he was down to earth, rooted and steady. He was the towering oak tree, planted firmly in the earth. I was the bird, flying in the sky above, and the wind had carried me too far to turn back now.

Maybe I'd write a song about goodbyes since I couldn't

speak the words.

The next morning, as promised, Nixon returned to Bozeman with my airplane. And for the second time in a decade, I left home.

And though I'd told my family I'd return, maybe it would be easier for us all if I stayed away.

"WHAT?" I snapped as I flung open the door to my penthouse.

"Ahh. There she is." Nixon strolled past me wearing a pair of sunglasses, jeans and a rumpled shirt—last night's clothes. The stench of booze and a sweaty club wafted in my face, making me gag. "You were so *nice* in Montana that I was worried your trip home had dulled that delightful, bitchy sass."

"It's four o'clock in the morning." I slammed the door. "Of course, I'm bitchy. And you stink."

He shrugged and pulled off his sunglasses. His eyes were bloodshot. His hands were shaky and his skin pale.

My irritation subsided as worry took its place. Nix was coming down from a high.

At least he'd come here to crash instead of another *friend's* house who'd only get him high again as soon as he woke up.

"Come in." I walked past him, leading the way to the kitchen. "Are you hungry? I ordered Chinese last night and have some leftovers." I'd been missing Graham and Colin so I'd gone for sweet and sour pork.

"Nah. Mind if I crash for a while?"

"Shower first."

"Yes, dear." He chuckled, tossing his sunglasses on the counter before striding away toward the guest bedroom suite.

I sighed and trudged to the coffee maker, rubbing the sleep from my eyes as I made a cup.

Nix might sleep all day, but now that I was up, I wouldn't be able to go back to bed. I'd only toss and turn, like I had last night, wondering why that sense of *home* I had in my apartment was missing.

The coffee dripped and I closed my eyes, searching for that sense of peace. *Nothing.* Just as it had been since I'd walked through the door.

The penthouse was clean and smelled like roses. I'd come home to a bouquet in the dining room, another in the living room and another in my bedroom. Ethan's touch, no doubt. He was clearly bored, not having us on tour to babysit.

With my coffee in hand, I padded into the living room, sinking into my favorite charcoal leather chair.

My interior decorator had gone for dark and cozy. The walls in the living room were painted a deep taupe. The black curtains made it so I could block out any light from outside. The floors were a chocolate wood with thick rugs placed strategically to break up the open concept and add warmth.

It had always felt more bachelor than female. But then, she hadn't asked me about my style. She'd decorated my place at the same time she'd done Nixon's and must have assumed that as a drummer, I wanted the same vibe. It hadn't been the first time I'd been lumped in with the guys and it wouldn't be the last.

The decor hadn't bothered me much until yesterday. I'd sat in this same chair, staring at my dark furnishings and abundance of space and wished to be sitting in a charming home instead. One with an outdated kitchen, bright bedrooms and two guys who were stuck on my mind.

Where had Graham put that plaid chair? By his fireplace in the living room? Or in the basement? That chair would probably become his football chair. I could picture him sitting there, grumbling about the lime green, drinking a beer watching the game on a Sunday evening. Colin would race around until he was older and got interested in football. Someday, there'd probably be a woman curled in Graham's lap.

"Ugh." Just the thought made my stomach churn.

What was wrong with me? Did I want him to be happy? Obviously. But in my heart, Graham would always be mine.

Seattle's city lights shimmered through the windows as I sipped my coffee and the sun began to rise. Dad was probably already at church, preparing for his service. Mom would be cleaning. And everyone else would be waking up and getting ready for a Sunday.

We'd had a Montgomerys-only family dinner on Friday night before I'd left. Walker and Mindy had brought over fried chicken. Brooklyn and Pete had brought cookies from a local bakery. The adults had visited. The kids had played, and Maya had even called me Aunt Quinn.

My sister hadn't snarled or glared as we'd worked together to set the table. Mindy had been fascinated by the recording process and had asked me question after question over the meal. After dinner and dessert, we'd said our good-byes and then . . . the next day I came home.

To my sanctuary.

That was oddly uncomfortable and not-so-serene.

There wasn't a sound coming from the guest room.

Nixon had showered and was probably snoring, so with my coffee refilled, I went to my master suite and took a shower of my own. I didn't bother blow-drying my hair or putting on makeup. I had no plans to leave the penthouse today. The refrigerator was empty, but anything I wanted would be delivered with a single call.

I put on a pair of sweats, a camisole and a Black Sabbath hoodie—one of the few items in my closet I'd actually purchased myself—then retreated to my music room and flipped on the lights.

I paid the owners of the building extra for this room. Rather, I paid to rent the apartment below this room. The last thing I needed when I was working out some stress on my drum kit was downstairs neighbors bitching about the noise. So I had nice buffer between me on floor eighteen and whoever lived on sixteen.

The piano beckoned and I sat down, running my hands over the surface. How long had it been since I'd been home? *Two months.* It felt like a lifetime.

The glossy black surface of my Sauter concert grand gleamed. Whether I was here or not, I hired a crew to clean the penthouse weekly and they had a special polish for the instruments in this room, my treasures.

My fingers skimmed the keys, and I set my mug on the floor to not risk a coffee ring. Then I closed my eyes and played, not worrying about Nixon on the other end of the apartment who was likely passed out.

Song after song, I let the music seep into the empty voids. It soaked into my heart, and when the notes shifted to the new song, my grandfather's song, tears streamed down my face.

Everything was wrong. Why? I was here, wasn't I?

Living in the penthouse I'd always adored and had always thought suited me perfectly. I was finally working on the album and the music held so much promise.

"So why the fuck am I crying?" I wiped furiously at my eyes.

"Because things are changing."

My heart leaped into my throat as I gasped, spinning around to find Nixon leaning against the door. "You scared me."

"Sorry." He walked across the room, his hands in his pockets.

His hair was damp and he'd changed into sweats of his own. The guest suite was stocked with extras because there'd been plenty of nights when Jonas, Nix and I would be messing around and it would get late so the guys would crash here. I had my own clothes at each of their places too.

As Nix sat beside me on the bench, I gave him an exaggerated sniff. "Much better."

He laughed and splayed his hands on the keys. He wasn't as good on the piano as I was, he mostly worked on his guitar, but he could hammer his way through a song if necessary. "What were you playing?"

"Something new," I told him, then launched into the story of Nan's letters and my grandfather's song.

"Sing it for me," he said, standing from the bench to grab the acoustic from the corner. I kept that guitar here for him and Jonas. Keys and drums were no problem, but I'd given up mastering the guitar a long time ago.

As I began playing, Nix took a seat on one of the room's stools, and at the second chorus, he joined in, playing until the last note echoed in the room.

I held his gaze, my heart in my throat, hoping that he

liked it. "Well?"

"Well, damn. That was awesome."

Thank God. If Nix liked it, he'd help me sell it. "Lyrics are Jonas's thing, but I want to pitch this to him and Harvey."

"They'll go for it. No question."

"You think?"

He nodded. "Especially when you agree to sing it."

"What? No. Jonas can sing it."

"It's your song, Quinn. Part of what makes it so powerful is *you.*"

Could I sing this? A thrill of possibility raced through my veins. "Would it throw the album off to add female vocals?"

Nixon grinned. "Not if we build the album around it."

I ran my hand down the keys, filling the room with a random string of notes as I sighed. "I have three others penciled that I'm really liking at the moment. You?"

"One." He stood and put the guitar aside, then stalked to the windows. "And it's shit."

I stood and joined him beside the glass, watching the street below as people bustled along the sidewalks and cars navigated the streets. Nixon, like me, had never had a block when it came to the music. "What's wrong? What can I do?"

"Nothing. I'll be fine."

"Will you?"

"Will you?"

"We're not talking about me, Nix."

He lifted his chin. "Maybe we should talk about you. Why are you here? What are you doing?"

"Um . . . I live here."

"You know what I mean." He arched an eyebrow, and my stomach dropped. Yeah, I knew what he meant. "I saw you with Graham. You look at him in a way that makes the

274

rest of us wish we had something half as strong. So what happened?"

I sighed. "We ended it. He doesn't want this lifestyle and I-I'm not quitting the band. So we're done. It's for the best."

"Wow." He scoffed. "Harsh. You cut the poor guy out before he had a chance."

"Excuse me?" I glared, shoving at his shoulder. "I didn't cut him out. We agreed on it. Together. He has a son. This lifestyle—the travel, the schedules—it's not steady. They have a good thing going and don't need me complicating it."

"So now you're a martyr. That's a new look for you."

"What is your problem?" I barked.

"I gave you an extra week to figure it out and you still didn't see it. So let me spell it out. I liked Montana Quinn. She was happy."

Montana Quinn? "There's only one Quinn. *Me*. And I am happy."

"No, you're not. You love him. You miss your family. And if you'd finally stop being so damn stubborn, you'd see that you're shutting them out, using us, the band, as an excuse because you're afraid of getting your heart broken again."

"I—" Fuck. He'd hit that one straight on. "How would it work? I look at Kira and Vivi and how they can go with Jonas. I don't see that happening with Graham."

"You haven't given him the time to figure it out."

"Ugh." I walked to the piano. "I hate when you're right."

"Doesn't happen much." He chuckled. "Better write it down."

"So I just go to Montana and, what, live there? How will that work?"

"It just will." He shrugged. "We're rock stars."

CHAPTER TWENTY-ONE

GRAHAM

"I want that gray stain. The light one that we used in my bathrooms. What's it called?"

"Lancaster."

"That's it." I nodded. "Flat panel style. Soft close."

"Can do." My cabinet guy Drew scribbled on his notepad. "Do you want us to build them for you? Or just deliver the boxes when they show up?"

"I'll build them." Doing it myself would save me some money even if it would take my time. I was already into this place more than it would resell for and I wanted to keep my costs down.

"Great." He clicked his pen closed and stuck it in his shirt pocket, stretching his other hand for a shake. "I'll give you a call when they show. Probably about four weeks."

Four weeks. I stifled a groan. "Thanks, Drew."

I'd thought about using an online supplier to get them faster, but with shipping costs and the discount Drew gave us at his shop, I'd take the delay, let him deal with the hassle and have his one-year guarantee in my pocket.

276

He waved and let himself out the front door, and I waited until he was gone to curse. "Fuck."

Why exactly had I destroyed my kitchen before I had the new cabinets ordered? This was a mistake not even the most novice DIYer would make. How the hell were we going to survive for over a month without a kitchen?

Eating out was going to get old fast. Grilling too. This was a clusterfuck all because I'd been so messed up about Quinn that I'd lost the ability to think logically.

Colin had come home after the Fourth and muttered a *whoa* when he'd stepped into the kitchen.

Whoa. Fucking whoa.

But this was my mess. I'd clean it up and was determined to get life back to normal. Normal, with a new kitchen. And a new floor.

The bright side of the cabinet delay was that I had four weeks to get the hardwoods installed. It was going to be my nighttime project when I couldn't stop thinking about Quinn. Hopefully, Colin could sleep through the noise of my nail gun.

I walked to the fridge that I'd pushed into the living room and took out a Mountain Dew—we'd call this lunch. After three shitty, sleepless nights, I'd been surviving on caffeine and sugar to keep me moving.

Walker was at the job site, finishing up with the inspector, so I'd come home to meet with Drew. I was going to chug this pop and sit down at my computer—where, I wasn't sure because my normal workspace at the dining room table was crowded with kitchen shit—to work on a bid.

We had two projects lined up after the Bridger mountain house. Neither Walker nor I liked looking into the future without three or four jobs stacked. If we won the bid we'd put in last month on a custom home in town, plus the one I was working up today, that would take us through the winter.

I crushed the empty can and took it to the recycling bin in the garage just as the doorbell rang. Drew must have forgotten a measurement.

My boots thudded across the subfloor—I'd torn out the carpet yesterday—and I set my can aside before swinging the door open.

It wasn't Drew.

"Hey." Quinn looked small on my porch. Nervous. Beautiful. Her hair was swept into a bun and she was wearing a dress. A simple, green sundress that made the blue in her eyes sparkle.

I blinked, making sure she was real. Had the delirium of no sleep conjured her from my dreams? "Thought you left."

"I came back."

I swallowed hard. "Why?"

"I'm a rock star."

"Uh, yeah. I know." Was that supposed to mean something to me? "So?"

"So, I'm a rock star. The Golden Sticks, though I've never been crazy about that nickname. Whatever. I'm rambling. The point is, I'm a rock star. Dream accomplished."

"Right. Wasn't that why you left? So you could go and be a rock star?"

"No. I *am* a rock star. I've been working so hard to become one, to get to the next level, that I missed the fact that I am one already. We're at the top."

"You didn't realize you were a rock star." I shook my head, not understanding a damn thing she was saying.

278

Mom always said, Mountain Dew will rot your brain. "Huh?"

"I thought this was it. The endless tours. The hours we'd spend in the studio, recording and adjusting and recording again. Making album after album without a break in between so we could make it big. That's what my life has been."

The life I'd spent nights contemplating. Trying to find a way to give Colin what he needed and still hold on to Quinn.

Sure, her lifestyle wasn't what I had imagined ever wanting for myself and Colin. She didn't have a quiet, small-town house with routine mealtimes and regular pop-ins from family. But kids could thrive in a city. I'd never been to Seattle, but I was sure it had redeeming qualities. As hectic as it might be, the touring and the concerts would give Colin a unique lifestyle.

It was different.

But possible.

And if it meant a life with Quinn . . .

"I get it," I said. "That's your life."

"No, that's—"

"Just let me get this out." I held up a hand. I'd planned to have this conversation next week, but for whatever reason, she'd come back and I wasn't wasting a moment. "I've thought a lot about it the last couple of days. What you said under the stars. What I said about the life I wanted for Colin. And I think we were both wrong."

She blinked, her mouth opening, but I kept going before she could interrupt.

"You have a special life. You have a gift. I'd never take that away from you, but I'm not losing you again. We belong together, Quinn."

"Graham—"

"If that means we move to Seattle and follow you around the world, we'll do it. Colin can have tutors. He'll get to see the world, something most kids wouldn't have the chance to do. And I'll be there. With you. I'll be front row during every magic hour, because if it makes you happy, I'll be happy. As long as we're together."

Her chin began to quiver. "And I'd be happy here, with you. Living in this house. Playing drums with Colin or watching him play baseball or reading books. As long as I can sleep in your bed each night, I'll be happy."

It took a flash for my brain to register what she was saying. But this was it. Us.

"I want—"

I hauled her into my arms and sealed my mouth over hers, swallowing her words. Whatever she wanted; she could tell me later. She could tell me day after day, year after year, and I'd do my best to make it happen.

The sweet sound of her moan rang in my ears. The taste of her lips soothed the fears that I'd lost her again.

By some miracle, she was here, and I wasn't letting go.

Not this time.

Quinn clung to me as I hauled her inside, kicking the door shut behind us as we shuffled toward my bedroom. A trail of clothes marked our path and when I laid her on my bed, the touch of her bare skin put the last of my worries at ease.

She'd come back.

Not that it mattered.

I'd already planned a trip next weekend to drive to Seattle and chase her down.

"I love you." I kissed the long column of her neck.

"I love you too," she whispered in my ear, her hands running down my spine.

I gripped my shaft, running it through her wet folds, then rocked us together, savoring the hitches in Quinn's breath as I eased inside, inch by inch, until I was rooted deep. "You're mine."

"Yes." She arched her hips. "Move, baby."

I glided out and thrust inside, hard and fast. "I missed you."

Her legs wrapped around my hips and her hands came to my ass, urging me deeper. My lips covered hers and we kissed, long and slow, in a rhythm that matched the motion of my hips, the slide of our bodies together. When the build and the heat became too much, our mouths broke apart. I lost myself in her stormy gaze, the dark swirls of blue dragging me with her as she toppled over the edge.

I collapsed, trapping her beneath me as the roar of blood subsided in my ears and the white stars in my eyes vanished. Then I buried my face in her neck, breathing in the sweet scent of her hair that had escaped its pins, and held her tight. "We'll make this work."

"You'd really follow me around the world?"

I shifted, rolling to my side so I could face her. "You'd really move here and give up the band?"

She nodded and clutched my hand to her chest. "For you."

"I'm never going to make you choose me or the band, Quinn."

Her eyes softened. "And I'm not going to make you give up what you have here. You didn't let me finish explaining outside. I'm a rock star."

"This is not new information, babe."

"Would you be quiet?" She laughed. "I'm saying that I'm a rock star. That status we've been chasing, the fame and the notoriety, we made it. We can stop chasing it now. I don't need to be glued to the studio. I don't need to be on tour all the time. We made it. I'm a rock star, and it's time to make space for the people missing in my life."

"What about Jonas and Nixon? Are they going to be okay taking a step back?"

"I haven't talked to Jonas, but I can't imagine he's going to be mad. He's already pushing for more family time in our schedule. And Nix was the one who put my ass on a plane this morning to come home."

"I knew I liked that guy."

She took my hand, kissing my knuckles. "We're burning out. It's time to slow down. I can be in Hush Note and live here. I can fly off for shows and then come home. Maybe we can do mini-tours in the summers so you and Colin can come with me."

She'd have the band.

I'd have roots.

But most importantly, we'd have each other.

"You're sure? I don't want you to look back in ten years and realize you sacrificed your career for us."

"I've spent the past two weeks looking back, Graham. I know exactly what's been missing. This time around, we do it together. I have no idea what it will look like, but I have faith that we'll figure it out."

I rolled on top of her, searching her eyes for any hesitation or fear. But they were clear and bold and true.

This was our second chance.

"You set me free once, Graham. You let me fly. Now I'm coming home."

If a home is what she wanted, a home is what she'd find.

―――――

"QUINN?" I called into the house.

"Downstairs!" she hollered back.

I grinned at Colin and followed him through the kitchen. We both kept our shoes on since I'd made no progress on the floor in the past week since Quinn had surprised me on my doorstep. The free time I'd expected each evening was suddenly nonexistent. Quinn, naked in my bed, took priority over home remodeling.

"Go grab your backpack," I told Colin.

"Okay." He smiled and raced to his room.

"Quinn! We gotta go."

"I'm coming." She jogged up the stairs. "Five minutes."

"You need to wear shoes, babe." I frowned at her bare feet as she tiptoed into the bedroom.

"I'm fine."

"Yeah, until you step on a nail I missed when I ripped up the carpet." I followed her, leaning against the door as she sat on the edge of the bed to pull on her Chucks. "How was your day?"

"Good. My parents came over this morning to deliver a latte and say hello. Then I spent a few hours writing. How would you feel about a piano in the basement? The keyboard isn't cutting it."

"Whatever you want is fine by me." Though in about an hour, we'd be talking about which house to have said piano delivered.

"Thanks." She hopped up and crossed the room, standing on her toes to give me a kiss. "How was your day?"

"Good. Better now."

It was amazing how good it felt to have someone ask about your day. To kiss you when you got home. And not just someone.

Quinn was *the one*.

"Ready!" Colin raced to us, strapping on his backpack.

"Did you get your flashlight?" Quinn asked.

"Yep."

"And your pajamas?"

"Yep," he answered her with a nod.

"And your toothbrush?"

"Uh . . ." He darted into the bathroom. "Got it."

"Then let's load up," I said. "There's a cheeseburger at Grandpa's with my name on it."

Quinn kissed me again, then walked beside Colin through the house and to the garage.

I hadn't had to sit Colin down and talk to him about Quinn. How she'd meld into our house, and how we'd go about making a two-person family into three. It had just happened seamlessly.

The day Quinn had returned, I'd kept her in bed all afternoon until it was time to pick up Colin from Vacation Bible School. On the drive home, I'd promised him a surprise when we got to the house.

Quinn had been sitting outside, waiting. The moment he'd spotted her, he'd bolted from the truck—before I'd fully parked, we'd had words about that—and crashed into her arms. He'd pulled her inside, talked her into a game of checkers and hadn't even blinked when he'd woken up the next morning to her in the living room wearing one of my T-shirts.

He'd crawled onto the couch beside her, yawning, and asked if he could have a donut for breakfast.

I'd said yes.

Quinn had said no.

She was unofficially living here, sleeping in my bed. The clothes she'd brought to Bozeman hung in my closet. Her makeup was on the counter in my bathroom.

No announcement necessary.

Colin hadn't asked questions. He was simply glad that she was here. But today, I'd snuck away from the job site a couple hours early to pick him up from day camp.

We'd had some shopping to do. And some talking.

"Did you use my drums today?" Colin asked Quinn as we climbed into the truck.

"Yes. I wrote the part for that song I played you last night."

"Cool."

"It is cool." Quinn beamed a smile my way. "And guess what else? I'm going to sing "Love, Always" for the album. Jonas called me today after talking with Harvey and they both love the idea. I've been waiting for Nixon to call me and rub it in, but I haven't heard from him all week. I'm starting to get worried."

"Call him."

"I'll text Ethan first." Her fingers flew over the screen as we drove.

I was beginning to see how these people fit as an extension of her family, how they loved and protected her like she did with them.

Which was why I'd made my own phone call to Jonas today.

285

Quinn clutched the phone in her lap as she waited for Ethan's reply, the *ding* coming seconds later. She read it and gasped.

"What?"

She closed her eyes and whispered, "Thank God."

"What?" I asked again, but instead of answering, she held up the phone for me to read Ethan's reply.

Rehab.

Nixon had gone to rehab.

"This is a good thing." She relaxed into the seat. "A really good thing."

"What is?" Colin asked from his seat.

"Grown-up stuff, bud."

"When will I be old enough for grown-up stuff? When I'm twelve?"

"Eighteen," I answered at the same time Quinn said, "Twenty-one."

Her protectiveness over my son was undeniably sexy.

"Where are we going?" Quinn asked when I hit Main Street and turned the opposite direction from our parents' neighborhood.

"It's a surprise."

She looked at me, then twisted to glance at Colin, who was wearing an enormous smile. "I thought we were having a family backyard campout."

It was something we'd done often as kids. My parents and her parents would set up some tents in their backyards and we'd all sleep outside. Or in my mother's case, pretend she was going to sleep outside until everyone else was tucked in for the night and then sneak inside to her soft bed.

"Change of plan," I said. "We are camping. Just us."

"Ah." She nodded. "That sounds good. What about your cheeseburger?"

"Coolers are already at camp."

"We picked up hot dogs, chips and s'mores," Colin added. "*No* vegetables."

She laughed. "Where are we camping?"

"You'll see."

She squirmed in her seat, her eyes tracking our every turn as we drove ten miles out of town and pulled off a gravel road into a bare lot. A two-wheel trail had been flatted in the grass and I followed it to a copse of quaking aspens. In the distance, the mountains towered bold and blue, the color nearly as stunning as Quinn's eyes.

"Here?" she asked as I shut off the truck.

I nodded and climbed out, opening the back door for Colin.

He scrambled out, his backpack forgotten, and raced around the truck to capture Quinn's hand as she stepped out. "Check out our fire pit."

"What is this place?"

"Ours." I breathed in the clean air and let the summer sunshine warm my face. "I got a tip about this property about four weeks ago. The real estate agent is a buddy of mine and he thought we might be interested in building a spec home on it." The tip had come right before Quinn returned to Bozeman for Nan's funeral. "Walker and I decided to let it go. We've been too busy with custom work to think about a spec. But I called the agent yesterday and put in an offer. It got accepted an hour later. What do you think?"

If she hated it, I'd transfer it into the company's assets, and Walker and I would build a spec house after all. But if

Quinn loved it, this would be home. I loved my house in town, but with three of us, hopefully more one day, we needed space.

"It's beautiful." She smiled and pointed to the mountains. "I want a window with that view."

"You can have whatever you want." I took her hand and walked her to the fire pit Colin and I had built after stopping by the grocery store to fill the coolers and bring them to the lot.

"I'm not letting you pay for all this yourself. Not if it's ours."

"Fine by me." We'd figure out the money later. I wasn't going to tell her how to spend her money, and I wasn't going to pretend she didn't make more than I ever could either. But that wasn't a conversation for today. "I'd like to build a home here with some space for our family to grow. We haven't talked about kids but—"

"Three. Plus Colin. Four total. I like even numbers."

God, I loved this woman. "Four total."

She leaned into my arm. "I'm glad we're camping here. It's like the first night in a new home."

"Me too." I dropped a kiss to her hair, then left her with Colin as I started to unload the rest of our supplies.

We set up our tent, spreading out our sleeping bags—Quinn zipped ours together. Then we explored the five acres, earmarking different spots for a potential homesite. When our stomachs growled, I lit a fire and we cooked hot dogs and ate s'mores. And as the night sky faded from blue to black, Colin's sugar high wore off and I tucked him into bed.

"Is he asleep?" Quinn asked as I zipped the tent closed.

"Just about."

She yawned and turned her face to the sky. The glow from the fire danced across her skin.

"Come on." I waved her out of her camp chair as I hopped up on the open tailgate of my truck. The blankets were already in place.

She climbed up beside me and we lay down, her tucked into my side, like we'd done time and time again.

"I called Jonas today."

"My Jonas? Why?"

"Because I'm going to steal a part of you from them. Man to man, I thought it was appropriate to give him a head's up. Same reason I swung by and paid your dad a visit today too."

"Graham . . ."

I reached over her body and captured her left hand, finding a certain finger, then sliding on a diamond solitaire ring.

A ring that Nan had left me along with that ugly fucking green chair now in my basement.

"Oh my god. This is Nan's ring." She lifted her hand, staring at the jewel. "She gave it to you? When?"

"Your dad brought it over today. It was on her list, I guess. She knew it was real. Even when we didn't, Nan knew."

Quinn smiled, a tear dripping from her eye and into her hair.

"Marry me." I ran my knuckles over her cheek. "Count stars with me until we're too old to climb in the back of my truck."

"Yes." She nodded, shifting closer for a kiss. "Yes."

"I love you."

"I love you too." She laced her fingers with mine, then

turned to the sky with a smile stretched across her beautiful face. "One."

"Two."

She kissed me again. "Three."

We didn't make it to four.

EPILOGUE

QUINN

O*ne year later ...*
        "Good luck!" Dad shouted over the roar of the
crowd.

"Thanks," I mouthed, not even trying to compete against
the noise.

We were backstage and our opener, a band who'd been
gaining fame quickly since joining our tour, had the arena
rocking. They'd just walked off stage, but the crowd was still
cheering as the crew raced to prepare for our set.

It was the end of another tour and my parents' first show.
They'd been wide-eyed since they'd arrived two hours ago.
Soon, Ethan would escort them to a section of seats he'd
roped off for my family.

Walker and Mindy each had beaming smiles on their
faces. Evan and Maya had the same awe in their expressions
as they looked around, seeing but not hearing much thanks to
the noise reduction earmuffs I'd given them in my dressing
room.

Colin was wearing the same, something he grumbled

about at each show, but the alternative was he missed the concert, so he wore them begrudgingly.

This wasn't Colin's first time on the tour, and he was enjoying being the resident expert, telling his cousins exactly what to do and bossing his grandparents around. Ethan loved that Colin was his shadow and adored the attention as much as my son.

My son.

Three months ago, Colin had officially become mine. The judge had approved the adoption, and though we'd been a family for a year, there was something settling about it being legal.

"Good luck, Mom!" Colin shouted.

My heart swelled. He'd been calling me Mom since the judge's ruling, but I wasn't used to it yet. "Thanks, buddy."

"We'll meet you after?" Dad asked.

I nodded, leaning in to speak loud enough for him to hear. "Just stick with Ethan. He'll take you to the dressing room when it's over and we'll regroup there."

Graham's arm slid around my shoulders and he pulled me into his side. His lips brushed the shell of my ear and his beard tickled my cheek. "Have fun."

"Thanks." I blew out a shaking breath and leaned into his strength. My stomach was in knots. My hands were trembling. Whether it was the fact that my family was here or that this was the last show or that we were about to start on a new adventure, I wasn't sure, but I was nervous.

Luckily, Graham was here to help me through it. Like he'd been at Nan's funeral. Like he had been on the start of this tour, standing behind the curtains where I could see him when I sang "Love, Always" for the first time to a live audience.

It was the second best-selling hit from our new album.

The first was a song Nixon and Jonas had written after Nix got out of rehab. They'd spent a month together at Jonas's home in Maine writing. "Mad Alibi" was on track to be our biggest hit to date.

It was a kickass song with a kickass beat, and when I started it off tonight with the slam of the bass drum, the crowd would explode.

"Good luck, Quinn!" Mindy waved as Ethan arrived to usher everyone to the VIP section.

I bent to kiss Colin's cheek before he started head-banging with his tongue sticking out. It was going to take forever for him to wind down and sleep tonight. That would be my parents' problem since he was bunking with them. Mom and Dad adored having all of their grandchildren close, so tonight they were having a campout in their hotel suite.

Ethan had arranged for child-size tents and sleeping bags to be waiting when they arrived after the show.

My husband and I would have a night alone.

The morning after Graham proposed, we told Colin the news over a campfire breakfast, and we asked if he would like me to legally become his mother. He screamed *yes* without hesitation before throwing his arms around my neck.

So Graham and I married the next weekend. We didn't want to delay the adoption process, worrying the family justice system might be difficult to navigate. We exchanged vows in my parents' backyard. I wore a simple, white strapless gown and went barefoot. Graham wore jeans and a white button-up.

My father was the officiant, and with our family and friends as witnesses, we signed our license without fanfare or fuss. A photo of Graham sweeping me into his arms for a kiss was framed on the fireplace mantel at home.

"Last show of the tour." Graham took my face in his hands, dropping his forehead to mine. "Enjoy it, babe. You deserve it."

Every nerve ending in my body was alive, sparked with excitement and adrenaline. Each show was fun, but some were out of this world. "It'll be a good one. I can feel it. Then we're taking a year off. Minimum."

"A year? What about next summer?"

I leaned back so I could watch the expression on his face. "I'm not taking a newborn baby on the road."

"A baby." He swallowed hard. "You're pregnant?"

"I took the test this morning."

Graham crushed me against him, burying his face in my hair as his arms banded tight. "I love you."

"Love you too." I breathed in the scent of his shirt and melted into his chest.

Thank you, Nan. I sent my gratitude to the heavens, hoping she was close enough tonight to hear. She'd brought Graham and me together. She'd returned me to my family. From now until I saw her again, I'd keep sending her my thanks.

"If it's a girl—"

"We're naming her Nan." Graham didn't let me go until our stage manager cleared her throat behind us, signaling it was time.

"Go." My husband winked. "Enjoy the magic hour. Then later, we'll have a little magic of our own."

I pressed my lips to his, lingering for a long moment before stepping away. "Make sure I can see you in the crowd tonight." I wanted to see him while I sang.

"I will." He nodded and disappeared down the hallway, walking behind Kira and the kids.

One more show.

After this concert in Seattle, Hush Note was officially on vacation.

We'd had a hectic summer, traveling and performing. Graham and Colin had joined me when they could, but we'd had too many nights apart. Graham had been working tirelessly, along with Walker, to finish up our home. When we returned to Bozeman tomorrow morning, we'd be moving into *our house.*

I was ready for this break. Colin was starting a new school year and I wanted to be the one to chauffeur him around this fall. I wanted some time to just be a mom and relax into the role.

And my sticks wouldn't be far away.

The guys and I had some new ideas for the next album. We'd already informed Harvey that we wouldn't be creating this one on a deadline. Our plan was to write through video chats and the occasional visit. We were reinventing our process to fit our changing lifestyles. To fit our families.

Without the pressure, we'd already polished two songs. If we kept it up, we'd have an album wrapped before the baby was born.

"Ready?" Jonas asked from where he stood with Nixon.

"Yeah." I walked over and took his outstretched hand, then I took Nixon's.

They clasped grips and tightened our circle. My eyes drifted shut and the noise from the crowd outside faded for just a moment.

This was our tenth year together. We'd changed a lot in that time. As individuals. As a band. But we fought for this

295

life. We fought for each other. We fought for the music that came from our souls.

I wasn't sure what was in store for Hush Note's future. But together, we'd navigate the way. We'd break the mold for a rock star life and have it all.

Jonas squeezed my hand before dropping it, and I met his smile with one of my own.

Here we go.

I was the first to walk on stage. I sat on my stool and scanned the crowd, finding Graham's eyes.

This was the magic. Not the fame or the fortune but finding his face in a crowd of thousands and letting the rest of the world fade away.

Maybe our melody hadn't come easily. There'd been times when our rhythm had been out of sync. None of it mattered.

Because our beauty was in the refrain.

PLAYLIST

"Good Things Fall Apart" (Travis Barker Remix) – Illenium,
Jon Bellion & Travis Barker

"Ocean" – Lady Antebellum

"Finally // beautiful stranger" – Halsey

"Tom Sawyer" – Rush

"Life is a Highway" – Tom Cochrane

"All The Small Things" – blink-182

"Interstate Love Song" – Stone Temple Pilots

"To Make You Feel My Love" – Mathilde Holtti

HUSH NOTE SERIES

"Lies and Lullabies" by Sarina Bowen
"Rifts and Refrains" by Devney Perry
"Muses and Melodies" by Rebecca Yarros

PREVIEW TO THE BIRTHDAY LIST

POPPY

"Are you ready for this?" Molly asked.

I looked around the open room and smiled. "Yeah. I think so."

My restaurant, The Maysen Jar, was opening tomorrow. The dream I'd had since I was a kid—the dream Jamie had shared with me—was actually coming true.

Once an old mechanic's garage, The Maysen Jar was now Bozeman, Montana's newest café. I'd taken a run-down, abandoned building and turned it into my future.

Gone were the cement floors spotted with oil. In their place was a hickory herringbone wood floor. The dingy garage doors had been replaced. Now visitors would pull up to a row of floor-to-ceiling black-paned windows. And decades of gunk, grime and grease had been scrubbed away. The original red brick walls had been cleaned to their former glory, and the tall, industrial ceilings had been painted a fresh white.

Good-bye, sockets and wrenches. Hello, spoons and forks.

"I was thinking." Molly straightened the menu cards for the fourth time. "We should probably call the radio station and see if they'd do a spotlight or something to announce that you're open. We've got that ad in the paper but radio might be good too."

I rearranged the jar of pens by the register. "Okay. I'll call them tomorrow."

We were standing shoulder to shoulder behind the counter at the back of the room. Both of us were fidgeting—touching things that didn't need to be touched and organizing things that had been organized plenty—until I admitted what we were both thinking. "I'm nervous."

Molly's hand slid across the counter and took mine. "You'll be great. This place is a dream, and I'll be here with you every step of the way."

I leaned my shoulder into hers. "Thanks. For everything. For helping me get this going. For agreeing to be my manager. I wouldn't have come this far without you."

"Yes, you would have, but I'm glad to be a part of this." She squeezed my hand before letting go and running her fingers across the black marble counter. "I was—"

The front door opened and an elderly man with a cane came shuffling inside. He paused inside the doorway, his gaze running over the black tables and chairs that filled the open space, until he saw Molly and me at the back of the room.

"Hello," I called. "Can I help you?"

He slipped off his gray driving cap and tucked it under his arm. "Just looking."

"I'm sorry, sir," Molly said, "but we don't open for business until tomorrow."

He ignored Molly and started shuffling down the center aisle. My restaurant wasn't huge. The garage itself had only been two stalls, and to cross from the front door to the counter took me exactly seventeen steps. This man made the trip seem like he was crossing the Sahara. Every step was small and he stopped repeatedly to look around. But eventually, he reached the counter and took a wooden stool across from Molly.

When her wide, brown eyes met mine, I just shrugged. I'd poured everything I had into this restaurant—heart and soul and wallet—and I couldn't afford to turn away potential customers, even if we hadn't opened for business yet.

"What can I do for you, sir?"

He reached past Molly, grabbing a menu card from her stack and rifling the entire bunch as he slid it over.

I stifled a laugh at Molly's frown. She wanted to fix those cards so badly her fingers were itching, but she held back, deciding to leave instead. "I think I'll go finish up in the back."

"Okay."

She turned and disappeared through the swinging door into the kitchen. When it swung closed behind her, I focused on the man memorizing my menu.

"Jars?" he asked.

I grinned. "Yes, jars. Most everything here is made in mason jars." Other than some sandwiches and breakfast pastries, I'd compiled a menu centered around mason jars.

It had actually been Jamie's idea to use jars. Not long after we'd gotten married, I'd been experimenting with recipes. Though it had always been my dream to open a restaurant, I'd never known exactly what I wanted to try. That was, until one night when I'd been experimenting with ideas I'd found on Pinterest. I'd made these dainty apple pies in tiny jars and Jamie had gone crazy over them. We'd spent the rest of the night brainstorming ideas for a jar-themed restaurant.

Jamie, you'd be so proud to see this place. An all-too-familiar sting hit my nose but I rubbed it away, focusing on my first customer instead of dwelling on the past.

"Would you like to try something?"

He didn't answer. He just set down the menu and stared, inspecting the chalkboard and display racks at my back. "You spelled it wrong."

"Actually, my last name is Maysen, spelled the same way as the restaurant."

"Huh," he muttered, clearly not as impressed with my cleverness.

"We don't open until tomorrow, but how about a sample? On the house?"

He shrugged.

Not letting his lack of enthusiasm and overall grouchy demeanor pull me down, I walked to the refrigerated display case next to the register and picked Jamie's favorite. I popped it in the toaster oven and then set out a spoon and napkin in front of the man while he kept scrutinizing the space.

Ignoring the frown on his face, I waited for the oven and let my eyes wander. As they did, my chest swelled with pride. Just this morning, I'd applied the finishing touches. I'd hung the last of the artwork and put a fresh flower on each table. It was hard to believe this was the same garage I'd walked into a year ago. That I'd finally been able to wipe out the smell of gasoline in exchange for sugar and spice.

No matter what happened with The Maysen Jar—whether it failed miserably or succeeded beyond my wildest dreams—I would always be proud of what I'd accomplished here.

Proud and grateful.

It had taken me almost four years to crawl out from underneath the weight of Jamie's death. Four years for the black fog of grief and loss to fade to gray. The Maysen Jar had given me a purpose this past year. Here, I wasn't just a twenty-nine-year-old widow struggling to make it through each day. Here, I was a business owner and entrepreneur. I was in control of my life and my own destiny.

The oven's chime snapped me out of my reverie. I pulled on a mitt and slid out the small jar, letting the smell of apples and butter and cinnamon waft to my nose. Then I went to the freezer, getting out my favorite vanilla-bean ice cream and placing a dollop atop the pie's lattice crust. Wrapping the hot jar in a black cloth napkin, I slid the pie in front of the grumpy old man.

"Enjoy." I held back a smug smile. Once he dug into that pie, I'd win him over.

He eyed it for a long minute, leaning around to inspect all sides of the dish before picking up his spoon. But with that first bite, an involuntary hum of pleasure escaped from his throat.

"I heard that," I teased.

He grumbled something under his breath before taking another steaming bite. Then another. The pie didn't last long; he devoured it while I pretended to clean.

"Thanks," he said quietly.

"You're welcome." I took his empty dishes and set them

in a plastic bussing tub. "Would you like to take one to go? Maybe have it after dinner?"

He shrugged.

I took that as a yes and prepared a to-go bag with a blueberry crumble instead of the apple pie. Tucking a menu card and reheating instructions inside, I set the brown craft bag next to him on the counter.

"How much?" He reached for his wallet.

I waved him off. "It's on the house. A gift from me to you as my first customer, Mister . . ."

"James. Randall James."

I tensed at the name—just like I always did when I heard Jamie or a similar version—but let it roll off, glad things were improving. Five years ago, I would have burst into tears. Now, the bite was manageable.

Randall opened the bag and looked inside. "You send to-go stuff in a jar?"

"Yes, the jar goes too. If you bring it back, I give you a discount on your next purchase."

He closed the bag and muttered, "Huh."

We stared at each other in silence for a few beats, every ticking second getting more and more awkward, but I didn't break my smile.

"Are you from here?" he finally asked.

"I've lived in Bozeman since college, but no, I grew up in Alaska."

"Do they have these fancy *jar* restaurants up north?"

I laughed. "Not that I know of, but I haven't been home in a while."

"Huh."

Huh. I made a mental note never to answer questions with "huh" ever again. Up until I'd met Randall James, I'd never realized just how annoying it was.

The silence between us returned. Molly was banging around in the kitchen, probably unloading the clean dishes from the dishwasher, but as much as I wanted to be in there to help, I couldn't leave Randall out here alone.

I glanced at my watch. I had plans tonight and needed to get the breakfast quiches prepped before I left. Standing here while Randall pondered my restaurant was not something I'd figured into my plans.

"I, um—"

"I built this place."

His interruption surprised me. "The garage?"

He nodded. "Worked for the construction company that built it back in the sixties."

Now his inspection made sense. "What do you think?"

I normally didn't care much for the opinions of others—especially from a crotchety stranger—but for some reason, I wanted Randall's approval. He was the first person to enter this place who wasn't a family member or a part of my construction crew. A favorable opinion from an outsider would give my spirits a boost as I went into opening day.

But my spirits fell when, without a word, Randall pulled on his cap and slid off the stool. He looped the takeout bag over one wrist while grabbing his cane with his other hand. Then he began his slow journey toward the door.

Maybe my apple pie wasn't as magical as Jamie had thought.

When Randall paused at the door, I perked up, waiting for any sign that he'd enjoyed his time here.

He looked over his shoulder and winked. "Good luck, Ms. Maysen."

"Thank you, Mr. James." I kept my arms pinned at my

sides until he turned back around and pushed through the door. As soon as he was out of sight, I threw my arms in the air, mouthing, *Yes!*

I wasn't sure if I'd ever see Randall James again, but I was taking his parting farewell as the blessing I'd been craving.

This was going to work. The Maysen Jar was going to be a success.

I could feel it down to my bones.

Not thirty seconds after Randall disappeared down the sidewalk, the door flew open again. This time, a little girl barreled down the center aisle. "Auntie Poppy!"

I hurried around the counter and knelt, ready for impact. "Kali bug! Where's my hug?"

Kali, my four-year-old niece, giggled. Her pink summer dress swished behind her as she raced toward me. Her brown curls—curls that matched Molly's—bounced down her shoulders as she flew into my arms. I kissed her cheek and tickled her sides but quickly let her go, knowing she wasn't here for me.

"Where's Mommy?"

I nodded toward the back. "In the kitchen."

"Mommy!" she yelled as she ran in search of Molly.

I stood just as the door jingled again and my brother, Finn, stepped inside with two-year-old Max in his arms.

"Hi." He crossed the room and tucked me into his side for a hug. "How are you?"

"Good." I squeezed his waist, then stood on my tiptoes to kiss my nephew's cheek. "How are you?"

"Fine."

Finn was far from fine but I didn't comment. "Do you

want something to drink? I'll make you your favorite caramel latte."

"Sure." He nodded and set down Max when Molly and Kali came out of the kitchen.

"Mama!" Max's entire face lit up as he toddled toward his mother.

"Max!" She scooped him up, kissing his chubby cheeks and hugging him tight. "Oh, I missed you, sweetheart. Did you have a fun time at Daddy's?"

Max just hugged her back while Kali clung to her leg.

Finn and Molly's divorce had been rough on the kids. Seeing their parents miserable and splitting time between homes had taken its toll.

"Hi, Finn. How are you?" Molly's voice was full of hope that he'd give her just a little something nice.

"Fine," he clipped.

The smile on her face fell when he refused to look at her but she recovered fast, focusing on her kids. "Let's go grab my stuff from the office and then we can go home and play before dinner."

I waved. "See you tomorrow."

She nodded and gave me her biggest smile. "I can't wait. This is going to be wonderful, Poppy. I just know it."

"Thanks." I smiled good-bye to my best friend and ex-sister-in-law.

Molly looked back at Finn, waiting for him to acknowledge her, but he didn't. He kissed his children good-bye and then turned his back on his ex-wife, taking the stool Randall had vacated.

"Bye, Finn," Molly whispered, then led the kids back through the kitchen to the small office.

The minute we heard the back door close, Finn groaned and rubbed his hands over his face. "This fucking sucks."

"Sorry." I patted his arm and then went behind the counter to make his coffee.

The divorce was only four months old and both were struggling to adjust to the new normal of different houses, custody schedules and awkward encounters. The worst part of it all was that they still loved each other. Molly was doing everything she could to get just a fraction of Finn's forgiveness. Finn was doing everything he could to make her pay.

And as Molly's best friend and Finn's sister, I was caught in between, attempting to give them both equal love and support.

"Is everything set for tomorrow?" Finn propped his elbows on the counter and watched me make his latte.

"Yes. I need to do a couple of things for the breakfast menu, but then I'm all set."

"Want to grab dinner with me tonight? I can wait around for you to finish up."

My shoulders stiffened and I didn't turn away from the espresso drip. "Um, I actually have plans tonight."

"Plans? What plans?"

The surprise in his voice wasn't a shock. In the five years since Jamie had died, I'd rarely made plans that hadn't included him or Molly. I'd all but lost touch with the friends Jamie and I'd had from college. The only girlfriend I still talked to was Molly. And the closest I'd come to making a *new* friend lately had been my conversation earlier with Randall.

Finn was probably excited, thinking I was doing something social and branching out, which wasn't entirely untrue. But my brother wasn't going to like the plans I'd made.

"I'm going to a karate class," I blurted and started steaming his milk. I could feel his frown on my back, and sure enough, it was still there when I delivered his finished latte.

"Poppy, no. I thought we talked about giving up this list thing."

"We talked about it, but I don't remember agreeing with you."

Finn thought my desire to complete Jamie's birthday list was unhealthy.

I thought it was necessary.

Because maybe if I finished Jamie's list, I could find a way to let him go.

Finn huffed and dove right into our usual argument. "It could take you years to get through that list."

"So what if it does?"

"Finishing his list isn't going to bring him back. It's just your way of holding on to the past. You're never going to move on if you can't let him go. He's gone, Poppy."

"I know he's gone," I snapped, the threat of tears burning my throat. "I'm well aware that Jamie isn't coming back, but this is my choice. I want to finish his list and the least you can do is be supportive. Besides, you're one to talk about moving on."

"That's different," he countered.

"Is it?"

We went into a stare-down, my chest heaving as I refused to blink.

Finn broke first and slumped forward. "I'm sorry. I just want you to be happy."

I stepped to the counter and placed my hand on top of

his. "I know, but please, try and understand why I need to do this."

He shook his head. "I don't get it. I don't know why you'd put yourself through all that. But you're my sister and I love you, so I'll try."

"Thank you." I squeezed his hand. "I want you to be happy too. Maybe instead of dinner with me, you should go to Molly's? You could try and talk after the kids go to bed."

He shook his head, a lock of his rust-colored hair falling out of place as he spoke to the countertop. "I love her. I always will, but I can't forgive what she did. I just . . . can't."

I wished he'd try harder. I hated to see my brother so heartbroken. Molly too. I'd jump at the chance to get Jamie back, no matter what mistakes he might have made.

"So, karate?" Finn asked, changing subjects. He might disapprove of my choice to finish Jamie's list, but he'd rather talk about it than his failed marriage.

"Karate. I made an appointment to try a class tonight." It was probably a mistake, doing strenuous physical exercise the night before the grand opening, but I wanted to get it done before the restaurant opened and I got too busy—or chickened out.

"Then, I guess, tomorrow you'll get to cross two things off the list. Opening this restaurant and going to a karate class."

"Actually." I held up a finger, then went to the register for my purse. I pulled out my oversized bag and rifled around until my fingers hit Jamie's leather journal. "I'm going to cross off the restaurant one today."

I hadn't completed many items on Jamie's list, but every time I did, waterworks followed. The restaurant's opening tomorrow was going to be one of my proudest moments and I didn't want it flooded with tears.

"Would you do it with me?" I asked.

He smiled. "You know I'll always be here for whatever you need."

I knew.

Finn had held me together these last five years. Without him, I don't think I would have survived Jamie's death.

"Okay." I sucked in a shaky breath, then grabbed a pen from the jar by the register. Flipping to the thirtieth-birthday page, I carefully checked the little box in the upper right corner.

Jamie had given each birthday a page in the journal. He'd wanted some space to make notes about his experience or tape in pictures. He'd never get to fill in these pages, and even though I was doing his list, I couldn't bring myself to do it either. So after I finished one of his items, I simply checked the box and ignored the lines that would always remain empty.

As expected, the moment I closed the journal, a sob escaped. Before the first tear fell, Finn had rounded the corner and pulled me into his arms.

I miss you, Jamie. I missed him so much it hurt. It wasn't fair that he couldn't do his own list. It wasn't fair that his life had been cut short because I'd asked him to run a stupid errand. It wasn't fair that the person responsible for his death was still living free.

It wasn't fair.

The flood of emotion consumed me and I let it all go into my brother's navy shirt.

"Please, Poppy," Finn whispered into my hair. "Please

think about stopping this list thing. I hate that it makes you cry."

I sniffled and wiped my eyes, fighting with all my strength to stop crying. "I have to," I hiccupped. "I have to do this. Even if it takes me years."

Finn didn't reply; he just squeezed me tighter.

We hugged each other for a few minutes until I got myself together and stepped back. Not wanting to see the empathy in his eyes, I looked around the restaurant. The restaurant I'd only been able to buy because of Jamie's life insurance money.

"Do you think he'd have liked it?"

Finn threw his arm over my shoulders. "He'd have loved it. And he'd be so proud of you."

"This was the one item on his list that wasn't just for him."

"I think you're wrong about that. I think this *was* for him. Making your dreams come true was Jamie's greatest joy."

I smiled. Finn was right. Jamie would have been so excited about this place. Yes, it was my dream, but it would have been his too.

Wiping my eyes one last time, I put the journal away. "I'd better get my stuff done so I can get to that class."

"Call me afterward if you need to. I'll just be home. Alone."

"Like I said, you could always go eat dinner with your family." He shot me a glare and I held up my hands. "Just an idea."

Finn kissed my cheek and took another long drink of his coffee. "I'm going to go."

"But you're coming by tomorrow?"

"I wouldn't miss it for the world. Proud of you, sis."

I was proud of me too. "Thanks."

We walked together to the door, then I locked it behind him before rushing back to the kitchen. I dove into my cooking, making a tray of quiches that would sit overnight in the refrigerator and bake fresh in the morning. When my watch dinged the minute after I'd slid the tray into the fridge, I took a deep breath.

Karate.

I was going to karate tonight. I had no desire to try martial arts, but I would. For Jamie.

So I hurried to the bathroom, trading my jeans and white top for black leggings and a maroon sports tank. I tied my long red hair into a ponytail that hung past my sports bra before stepping into my charcoal tennis shoes and heading out the back.

It didn't take me long to drive my green sedan to the karate school. Bozeman was the fastest-growing town in Montana and it had changed a lot since I'd moved here for college, but it still didn't take more than twenty minutes to get from one end to the other—especially in June, when college was out for the summer.

By the time I parked in the lot, my stomach was in a knot. With shaking hands, I got out of my car and went inside the gray brick building.

"Hi!" A blond teenager greeted me from behind the reception counter. She couldn't have been more than sixteen and she had a black belt tied around her white uniform.

"Hi," I breathed.

"Are you here to try a class?"

I nodded and found my voice. "Yes, I called earlier this week. I can't remember who I talked to but he told me I could just come over tonight and give it a shot."

"Awesome! Let me get you a waiver. One sec." She disappeared into the office behind the reception counter.

I took the free moment to look around. Trophies filled the shelves behind the counter. Framed certificates written in both English and Japanese hung on the walls in neat columns. Pictures of happy students were scattered around the rest of the lobby.

Past the reception area was a wide platform filled with parents sitting on folding chairs. Proud moms and dads were facing a long glass window that overlooked a class-room of kids. Beyond the glass, little ones in white uniforms and yellow belts were practicing punches and kicks—some more coordinated than others but all quite adorable.

"Here you go." The blond teenager returned with a small stack of papers and a pen.

"Thanks." I got to work, filling out my name and signing the necessary waivers, then handed them back. "Do I need to, um, change?" I glanced down at my gym clothes, feeling out of place next to all the white uniforms.

"You're fine for tonight. You can just wear that, and if you decide to sign up for more classes, we can get you a gi." She tugged on the lapel of her uniform. "Let me give you a quick tour."

I took a deep breath, smiling at some of the parents as they turned and noticed me. Then I met the girl on the other side of the reception counter and followed her through an archway to a waiting room. She walked straight past the open area and directly through the door marked *Ladies*.

"You can use any of the hooks and hangers. We don't wear shoes in the dojo, so you can leave those in a cubby with your keys. There aren't any lockers, as you can see," she laughed, "but no one will steal anything from you. Not here."

"Okay." I toed off my shoes and put them in a free cubby with my car keys.

Damn it. I should have painted my toenails. The red I'd chosen weeks ago was now chipped and dull.

"I'm Olivia, by the way." She leaned closer to whisper. "When we're in here, you can just call me Olivia, but when we're in the waiting area or dojo, you should always call me Olivia Sensei."

"Got it. Thanks."

"It'll just be a few more minutes until the kids' class is done." Olivia led me back out to a waiting area. "You can just hang out here and then we'll get started."

"Okay. Thank you again."

She smiled and disappeared back to the reception area.

I stood quietly in the waiting room, trying to blend into the white walls as I peeked into the dojo.

The class was over and the kids were all lining up to bow to their teachers. *Senseis.* One little boy was wiggling his toes on the blue mats covering the floor. Two little girls were whispering and giggling. An instructor called for attention and the kids' backs all snapped straight. Then they bent at the waist, bowing to the senseis and a row of mirrors spanning the back of the room.

The room erupted in laughter and cheers as the kids were dismissed from their line and funneled out the door. Most passed me without a glance as they went to find their parents or change in the locker rooms.

My nerves spiked as the kids cleared the exercise room, knowing it was almost time for me to go in there. Other adult students were coming in and out of the locker rooms, and I was now even more aware that I would be the only person tonight not wearing white.

I hated being new. Some people enjoyed the rush of the first day of school or a new job, but not me. I didn't like the nervous energy in my fingers. And I really didn't want to make a fool of myself tonight.

Just don't fall on your face.

That was one of two goals for tonight: survive, and stay upright.

I smiled at another female student as she emerged from the locker room. She waved but joined a group of men huddled on the opposite wall.

Not wanting to eavesdrop on the adults, I studied the children as they buzzed around until a commotion sounded in the lobby.

Determined not to show fear to whoever came my way, I forced the corners of my mouth up. They fell when a man stepped into the waiting area.

A man I hadn't seen in five years, one month and three days appeared in the room.

The cop who'd told me my husband had been murdered.

ACKNOWLEDGMENTS

Thank you for reading *Rifts and Refrains*! I loved writing this Hush Note story. If you haven't read Jonas and Kira's book, don't miss *Lies and Lullabies* by Sarina Bowen. And follow Nixon to *Muses and Melodies* by Rebecca Yarros.

Thanks to my incredible editing and proofreading team: Karen Grove, Julie Deaton, Karen Lawson and Kaitlyn Moodie. Thank you to Sarah Hansen for this gorgeous cover.

To the bloggers who take the time to read and post about my books, thank you from the bottom of my heart. A huge shout-out to the members of Perry Street for all your love and support. And a special thank you to my wonderful family and friends for encouraging me through another project.

And lastly, to Sarina and Rebecca. Thank you for sharing Hush Note with me. You rock!

ABOUT THE AUTHOR

Devney is a *USA Today* bestselling author who lives in Washington with her husband and two sons. Born and raised in Montana, she loves writing books set in her treasured home state. After working in the technology industry for nearly a decade, she abandoned conference calls and project schedules to enjoy a slower pace at home with her family. Writing one book, let alone many, was not something she ever expected to do. But now that she's discovered her true passion for writing romance, she has no plans to ever stop.

Don't miss out on Devney's latest book news.
Subscribe to her newsletter!
www.devneyperry.com